I0726713

Books by Shirleen Davies

Historical Western Romance Series

MacLarens of Fire Mountain

Tougher than the Rest, Book One
Faster than the Rest, Book Two
Harder than the Rest, Book Three
Stronger than the Rest, Book Four
Deadlier than the Rest, Book Five
Wilder than the Rest, Book Six

Redemption Mountain

Redemption's Edge, Book One
Wildfire Creek, Book Two
Sunrise Ridge, Book Three
Dixie Moon, Book Four
Survivor Pass, Book Five

MacLarens of Boundary Mountain

Colin's Quest, Book One,
Brodie's Gamble, Book Two, Releasing 2016

<u>Contemporary Romance Series</u>

MacLarens of Fire Mountain

Second Summer, Book One
Hard Landing, Book Two
One More Day, Book Three
All Your Nights, Book Four
Always Love You, Book Five
Hearts Don't Lie, Book Six
No Getting Over You, Book Seven
'Til the Sun Comes Up, Book Eight, Releasing 2016

Peregrine Bay

Reclaiming Love, Book One, A Novella
Our Kind of Love, Book Two

The best way to stay in touch is to subscribe to my newsletter.
Go to *www.shirleendavies.com* and subscribe in the box at the top of the right column that asks for your email. You'll be notified of new books before they are released, have chances to win great prizes, and receive other subscriber-only specials.

Survivor Pass

Redemption Mountain

Historical Western Romance Series

SHIRLEEN DAVIES

Book Five in the Redemption Mountain

Historical Western Romance Series

Copyright © 2016 by Shirleen Davies

All rights reserved. No part of this publication may be reproduced, distributed, or transmitted in any form or by any electronic or mechanical means, including information storage and retrieval systems or transmitted in any form or by any means without the prior written permission of the publisher, except by a reviewer who may quote brief passages in a review. Thank you for respecting the author's work.

For permission requests, contact the publisher.

Avalanche Ranch Press, LLC
PO Box 12618
Prescott, AZ 86304

Survivor Pass is a work of fiction. Names, characters, places, and incidents are either products of the author's imagination or used facetiously. Any resemblance to actual events, locales, or persons, living or dead, is wholly coincidental.

Book design and conversions by Joseph Murray at 3rdplanetpublishing.com

Cover design by the Kim Killion, The Killion Group

ISBN: 978-1-941786-33-8

I care about quality, so if you find something in error, please contact me via email at shirleen@shirleendavies.com.

Description

Survivor Pass, Book Five, Redemption Mountain Historical Western Romance Series

"The Redemption Mountain series is as good as historical romance gets—vivid settings, memorable characters, love, and lots at stake. Shirleen Davies knows how to bring the old west to life. You feel as if you've traveled, with the characters, to the frontier. I hope there will be more to come!" Book Review

He thought he'd found a quiet life...

Cash Coulter settled into a life far removed from his days of fighting for the South and crossing the country as a bounty hunter. Now a deputy sheriff, Cash wants nothing more than to buy some land, raise cattle, and build a simple life in the frontier town of Splendor, Montana. But his whole world shifts when his gaze lands on the most captivating woman he's ever seen. And the feeling appears to be mutual.

But nothing is as it seems...

Alison McGrath moved from her home in Kentucky to the rugged mountains of Montana for one reason—to find the man responsible for murdering her brother. Despite using a false identity to avoid any tie to her brother's name, the citizens of Splendor have no intention of sharing their knowledge about the bank robbery which killed her only sibling. Alison knows her circle of lies can't end well, and her growing for Cash threatens to weaken the revenge which drives her.

And the troubles are mounting*...*

There is danger surrounding them both—men who seek vengeance as a way to silence the past...by any means necessary.

Survivor Pass is book five in the Redemption Mountain historical western romance series. It is a full length novel with an HEA.

From the Author

Join Shirleen Davies' Newsletter to Receive Notice of:

- New Releases
- Contests
- Free Reads & Sneak Peeks

Visit my website for a list of characters for each series.

http://www.shirleendavies.com/character-list.html

Acknowledgements

A special thank you to my husband and chief inspiration, Richard, who spends endless hours reading and re-reading my manuscripts to ensure accuracy and content flow. His help is instrumental in providing my readers with solid stories and engaging characters.

As always, many thanks to my wonderful resources, including my editor, Kim Young, proofreader, Alicia Carmical, Diane Lebow, who is a whiz at guiding my social media endeavors, my cover designer, Kim Killion, The Killion Group, and Joseph Murray, who is a genius at formatting my books for both print and electronic versions.

Survivor

Pass

Prologue

Battle of Atlanta
July 1864

Years later, he'd look back on today, believing these were how nightmares were created.

"General Hood's orders are clear, Captain Coulter. Your men will drop back from their outer lines, march through and out of the city. You'll leave tonight and position your men to jump into General McPherson's left flank while General Wheeler attacks McPherson's wagon trains." As he spoke, Confederate Lieutenant General William Hardee thrust a finger, pointing to locations on the map, emphasizing the severity of the campaign. "It is critical we stop their advance. Am I clear, Captain?"

Captain Cash Coulter knew Union General McPherson's men would be a tough opponent. Under the command of Union General William Tecumseh Sherman, the Army of the North continued their march toward Atlanta, winning one battle after another in their attempt to destroy a major industrial center and railroad hub in the heart of the South. Any success by the Union troops would be disastrous to the South's strategy.

"Yes, sir. My men will hold the line." Cash's gaze shifted from the map, focusing on Hardee's stern features. "I'll need at least six hours to get into position."

"You have three, Captain. Hood's men are five miles north of Atlanta. Delays can mean the difference between saving the city and letting it fall into enemy hands."

General Hardee's words played over and over in Cash's mind as he encouraged his men during the grueling march. Exhaustion, the sweltering night, and dusty roads contributed to the slower than anticipated progress. Before his men could gain position, word came from Hardee. He could wait no longer, deciding to deploy.

Cursing the decision, knowing his men weren't far enough into McPherson's flank to achieve their goal, he positioned his troops.

"Captain, we need more time." First Lieutenant Stephen Ramsey kept his voice low, although the urgency was clear. "Captain Davis is to our east and already experiencing fire from Union sharpshooters." Ramsey had become indispensable as a tracker and tactical leader. The only man Cash trusted more was Captain Beauregard Davis, who led another division under the command of Hardee.

"We have no more time, Ramsey. Get the men into position."

The sounds of artillery and the screams of the injured split the air for hours as morning turned to afternoon, then evening. Gunfire gave way to war cries and shouts as the forces met in savage hand-to-hand combat, neither side giving up as evening turned to the dark of night. When advancement proved futile, Cash searched for Ramsey, determined to move his remaining men south.

"Captain Coulter!"

The shout from an infantryman went up to his right. Crouching, Cash ran toward the man, dropping to his knees where one of his men lay injured, curses streaming from the man's lips. Dirt and blood covered his clothing, his left leg bent at an odd angle. Taking a closer look, Cash sucked in a breath when he saw two bars, indicating a first lieutenant.

"Ramsey..." Rolling his friend over, Cash swallowed at the damage to his left leg and arm. "Get help. Now!" Staunching the flow of blood, he waved to another lieutenant. "Move the men south. Take a position, and damn it to hell, hold it."

"You need to go." Ramsey spoke through gritted teeth, trying unsuccessfully to move his left arm. "Leave me, Captain."

Cash continued to wrap the wound on Ramsey's left leg, fearing the worst. He glanced around, torn between his duty to lead his men and loyalty to a friend.

Ramsey tried to rise, then fell back. "Hear me, Cash. Go." Sucking in a ragged breath, he closed his eyes against the pain. "Either I'll make it or I won't. There's no more you can do."

Hearing the pounding of boots, Cash glanced over his shoulder to see two men drop a stretcher next to him.

"We'll take care of him, Captain," one of the men said as they shouldered their way past Cash. They grasped Ramsey by his shoulders and good leg, then unceremoniously dropped him on the stretcher.

"Damn it, men. Be careful." Cash stayed next to them as they ran toward a waiting wagon. Stepping aside, he watched as they laid Ramsey inside. "Hold," Cash yelled as the wagon began to lurch forward. Gripping Ramsey's hand, he leaned over the sideboards. "Whatever you need, I'm here for you."

Ramsey nodded, his eyes beginning to roll back.

"Anything, Stephen. Don't forget," Cash whispered as he took one last look at the wagon, praying he'd see his friend again.

Chapter One

Splendor, Montana
February 1868

"This is your stop, ma'am." The driver held out his hand, glancing around to see if anyone waited for the lone passenger in his stagecoach. He turned his head to spit the trail dust from his mouth. "Sorry, ma'am."

"Quite understandable." Alison Burns McGrath took the driver's hand, glancing down at the mud, grimacing as she thought of her one good pair of shoes landing in the muck.

"Stand aside, Charlie. I'll take care of the lady."

Before she had a chance to react, strong hands grasped her waist, swinging her toward the boardwalk, holding steady as her feet touched the ground. Stepping back, he tipped his hat.

"I'm Sheriff Gabe Evans, ma'am." His eyes narrowed when she stared up at him, saying nothing and showing no interest in those standing around. "Is someone meeting you?"

Clearing her throat, Alison took a step back, adjusting her hat as she gripped her reticule in the other hand. "I believe Mr. Horace Clausen planned to meet me." She dug into her handbag, checking the piece of paper with the banker's name. "Perhaps he doesn't know the stage has arrived."

Gabe peered down the street toward the bank before a shout caught his attention. "There he is." He nodded at a tall, slender man with graying hair and a short beard walking toward them.

"Mrs. Burns?" Horace asked, making a slight bow when she nodded. "I'm Horace Clausen. I hope your journey wasn't too difficult."

"Long, but uneventful, Mr. Clausen." She looked between the two men, then focused her attention on Gage. "Thank you for coming to my aid, Sheriff."

"My pleasure, Mrs. Burns, and welcome to Splendor. I'll leave you two to your business." Touching the brim of his hat, Gabe crossed the street, disappearing into the Dixie Saloon.

Horace chuckled at his hasty departure. "You'll have to excuse the sheriff, Mrs. Burns. He married a couple months ago and can't seem to stay away from his wife for more than a few hours." He sobered at the confusion on her face.

"The sheriff's wife works in a saloon?" Alison clamped her mouth shut, wishing she could take the words back.

"Yes, she does. She's one of the owners." He picked up the traveling bag Charlie had deposited on the boardwalk before taking her elbow to guide her toward the bank. "You'll have plenty of time to get to know the people in town. I'm sure you'll be quite pleased with the people of Splendor."

She narrowed her gaze at him, not responding. Being pleased wasn't in Alison's plans. She'd left Kentucky for one purpose, which didn't include becoming close with the people of Splendor.

"Thank you, Mr. Clausen. I'm certain you're right."

"Don't forget this, Mrs. Burns." Charlie lumbered toward them, balancing an odd-shaped crate in his arms. Setting it next to Clausen, he swiped his arm across his forehead. "I'll be getting lunch, then heading out."

"Thank you so much. You've been a great help." Alison smiled, seeing Charlie's face redden before he turned to leave.

"May I assume this is for your business?" Clausen asked.

"It's my sewing machine, Mr. Clausen. I was able to obtain it from a traveling merchant in Kentucky, who purchased it from one of the factories in New York after the war." She reached down to pat the crate. "It was my good fortune to secure it for my shop."

"I'd heard of the factories in the north that sprang up to make uniforms during the war. I've never seen one of those machines in operation, though."

"Well, Mr. Clausen, now's your chance."

Alison stood in the middle of her millinery and seamstress shop, her gaze moving over the hat forms, ribbon, bolts of fabric, thread, lace, buttons, and paper patterns left by the previous owner. It had been her good fortune to spot the newspaper ad Horace placed for the relatives of the woman who'd succumbed to consumption, leaving a good business in a growing town.

The timing had been perfect. The merchant coming through town had wanted nothing more than to rid himself of the cumbersome sewing machine. Although her mother objected, she'd paid the small amount he requested, then shooed him on his way before he realized the bargain he'd left behind. She smiled to herself.

"Hello. Are you the new owner?"

Alison turned at the cheery voice, seeing three women step inside.

"Yes, I am." She walked up to them. "Welcome to my shop. I'm Alison Mc...Burns." She'd almost slipped and used her surname of McGrath rather than her mother's maiden name, the one Alison chose as her married name. She had to be more careful. It wouldn't do to associate herself with her dead brother, Bobby McGrath. Not until she discovered the truth about his death.

"It's wonderful to meet you. I'm Abigail Brandt. These are my friends, Rachel and Ginny Pelletier.

We'd heard about the new owner and couldn't wait any longer to meet you." At that moment, the machine near the back caught Abby's attention. "Oh my. Is that what I think it is?" She moved to it, reaching out to touch the contraption.

"If you mean a sewing machine, then yes. I brought it with me from Kentucky."

"Rachel, have you ever seen one of these?" her sister-in-law, Ginny, asked.

"I have. I don't know how we would have fought the war without them." Rachel turned toward Alison, seeing the young woman's face pale. "I worked as a nurse in Union field hospitals during the war. Our soldiers would never have gotten uniforms without the factories using these machines."

"Yes, ma'am. My father fought for the North under General Benson. He died at the Battle of Richmond."

Rachel let out a sigh. "We lost many good men during the war."

"But it's over now. Time to move on, right?" Abby said, trying to shift the mood. "Are you taking customers yet?"

Alison shook off the memories of her father, wishing she could do the same when she thought of her brother.

"Yes. What can I do for you?"

An hour later, Alison watched the three women leave. She'd obtained orders for six dresses with hats to match, two apiece, and a promise to meet them for lunch in town the following Saturday. Lowering herself into a nearby chair, she held the order in her hand, still reeling from the changes in her life.

Her father had died fighting for the North in August of 1862, leaving Alison, her mother, and younger brother, Bobby, to take care of their farm. While Bobby tended the animals, Alison and her mother had taken laundry and seamstress work to keep the family going. They all took care of the crops, although weather and marauding troops from both sides had done all in their power to take them under.

In late 1864, Bobby had given into his anger, enlisting in the Southern Army. Afterwards, he'd joined a group of disenchanted Confederate soldiers, traveling west to make his fortune so he could support his mother and sister the way their father hadn't.

They'd heard little from Bobby, receiving few letters and no money, until a telegram came in late 1867 from the sheriff of Splendor. Gabe Evans, the man she'd met on her arrival, had been brief. Bobby had been shot and killed during an attempted bank robbery. If interested, his family could obtain his personal effects in person.

Alison's stomach still clenched whenever she thought of the curt message announcing her brother's death. He'd been seventeen, barely a man, and most certainly not a bank robber. With a shaky hand, she swiped a tear from her face, anger at the injustice surfacing again.

She'd made a promise to her mother, and herself, to find the man who had fired the gun. He'd shown Bobby no mercy, and she vowed he'd receive none from her. All she had to do was settle in, get to know the people of Splendor, and discover who murdered her brother. Alison would take care of business, then disappear without a shred of regret.

"Another telegram for you, Sheriff. It's from Cash. When do you think he'll be coming home?" Bernie Griggs had run the Western Union office for years, having no plans to ever retire.

"I wish I knew." Gabe Evans glanced at the message Bernie handed him. After reading it, he shook his head. Cash Coulter, ex-Confederate soldier, bounty hunter, and deputy sheriff in Splendor, had left town right after Gabe married Lena Campanel. He'd provided few details, saying he owed a friend and had to go.

"Do you want to send a reply?"

"Yeah. Tell him to finish up whatever he's doing and get his scrawny ass back to Splendor." Gabe tossed a coin on the counter and left, hearing Bernie chuckle before he closed the door.

Taking a few steps toward the jail, his head snapped up at the sound of gunfire coming from the Dixie Saloon. Drawing his gun, Gabe dashed across the muddy street, seeing Beau Davis, his other deputy, storm out of the jail. Their gazes connected. As if they read each other's mind, Beau crossed as quickly as he could given the tendency of the gooey muck they called a street to tug at his boots.

Getting as close as possible, listening to the continuing gunfire, Gabe nodded at Beau while holding up his fist. One...two...three fingers, then they charged into the saloon, coming to an abrupt stop at the scene before them.

"What the..." Gabe's gaze moved from the three men crouching under a table to the woman pointing a revolver at them. The look on his wife's face was feral as she glared at the men.

"Not one of you is welcome in the Dixie again. Do you understand?" She shot another two rounds into the air, then set the revolver on the bar, picking up the loaded one next to it. "Now, get out." Her voice remained low and strong, the gun not wavering.

Stepping up next to her, Gabe slid an arm around her waist. "Do you need any help?" he whispered in her ear.

"No. I think I can handle this." She didn't look at him, all her attention focused on the men still hiding under the table.

"She tried to kill us, Sheriff," one of the men growled. "You need to arrest her."

"Why don't you three come out from your hiding place and we'll talk." Gabe dropped his arm from around Lena's waist and stalked toward the men, still holding his gun in one hand.

"Come on. You heard the sheriff," Beau said, slapping his hand on the table. "And I'll take your guns while we sort this out."

"Hell no. I'm not giving you my gun." The largest of the three got to his feet, slamming his hat down on his head.

Another shot rang out. "You heard the deputy. Hand over your guns." Lena narrowed her eyes at the men.

"Lena, why don't you give me the gun? Beau and I will take it from here." Gabe reached out, wrapping his hand around the barrel of the gun as her finger moved from the trigger. "Good. Now tell me what happened." He nodded his appreciation at Paul when the bartender set two whiskeys in front of him. "Here, drink this," he said, handing a glass to Lena.

She downed it in one swallow before turning to face the three men Beau had lined up against one wall.

"Gina started today." She crossed her arms, trying to settle the anger still pulsing through her.

"The new server girl from Denver?"

"Yes. If you remember, she doesn't provide anything except drinks and conversation. She'd served those men drinks, then continued to serve other tables. On the second round, the big one grabbed Gina and settled her on his lap. She tried to stand, but he wouldn't let her go. He ran his hand up her leg and under her dress. When she slapped him and shoved herself up, he grabbed her arm and slapped her. Then the other two joined in. Neither Paul nor I could get to her fast enough."

Gabe cursed, understanding why Lena had gone after them.

"I didn't try to hurt them, but I needed to get their attention. When the big one pulled a gun, I shot close enough to him that he dropped it, but then he started toward me. That's when Paul grabbed the shotgun." Talking about it seemed to escalate her anger rather than control it. She took a deep breath. "They finally took cover under the table just before you and Beau got here."

"Do you know them?"

"I've never seen them before. Probably riding through—at least I hope that's their plan."

Gabe leaned over, giving Lena a kiss, then pushed away from the bar. "If not, it *will* be their plan now."

Alison walked into the boardinghouse dining room on Saturday, coming to a stop when she spotted the table filled with women. She'd met three—Abigail, Rachel, and Ginny. The other three were strangers. Straightening her shoulders, she took a deep breath and started forward, fidgeting with the drawstring of her reticule as she walked.

"Alison, we're so glad you could join us." Abby turned to the others. "Everyone, this is Alison Burns. She bought the millinery and seamstress shop next to the bank. Alison, this is Isabella Boucher, Caroline Iverson, and Magdalena Evans."

"Please, call me Lena," Magdalena said, offering a warm smile. "It's a pleasure to meet you."

"And you can call me Caro." Caroline offered Alison a warm smile.

Alison nodded, forcing her own smile as she took a seat next to Abby.

"We were just getting the story on what happened at the Dixie yesterday." Rachel glanced at Lena. "So you grabbed your gun, then what?"

Alison's eyes widened at the question.

"It really wasn't as bad as it sounds." Lena took a sip of her coffee, glancing over the rim at Alison, noting her discomfort. "Three men acted inappropriately toward one of the new girls, and I set them straight. That's all."

"That's all? From what Beau said, you took on the three men and they hid under a table." Caro looked at Alison. "Did you hear the commotion?"

"When I heard the gunshots, I stayed put. Where I come from, we had so many raiders come through town that we knew to stay inside when we heard shots. What happened to the men?"

"Gabe and Beau arrived and broke it up. Beau took them to the jail while Gabe stayed with me." Lena grinned, her face flushing pink. "He's so protective."

"Gabe Evans is your husband, right?" Alison asked, trying to recall what she'd heard about the various women.

"Yes, he is."

"You'll figure it all out, but a short version is Noah Brandt is my husband," Abby explained. "Rachel is married to Dax Pelletier, and Ginny is married to his brother, Luke."

"Isabella and I are widows," Caro added. She shifted toward Isabella, touching her arm.

"What she isn't saying is that each has a suitor." Ginny laughed at the surprised look on each woman's face. "You thought we didn't know about Travis and Beau?"

Caro cleared her throat. "Beau Davis is a wonderful man whom I'm proud to call a friend. There is nothing more between us."

"Uh-huh. Is that also true for you and Travis, Isabella?" Ginny asked.

"Yes, it is. He's been there for me during some rough times and I value his friendship." She shrugged. "He's a southern gentleman. As you all know, he's still dealing with the loss of his wife and daughter during the war." Isabella looked at Alison. "Travis works for Dax and Luke Pelletier."

"And he's one of our best men," Rachel added, wanting to change the subject. "So, tell us, Alison. Why did you pick Splendor?"

Alison's hands stilled at the question, her mind racing to form a response.

"It's simple. My mother didn't cope well with the death of my father. She became more and more withdrawn each year. Last summer, she took sick. The doctor said her heart gave out." Alison winced at the lie, knowing her mother might never recover from Bobby's death, but still lived on their Kentucky farm. "My husband was killed in the war." She bit her lower lip at the second lie in less than a minute, hoping they didn't question her further on her non-existent marriage. Before making the trip west, she'd made the decision to present herself as a widow without family. "I couldn't take care of the farm alone. A local family made an offer about the time I saw the ad Mr. Clausen placed in the newspaper. There was nothing keeping me in Kentucky, so..."

Her voice trailed off as an image of the farm took hold.

"And here you are." Ginny leaned forward, the corners of her mouth tilting upward. "I came in a wagon train with my younger sister. Our parents died on the journey and we had no funds to go further. Rachel came west to join her uncle in his clinic. Lena traveled here from back east to join her business partner."

"I came here after my husband died," Isabella added, surprising the other women by discussing her past. "I've known Lena since we were children. This seemed like the best place to be as I have no other family."

"It's the only place you should be." Lena wrapped an arm around Isabella's shoulders and squeezed.

"Where did you come from, Caro?" Alison asked.

"I grew up in New York. Gabe and I have known each other for years. When my husband died, I decided to break away from the suffocating attention of my family and travel west. As luck would have it, I encountered Gabe in Big Pine, where he had business. He encouraged me to come to Splendor."

"Are you glad you listened to him?" Alison leaned forward. She hadn't expected to like any of these women, yet the more they shared, the more she felt guilty about her true reasons for being in Splendor.

"Oh yes. This is a wonderful town with some of the most delightful people I've ever known. I hope you feel the same after you've been here a while."

Alison glanced at the other women, knowing she'd never truly fit in and would most definitely not be staying. "Perhaps I will, Caro. You never know what life has planned, do you?"

Chapter Two

Little Rock, Arkansas
April 1868

Cash Coulter paced back and forth in the small study at the home of his friend, Stephen Ramsey, hands on his hips as he thought about the situation. "It's obvious someone close to you is feeding the rustlers information. One of your men, or..." His voice trailed off, not liking the direction his thoughts were taking him.

"Or who?" Stephen turned from where he leaned against a window frame, looking out at the charred barn. Another reminder of the attacks he'd experienced over the last several months.

He'd fought off pitying looks, denials of work, and those who sought to take advantage of a man they considered a cripple since losing a leg at the Battle of Atlanta. Through it all, he'd married Helen, his childhood sweetheart, moved his growing family to Arkansas, and found contentment raising cattle and tending their farm. A few months ago, raiders began targeting his land, feeling secure a man such as him couldn't resist their attacks. It had taken Helen's prodding before he relented and contacted his old friend, requesting the help Cash had offered in those last moments before Stephen's service to the Confederacy ended.

Cash shoved his hands in his pockets, not wanting to voice the suspicions rooted in his gut.

"Are you going to tell me what's eating at you, Captain, or make me guess?"

Shaking his head, Cash stepped beside Stephen, clasping him on the shoulder. "I haven't been your captain for a long time. Just a friend."

The corners of his lips twitched. "Fine. As my friend, tell me who you think is behind the rustling."

"Who is the one person who'd like to see you fail?"

Stephen's face went slack as the implication of Cash's words sank in. Casting his gaze down to his missing leg, he fisted both hands.

He'd always been strong and determined to succeed. The loss of a leg and only partial use of his left arm didn't stop him from marrying the girl he'd loved since they were children, chasing each other around the schoolyard. His parents loved Helen. Her father tolerated Stephen, not hiding the fact he believed his daughter could do much better than the son of a poor dirt farmer.

Returning from battle as a cripple intensified the man's objections to Stephen wedding his only daughter. Nevertheless, the marriage happened, followed by one son and a life as far away from Helen's father as she'd allow.

"He's still in Tennessee. Never made a single attempt to visit Helen or his grandson. I can't imagine why he'd care after all this time."

Cash crossed his arms, leaning against the desk. "You can't? What of her grandmother's will?"

Stephen's face twisted in disgust as he pushed away from the wall. "Helen doesn't get the inheritance for four more years when she turns twenty-six. I've already told her I don't want any part of it. The money will be in her name to do with as she wants."

"I've been here almost a month. It's a small house, hard to ignore even private conversations. Helen's made no secret of her desire to be closer to her father now that her mother is dead. Maybe he's trying to make her wish a reality." Cash watched emotions play across Stephen's face, hating the pain he saw. "Think about it. The rustlers tend to scatter your herd rather than take them. The one time we ran across the gang, they shot over our heads. No one is as bad a shot as those men. The fires have all been set away from the house, causing little damage. And they've hit no other ranches. Maybe they don't want to harm you, but are just sending you a message—trying to frighten you into leaving."

"Sending me a message?"

"That's what my gut is telling me."

Stephen's breathing became labored as he absorbed Cash's words. He didn't believe Helen would be involved. The same belief didn't hold true for her father. If she'd written him, indicated how much she missed him, his father-in-law might take action, hiring thugs to intimidate Stephen into selling. He rubbed his eyes, feeling tired and beaten down.

"The only way to know for sure is to capture one of the men and make him talk," Cash continued. "At some point, you, Helen, or someone else will be a victim, whether intentional or not. I can track them and bring one back." He'd been a bounty hunter after the war, then became a deputy in Splendor, Montana. His tracking skills were sought after by lawmen and business owners who needed those services.

"You make it sound so easy."

"Trust me. Those men won't be hard to find. I'll leave after supper." Cash walked toward the door, turning at Stephen's response.

"No. If that's what is needed, we both go. This is my problem. I won't let you ride out alone."

"Son of a..." Stephen cursed when Cash pointed out the fire in a canyon not far from the ranch. He counted five men. "How did you know where to find them?"

"Their tracks were easy to follow. My guess is they move their camp after each raid." Cash's gaze followed one man in particular. He seemed to keep his distance from the others sitting around the fire playing cards and joking. Even when he settled near the campfire, he planted himself away from the rest of the gang. "The one closest to the horses is who we want."

"Why him?" Stephen turned toward Cash, his brows raised.

"He appears to be a loner. They may not notice him missing as soon as someone else." Cash thought a moment, his eyes focused on his target. "It may be hard to break him, though." His experience told him the quiet ones who kept to themselves were often the most difficult to crack. They had an internal pride, some private code which secured their silence.

Stephen nodded, understanding. They'd do what needed to be done in order to obtain the information they wanted, even if it meant extracting a little blood.

"You get some sleep, Stephen. I'll wake you after they've all bunked down. We'll make our move then."

Cash took a position so he could keep watch on the camp and the surrounding area. He watched his friend lower himself onto the ground, Stephen's right leg supporting his weight as he shifted on the wooden prosthesis he wore on his left. The hinged knee and ankle allowed him more stability when riding, but Cash knew the contraption slowed him down when performing many normal activities. Stephen preferred his crutch most of the time.

Observing how he struggled, Cash made a decision, knowing Stephen wouldn't like it. Then again, he wouldn't like many of the decisions Cash had made since the war.

If Stephen truly understood the man Cash had become, he wouldn't want him anywhere near his wife and son. The man Stephen knew during the war hadn't drawn a clean breath since the Battle of Atlanta. He'd been replaced by someone Cash seldom recognized. A darker, somber, damaged version of the man he'd been before all the battles, endless carnage, broken souls, and twisted humanity that greeted him each morning.

Only one man knew of the changes in Cash, the dark side no one else saw, and he'd take his knowledge to the grave. Beau Davis, his fellow deputy in Splendor, had lived through a similar hell. Unlike Cash, he'd been able to keep his inner rage under control, not letting it defeat him. His work as a bounty hunter hadn't lessened the violence buried within him. Neither had his work as a deputy in Splendor, a town he'd grown to love. If Gabe Evans and others in the town had any idea of the demons he kept hidden, he knew his days as a small town deputy would come to an end, along with any peace he'd been able to find.

Waiting until he heard Stephen's deep breathing and the men in the camp bedded down, Cash made his way through the thick stand of trees. They'd made their camp along the Arkansas River, a few miles downstream from Stephen's ranch. The dense brush provided the perfect cover for what he hoped would be an easy job of *convincing* the man hunched alone, yards from the others, to abandon his friends.

Getting to within a foot of the man, his gun drawn, Cash tapped him on the shoulder. His head whipped around, only to be greeted by a hard fist, then another. He dragged the unconscious man away from the camp, stopping once to stuff a bandanna in his mouth and tie his hands behind him.

Cash muttered a curse as he began to tire. The man was much larger and heavier than he first suspected. Breaking through the trees, he came to a halt at the look in his friend's eyes.

"What the hell? You should've woken me." Stephen stared at the unconscious man before locking his gaze on Cash. Standing, he shifted his weight to his right leg, adjusted the prosthesis on his left, then walked toward the man who now moaned as he regained consciousness. Yanking the bandanna from his mouth, he stepped back and waited.

Shaking his head, he looked up at the men towering over him. Staring, he focused on Cash's face.

"Captain?"

Cash's eyes widened. Dropping to a crouch, he took a good look at the man he'd disabled and dragged through the dirt, cursing when recognition hit.

"Wyatt?" He mumbled another curse. "What the hell are you doing riding with this bunch?" Cash stood, helping him up and untying his hands.

"Here." Stephen handed Wyatt a flask filled with whiskey.

Wyatt tipped it back, taking a swallow.

"Ramsey? I thought you died at the Battle of Atlanta." Wyatt took one more swig, then handed the flask back.

"Not hardly, Jackson. Those Union bastards took my leg, not my life." Stephen glared at him. They'd both been first lieutenants under Cash's command, although their duties couldn't have been more different. Stephen commanded an infantry platoon, while Wyatt Jackson handled special assignments known only to Cash and his superiors. Stephen always suspected the jobs included spying and assassinations, but he'd never asked.

"Wyatt, answer my question. What are you doing with those rustlers?" Cash's patience had ended. He needed answers.

"I'm not *with* them, Captain. I've been watching the gang for several weeks. There's a bounty out on one of them and I aim to collect it." He rubbed his jaw, wincing at the lump already forming. Swearing, he looked at Cash. "Did you have to hit me so hard?"

Cash ignored the question, letting the information Wyatt provided roll over in his mind.

"What's he wanted for?"

"Murder and robbery in Tennessee." Wyatt nodded toward the camp. "I couldn't get him alone and didn't want to face the entire gang, so I decided the best approach was to join them. I met up with them a few nights ago." He glanced over Cash's shoulder toward the camp. "You know, it won't be long before they notice I'm gone."

Cash moved so he could see the camp, watching as one man stood to toss another log on the fire, not bothering to look around before returning to his bedroll.

"What do you know about them?" Cash crossed his arms, narrowing his gaze at Wyatt.

"Besides being wanted for murder? Not much. All served the Confederacy, then banded up after the war ended. They rustle cattle, robbing a stage or bank when it suits them. Someone hired them to scare a local rancher—encourage him to sell out."

Cash shot a look at Stephen. It had been over a week since the last raid on his place.

"Do you have a name of who hired them?" Stephen asked.

"No. I didn't ask. I'm not here to dig into their business. All I want is to get the man I'm after and ride out." Wyatt scowled, then scrubbed a hand along his stubbled jaw. The last few months had been a nightmare. "He attacked my sister and murdered her husband." He let out a breath, taking a few steps away, his face showing the misery he felt. "I'd gone into town for a drink and a few hands of cards. I got tangled up with one of the women and didn't make it back to the farm until late. I found my sister huddled in a corner, her dress torn, blood all over her." He looked up, his eyes haunted in a way Cash had seen many times during the war. "He raped her, then murdered my brother-in-law. She killed herself a week later." His voice broke and he turned away from them.

During the war, Cash had given Wyatt orders that would haunt most men, but he carried them out without comment. He'd never shown an ounce of emotion—until this attack on his family. Cash didn't need to dig too deep to know how Wyatt felt. His family had also been slain by raiders while tending their Louisiana farm. Tracking them, he'd felt the initial satisfaction of revenge, followed by lengthy bouts of depression and anger. Even now, Cash fought to keep his demons from consuming his life.

"You don't intend to take him in, do you?" Cash already knew the answer.

Wyatt turned, his face contorted in pain. "No, Captain, I don't."

Cash walked up to him, placing a hand on his shoulder. "Trust me, Wyatt. Revenge won't help."

His tortured eyes met Cash's. "You won't talk me out of this, Captain."

"I'm no longer your captain, but I am your friend. We won't stop you from your mission, but I'm asking for something in return."

Wyatt's eyes widened. "What's that?"

"Stephen's farm is the one the gang is raiding. We need to know who put them up to it."

"We need a name," Stephen added.

Wyatt moved up to within inches of Cash's face. "If I get you a name, you'll let me ride out with my man?"

"Yes."

Wyatt nodded, saying nothing more. Turning away, he moved silently through the darkness to rejoin the men who still slept, unaware of his absence. Slumping against a tree, he stared at the man who'd caused the deaths of two people he loved. Glancing over his shoulder in the direction where Cash and Stephen kept watch, he vowed to get the name and ride out of Arkansas with the man he'd come for all within a few days. He'd grown weary of

the hunt. It was time to complete his duty and find
the justice he sought.

Chapter Three

Splendor, Montana
Several weeks later...

"Good morning, Mrs. Burns. What can I do for you today?" Horace Clausen held open the door of the bank, letting her pass.

"Hello, Mr. Clausen. I've a small deposit to make."

Horace chuckled. "Believe me, there are no small deposits."

As he moved to close the door, another man stepped inside.

"Morning, Horace." He nodded, then tipped his hat to Alison. "Ma'am."

Alison couldn't stop the slight intake of breath when she took a good look at the stranger. Tall with overlong blond hair and striking green eyes, he had a coarse appearance she found extremely appealing, but also strangely unsettling.

"Good to have you back in town. Cash, have you had a chance to meet our newest business owner?"

"No, I haven't had the pleasure." Cash removed his hat and took a step forward.

"Mrs. Burns, allow me to introduce Cash Coulter. He's one of Sheriff Evans' deputies."

"It's nice to meet you, Mr. Coulter."

"The pleasure is mine, Mrs. Burns. Welcome to Splendor." A weary smile crossed his face, his eyes crinkling a little at the corners as his gaze lingered on hers. "What business do you have?"

"I bought the millinery and seamstress shop next to the bank."

"I'm certain you'll be quite successful as the women in Splendor were vocal in their disappointment when it closed." He raised his brows at Horace, who nodded in understanding. The women in town allowed themselves few luxuries. For those who could afford it, the presence of a seamstress who could create hats, as well as alter clothes, made their lives much easier.

"So far, business has been beyond my expectations." She tightened her grip on her reticule, anxious to finish the deposit and return to her store, where she felt in control and safe. Something about Cash's presence produced strange feelings she had no desire to examine. "Well, I'll let you continue with your day, Mr. Coulter."

Cash tipped his hat, watching as she walked toward one of the tellers, then he turned to Horace. "I assume she's married."

"A widow," Horace answered. "From what I understand, her husband died during the war. She has no other family and decided to make a fresh start."

"Where did she come from?"

"Kentucky. A long way for a lone woman to travel."

Cash nodded at Alison as she finished her deposit and left the bank. "Yes, it certainly is."

Alison worked all afternoon, not even stopping to eat, as she finished the dresses for Rachel, Ginny, and Abby. Along with other orders, she already knew there'd be a profit at the end of the month. Completing the last stitch on one of the dresses, she glanced up at the sound of the bell above the entry door.

"Mrs. Burns?"

Alison moved to the front, her gaze taking in a young woman of average height with chestnut brown hair, bright green eyes, and freckles sprinkled across her nose and cheeks.

"Yes, I'm Alison Burns." She cocked her head, noting the package in the woman's hands.

"I'm Lydia Rinehart. I live at the Pelletier ranch and heard about you from Rachel." She shifted her weight from one foot to the other as she bit her bottom lip. Holding out the package, she hesitated a moment, as if deciding what to say.

"Is that something you'd like me to look at?" Alison asked, noting the discomfort on Lydia's face.

"Yes. It's just a simple store-bought dress."

"I'm sure it's lovely. May I?" Alison took the package from Lydia's outstretched hands, setting it on a table to remove the wrapping. Holding it up, she smiled at the pretty deep green calico print. "It's beautiful. What is it you'd like me to do?"

"The hem and sleeves are a little long, and..." Lydia didn't finish.

"And?" Alison tilted her head.

"Nothing. If you could fix the hem and sleeves that would be wonderful." Lydia clasped her hands in front of her. It had taken every penny she had to purchase the dress at Petermann's General Store. She'd need to do extra chores to have enough money to pay for the changes.

"Well, I can do that easily enough. When would you like it?"

"The Pelletiers are having a party in two weeks. Do you think it would be ready by then?"

Alison studied the dress, then placed it back on the table. "I can have it for you within a week."

"Only a week?" Lydia asked, her brows knitting together. "It may take me a few days longer to earn the money to pay you." She worried her lower lip, then cleared her throat. "I did some sewing when I was younger, but it's been a long time."

Alison's heart warmed at the hesitancy in Lydia's voice. "I understand. It will be ready next Monday. You come and get it whenever you're ready." She thought a moment, then quoted an amount. "If you don't quite have the money before the party, you can pay me when you do. All right?"

Lydia's eyes lit up at the low price. "Yes, that would be wonderful. Thank you, Mrs. Burns." For the first time, her face broke into a smile, her eyes sparkling. "It was nice to meet you."

The bell over the door caught both women's attention.

"I thought I might find you in here." Rachel closed the door behind her, taking the few steps needed to stand next to Lydia.

"You're right. Mrs. Burns is wonderful. She'll have the dress ready in time for the party."

Alison blushed at the compliment, feeling a renewed sense of guilt over the amount of deceit surrounding her. These were good people who'd accepted her without hesitating. She swallowed the lump in her throat, wishing it could all be different, knowing it couldn't.

"If you want to try them on, I have your dresses ready, Rachel." Alison moved to a wooden rack that held her completed work. "You can change in there." She pointed toward a curtain concealing a small dressing room.

A few minutes later, Rachel emerged wearing a stunning blue silk evening gown with a scooped bodice, capped sleeves, fitted waist, and separate peplum. Alison had decorated it with yards of white silk braid and white and blue silk ribbon.

"Oh my, Rachel. It's absolutely beautiful, but where will you wear it?" Lydia's brows lifted as her eyes widened.

"Dax and Luke have been invited to the Governor's Ball in Big Pine. Alison opening her shop came at the perfect time." Rachel skimmed her hands down the exquisite dress, looking at Alison. "What do you think?"

Alison walked around Rachel, taking in each seam and tuck. "I don't believe I'd change anything."

"Wonderful. I'll try on the other dress."

Half an hour later, Rachel and Lydia began their trip back to the Pelletier ranch, their wagon loaded with supplies, leaving Alison to her other jobs.

Hanging up the last of the dresses for Ginny and Abby, she heard her stomach growl, realizing she'd skipped lunch again. It seemed to be a habit with the increase in business.

She'd kept her rates low, hoping to garner more customers and compete with mail ordered clothing. Most women sewed, yet with their other chores, making a new dress never seemed a priority, especially when the only time available came after the children were asleep and they'd finished their regular mending.

"It appears you are in deep thought, Mrs. Burns."

Alison jumped, her hand coming to her chest as she spun around to see Cash standing a few feet away.

"Mr. Coulter, you startled me." A nervous laugh escaped as she dropped her hand and stepped toward him.

"My apologies. The bell over your door *did* ring, but it seems you were engrossed in your own world. I hope all is going well." His eyes narrowed in what Alison interpreted as concern.

"Yes, all is going quite well, thank you. May I help you with something?" She didn't often work on men's clothing, even though she had the skills to make pants, shirts, and coats.

He cleared his throat, fingering the brim of the hat he held in front of him. "I know it may seem presumptuous, but I would be honored if you would accompany me to supper tonight."

Her hands stilled in front of her, the invitation catching her unaware. She'd been courted before the war, never meeting a man who'd made her heart thump or blood heat. Her mother and father had been deeply in love, never hesitating to embrace each other, even in public. Alison wanted the same kind of love...uninhibited and devoted.

Looking at Cash, she noted the attractive combination of his thick hair, sun-browned skin, and broad shoulders. Then her gaze moved to his deep emerald eyes, which appeared distant and unemotional, as if he were looking through her instead of at her. She had the sudden urge to trace a finger down his face and across his full lips, learning the mysteries she felt certain he held deep inside.

"It would be my pleasure to have supper with you, Mr. Coulter. Let me get my coat and close up."

The sun finished its descent behind the mountains as Cash escorted Alison to a restaurant on the other side of the bank. He made no move to offer his arm as she kept a distance of no less than a foot between them.

"Have you eaten in here yet?" he asked, opening the door to let her pass.

"No, I haven't. I usually cook or go to the boardinghouse for meals." She glanced around the interior, noting the simple decorations and clean tables. "It smells wonderful."

"Suzanne's boardinghouse is very good, and I eat there most of the time. It's nice to have a place that isn't always crowded with my friends, though." He nodded at a woman walking toward them. "The owners used to be open for breakfast and dinner only. Now they offer supper. I come in about once a week. It spreads the business around." His mouth tilted up at the corners as he pulled out her chair.

"Hello, Cash. You must be Mrs. Burns, the seamstress." A woman of medium height, as broad as she was tall, stood next to their table. "I'm Betts Jones. My husband and I own this place."

"It's nice to meet you, Mrs. Jones."

"This is her first time in here, Betts. What's your special tonight?"

"Pot roast, and it's incredible, even if I'm the one who made it." She winked at Alison.

Cash laughed as he glanced at Alison. Seeing her nod, he ordered two of the specials.

"Horace Clausen told me you're from Kentucky. Tell me what brings you this far west." He sipped the coffee Betts set before him, leaning forward to get a better look at her face.

Alison conveyed the same story she'd told everyone about her husband dying in battle, her mother passing not long after. It had become ingrained in her, the lies now streaming from her mouth with ease.

"I'm sorry to hear about your husband. Many good people died during the war."

She'd glanced around the restaurant, not quite meeting his gaze. She needed to change the direction of their conversation. "Yes, they did. How long have you been here, Mr. Coulter?"

"Close to two years. I came here looking for friends I've known since we were boys."

"Did you find them?"

He chuckled. "I sure did. Dax and Luke Pelletier. They're the ones who convinced Beau and me to become Gabe's deputies. It's worked for us so far." His gaze never wavered from her face, making her squirm. Although his face held various expressions, his eyes never warmed or changed the way they appeared to slice right through her.

She leaned back in her chair, placing her hands in her lap. "Will you be staying?"

"Seems likely." Cash sat back as Betts set their plates down.

Alison ate slowly, glancing across the table at Cash. In her mind, he couldn't be described as handsome, yet the creases in his forehead and the way his eyes crinkled when he smiled gave him character she found captivating and quite appealing. She couldn't define what made her feel edgy, though, her body tensing the longer they sat in silence. Finishing her meal, she set her fork down, clasping her hands in her lap.

"What did you do before coming to Splendor?" she asked when he took his last bite.

"I fought for the South. When the war ended, Beau and I met up, traveling west as bounty hunters."

A shiver went up her back. "I don't recall ever meeting a bounty hunter. It's not a profession most men would choose." Wrapping her hands around a steaming cup of coffee, she took a sip, glancing over the rim to see his impassive expression.

"Perhaps not, but war changes men in ways that can't be predicted. We had the skills, needed the money, and the number of men with bounties was high. Still is." He shrugged. "We did what needed to be done."

"Such as?" Her brow quirked up, leaning forward in her seat.

When he remained silent, she thought he'd decided not to answer. Then he leaned toward her, resting his arms on the table.

"That's a story for another time."

Alison shook her head. She'd been right about him being a man of many secrets. She knew it would take time to gain his trust. Getting to know the people in Splendor could only help her as she identified the man who killed her brother. So far, she'd kept her questions about the bank robbery and killings to herself, not wanting to draw attention to her curiosity about an event happening months before. Having supper with Cash had been a nice distraction. The time had now come to get the answers she needed to give her mother peace, and mend the ache in her own heart.

Chapter Four

Cash sat on the edge of the desk in the sheriff's office as he rifled through wanted posters, recalling his conversation with Sheriff Parker Sterling in Big Pine. He'd stopped there on his way back to Splendor, expecting to say hello, then leave. Instead, he'd been given some unsettling news.

"Cash Coulter. You're a sight for sore eyes." Sheriff Sterling walked around his desk, extending his hand. "It's been too long. I heard you left Splendor a few months ago. Where've you been?" He moved to a nearby table, pouring coffee into two tin cups and handing one to Cash, then motioning to a chair.

"Thanks." Cash took the cup, sipping the hot liquid. He'd made good time after passing through a freak storm in the Dakotas. "Been helping a friend in Arkansas. We served together during the war."

"Yep, I know how that is. You carve a bond with men when you trust them to have your back during battle. Those bonds can last a long time." Parker sat back, his eyes focused on a spot across the room before looking once more at Cash. "I trust all went well."

"It did. It's time I got myself back to Splendor, though. I don't want Gabe to give away my badge."

"I doubt there's much chance of that." Parker chuckled. He set down his cup, then pulled open a drawer. "I have something here you might be interested in seeing." Sorting through a stack of paper, he pulled two out, sliding them across the desk to Cash. "Appears one of the men shot during the bank robbery in Splendor may have two brothers."

Cash studied the wanted posters, cursing when he noticed the names and resemblance to the oldest outlaw they killed months before during a failed bank robbery.

"Milton and Harrison Penderville. As I recall, the one who died was Chet Penderville. Same features as these two." Cash slid the posters back across the desk. "I figure you're showing these to me for a reason. What do you know about them?"

"I got a telegram from a friend who's a sheriff in the Dakota Territory. Seems these two, and a few others, came through town a week ago. Stirred up quite a fuss, roughed up some locals, and rode out without settling the hotel bill. He didn't know who they were until he searched his posters, finding these. He wanted to be sure I had them in case they came our way."

"Says they're from Virginia. Gabe, Beau, and I figured Chet Penderville and his gang were mostly disgruntled ex-Confederates, out for whatever they could get."

"A lot of them out there. Figure the government, even the people, owe them something." Parker stood, filling his cup, then tilted the pot toward Cash, who shook his head. "Can't blame them in some ways, but a man has no right to turn his hate on innocent people and take what isn't theirs. I thought you'd want to know...in case they show up in Splendor."

Cash scrubbed a weary hand down his face, his eyes red from lack of sleep. Pushing up from the chair, he handed his cup back to Parker, rubbing a hand behind his neck.

"Guess this isn't going to end anytime soon," he said, turning toward the door.

"Not in our lifetime anyway. I expect nothing but trouble from the east over the next several years. Too many people lost their homes, jobs, and families. Some are looking for revenge, others for a new start. Trouble is, you can't pick out the good from the bad much of the time." Parker followed Cash to the door, pulling it open.

"Not until it's too late." Cash's tired, road weary voice spoke as much about his current state as his appearance.

Now, a week later, he looked at each poster, trying to locate the ones of the bank robbers who died the previous summer. One by Cash's bullet. Gabe had a habit of keeping old posters, not wanting to forget the ones who'd been captured or killed for their misdeeds. Something about the youngest outlaw bothered him. He couldn't put his finger on what it was, but felt certain if he could see the image of the boy, it would help him figure out the mystery haunting him.

"Heard you had supper with the new seamstress last night." Beau walked toward him, hanging his hat on a hook, then turned a chair around, resting his arms on the back.

"News travels fast," Cash muttered, not looking up from the stack of posters.

"Some does. Other news takes time, such as what happened in Little Rock." Beau watched as Cash set the papers aside and crossed his arms.

"Not much to tell." He offered a shortened version of what happened at Stephen's ranch and his father-in-law's duplicity. "Finding Wyatt Jackson had been the turning point in our effort to rid the area of the raiders Helen's father had sent to drive Stephen out. Wyatt did what he promised—captured the leader who'd been accused of murder, gave us the name of the man who hired them, and left the others to fend for themselves. The fact is, I doubt the outlaw ever saw a jail or jury."

"That doesn't bother you?" Beau asked, watching Cash's face, seeing his jaw tense.

"Not one bit."

"Too much like what happened to your family in Louisiana." Beau stood, turning the chair back around and pacing to the old stove, picking up a tin cup. "Coffee?"

Cash nodded, accepting the cup as he thought about how he'd doled out justice to those who'd murdered his kin. He understood the type of justice Wyatt intended to impose. A life for a life, the same as Cash had delivered to the men who'd killed his family. In his world, a man took care of those he loved.

"What happened with the father-in-law?"

Cash set his cup down, remembering the results of Stephen's telegram to Helen's father.

"It took one telegram to get the lonely, embittered man to call off the rest of the gang. Thankfully, no additional raids had occurred and no one died. A miracle, considering the type of men the old man hired."

Cash's jaw hardened as he wondered about what possessed a man to rain vengeance down on the man his daughter loved, the father of his grandson. The death of his wife turned him from a man who disapproved of his daughter's choice into one who sought the kind of justice no one could explain. No amount of reason could ease his mind. Those who lost loved ones could become extreme in assuaging their pain, often placing blame where none existed.

He was glad to be home in Splendor and the life he'd begun with people who cared about one another and had each other's back.

"Hello, Mrs. Burns. We have the wood you ordered for your new shelves."

Alison smiled at the young man behind the counter at the lumber mill. Enthusiastic and friendly, he'd helped her when she'd first arrived in town and needed assistance setting up her store.

"Thank you, Monty. Will you be able to deliver it to me?" She counted out the amount he quoted, placing it in his palm.

"Sure thing, Mrs. Burns. I'll have the order over to you this afternoon."

Turning, Alison closed her reticule, almost bumping into the man standing behind her.

"Oh, pardon me..."

"Mrs. Burns. It's good to see you again." Cash tipped his hat, stepping aside to give her space. "What brings you here today?"

It had been a week since they'd had supper together, and she still felt an odd rush of uneasiness in his presence. He'd been a perfect gentleman, their conversation congenial. She didn't want to even consider her feelings for him might have more to do with attraction than caution.

"Monty made some shelves for my shop."

"I'd be happy to bring them over and put them together for you." He leaned against the counter, noticing Monty a few feet away, taking in every word.

"Thank you, but Monty is delivering them this afternoon. I'm not an expert, but I believe I can handle a hammer and nails well enough to create my shelves."

His gaze narrowed at her, a brow quirking up. "I'm sure you can, Mrs. Burns, but I have the time. Why don't I come by later and take care of it so you can concentrate on your work. There's no reason for you to lose income while building a shelf."

"As much as I appreciate your offer, it's not necessary." Although a part of her welcomed whatever help she could get, she knew being cooped up in her store with Cash for a few hours wouldn't help her concentrate on the work she needed to complete. In fact, he'd be a major distraction.

"I understand. In truth, you'd be helping me," he confessed, a sheepish grin tilting his lips up.

She cocked her head to one side, studying him. "How would it help you?"

"It would be a nice change to work with my hands. If you'd prefer to do it yourself, I'll understand. But if you could use the help..." He stared at her, waiting for a response.

His gentle voice, almost a plea, softened her feelings. Alison hadn't expected such an honest and sincere response. She let out a deep breath.

"If you're certain, then yes, I'd appreciate your help." She looked at Monty, who hadn't hidden his curiosity at their exchange. "Thank you again, Monty."

"Like I said, I'll bring over the wood early this afternoon." Turning, he walked toward a workbench, leaving them alone.

"I need to stop by the bank. May I escort you to your shop?"

She nodded, slipping her hand through the arm he offered. "Your offer is very generous, Mr. Coulter."

"I've learned a few things during my time in Splendor. One of them is the people in this town help each other."

"My experience is many people offer, but few respond when needed." Alison thought back to her mother and how no one offered any assistance when her mother went from farm to farm, asking for a few hours of their time to help with the crops. She'd been turned away by neighbor after neighbor. No one had time for the war widow or her needs.

"Then you've been living in the wrong place. Perhaps Splendor is what you're searching for."

She glanced at him, her gaze focusing on his ever observant eyes. "And what makes you think I'm searching?"

"Well, now, let's just say you have this look about you telling others you're not quite sure where you stand. Experience tells me it's a look of someone not ready to put down roots or make close friends." He looked down at her. "Am I right?"

The comment surprised her, causing her heart to race. Cash had read her so easily. *Had others?*

"Maybe it's the look of someone trying to fit in." Her mind whirled as they continued toward the shop. Her plans were set. She didn't need anyone in Splendor questioning her motives for being here.

Cash mulled her comment over for a brief moment, then chuckled. "I don't think so, but perhaps you'll prove me wrong." Stopping at the entrance to the shop, he waited while she pulled out her key. "I'll see you in a couple hours, Mrs. Burns."

Nodding, Alison disappeared inside, closing the door behind her. Shrugging out of her coat, she took a deep breath to calm the panic caused by Cash's comments. He'd somehow figured out there was more to her settling in Splendor than the need to move west. Or had it just been a lucky guess? Either way, she needed to squelch those thoughts and get him to believe her sole motivation for leaving Kentucky was to begin a new life, away from the ravages of war. The fact she planned to kill one of the locals could never come to light.

"All done." Cash stepped back after securing the shelving to the wall, checked his work, then made one more adjustment.

"It's perfect. I don't know how you were able to build it in such a short period of time." Alison studied it, then turned toward him, her eyes sparkling. "You've done so much better than I could've ever done."

Chuckling, he set the hammer down. "I would hope so. I used to help with the carpentry on my uncle's farm."

"You're hired for any other projects." Walking to her work table, she picked up her coin purse. "How much do I owe you?"

He looked as if she'd slapped him. "You don't owe me anything." He held up his hand when she started to protest. "I did it because we're neighbors, not because I expect anything in return." Looking out the window at the darkening sky, Cash grabbed his coat, slipping it on before walking toward her. "It felt good doing physical work, building something useful."

"Can I at least offer you more coffee? Or supper?"

"I don't believe I can drink one more cup, and as much as I'd like to stay and sample your cooking, Sheriff Evans asked me to make the rounds tonight. I'd best get going." He settled his hat down and smiled. "Thank you. It's been a good day."

"For me also, Mr. Coulter." She stepped to within a foot of him, feeling a pull she couldn't break. Staring up into his eyes, she watched as they widened and his face softened.

He closed the distance between them, tilting her chin up with his finger, deep hunger gripping him as her tongue slipped out to moisten her full, red lips. He let out a breath, then lowered his head, placing a soft kiss on her forehead before stepping back.

"Have a good evening, Mrs. Burns."

He walked out without another word. Alison had never known a man like him. There was something about him that drew her in, even as parts of her wanted to pull back. After studying him all day, she decided it was his eyes. Light green in the center with a circle of deep green rimmed with black, they never seemed to stop searching. They were almost haunting, holding tight onto whatever secrets Cash didn't want to share. Not too much different than her.

He was right to imply Alison held secrets. Watching him today, she had no doubt he held some, too.

Stepping into the crisp evening air, he looked up the street, then down, noting the progress on a couple new buildings. The town had grown since he'd left for Little Rock. He'd been gone a few short months, yet he'd still been surprised at the changes.

"Cash."

He turned at the familiar voice and smiled. "Noah."

"Thought I recognized Hunter outside the sheriff's office. Did you just get back?"

"Close to a week ago. I've stopped by the livery a few times to visit. Where have you been hiding?"

"Abby needed my help with some business in Big Pine. I saw Sheriff Parker while we were there and he told me you'd ridden out early that morning." Noah shook his head. "I'm surprised we didn't see you."

"I got in late and left early."

Noah chuckled. "Couldn't wait to get home?"

"Seems so." Cash started walking toward his horse, Noah keeping pace. "Hunter's favoring his right foreleg."

"Let me take a look." Noah skimmed his hand down the horse's flank, then picked up the leg. "Nothing in the shoe. He may have a sprain, but I doubt it's serious. Why don't you leave him with me a few days so I can keep watch over him?"

"I don't know why you don't hire someone to run the livery for you. You've got other projects and plenty of money—"

"It's not my money, Cash, and you know it. I have a little savings and a couple good businesses, but Abby's the wealthy one." Noah's jaw pulsed in frustration at the one characteristic of his marriage he'd never been able to fully reconcile. Muttering a curse, he led Hunter into the livery.

Cash didn't say any more on the subject as he removed the saddle and bridle. "I've got to make the rounds, then I'll be getting supper at Suzanne's. Why don't you join me?"

Noah let out a deep breath, letting the last of his irritation go. "I'd like to, but Abby's got supper waiting for me at home. Why don't you come out to our place instead? I know she'd like to see you."

Cash thought of Abby and the home Noah built her on the hill above Splendor. It was beautiful, yet nowhere near as large as the one she'd left behind.

Abby sold her ranch and house to the Pelletiers before marrying Noah. Her late father, King Tolbert, built the house years before, showcasing his position as a prominent citizen of Splendor. Luke and Ginny Pelletier lived there now, rolling the property into the original Redemption's Edge ranch where Dax and Rachel lived, making the Pelletier spread the largest in western Montana.

She still owned many other properties in Splendor, as well as investments in other industries, including mining and lumber. Even though he protested, Cash knew Noah adored his wife and accepted her extreme wealth, even if he didn't embrace it. They'd been through a lot before giving into the love the entire town knew drew them together.

"Another time, my friend. Think I'll eat in town tonight."

"No problem, but we'll expect you to visit soon." Noah walked over to another stall holding a buckskin with black mane and tail—an almost identical horse to Hunter. "You can ride Joker until I figure out what's going on with Hunter."

"I've seen Joker before and admired his lines. He's almost a twin to Hunter."

"That he is. Well, I'd best get cleaned up and head home. Abby gets worried if I'm gone too long."

"Thanks, Noah. I'll see you tomorrow."

Once Cash finished his rounds, he ate a solitary supper before taking a narrow road behind the buildings on Main Street toward the house he shared with Beau. It sat between Gabe's place and the house the town had built for the school teacher. Closing the door behind him and striking a lucifer, he lit lamps in his bedroom, Beau's room, the front room, and kitchen, giving the small space a warm glow as he started a fire in the fireplace. Beau made sure the place had a large woodpile out front, a good supply of whiskey, and a well-stocked kitchen, even though they ate at the boardinghouse restaurant as often as they cooked.

"How about a drink?" Beau asked as he entered the house, chuckling when he saw Cash already setting two glasses on the counter.

Filling each, Cash handed one to Beau. "To a quiet night." They sipped their whiskey, Cash lowering himself into a large chair near the fire. "Didn't see you tonight."

"Gabe had me ride south to check out some of the sheep ranches. Seems they're missing several head and have experienced a few strange *accidents*." Beau finished his drink, then poured another.

"Like what?"

"Fires, fences cut, a stolen wagon." Beau looked up. "It was found all busted up."

"No one's been hurt?"

"Not yet. I figure it's only a matter of time. Gabe tried to warn the sheep farmers about the risks of moving into cattle country, but they were determined to make it work. Seems someone is out to close them down."

Cash sipped his drink as he stared at the fire, trying to guess who might be trying to drive the sheepherders out. "Might be one of the ranchers closer to the Idaho border."

"Maybe. After your experience in Little Rock, I wondered if it might be raiders hired by ranchers who don't want to be tied to accidents or rustling."

"Doesn't matter. We just need to find out who's giving the orders and hope it isn't anyone we know."

Standing, Cash set his glass in the sink, stretching his arms above his head to loosen the ache in his back. "I'm worn out. See you in the morning."

He thought he'd be out within minutes of climbing into bed and closing his eyes. Instead, he couldn't get the image of a certain honey-haired woman, with almond shaped eyes the color of rich chocolate, out of his mind. Even as his instincts told him something wasn't right, that she had something to hide, he couldn't stop the wanting. It had been a battle to keep from pulling her to him, kissing her until they were both weak.

A woman like Alison deserved better than an embattled ex-Confederate soldier who still suffered from nightmares and bouts of rage. He hid his demons well. Still, he didn't have it in him to saddle an unsuspecting woman with the monsters in his soul. Maybe someday, when he learned to forget, he might have a chance. As far as he could tell, that day was years away.

Chapter Five

"Here you are, gentlemen." Suzanne Briar set supper plates in front of Cash and Beau a couple nights later. "Now, don't you go showing your food to anyone else in the restaurant. I prepared these special for the two of you." She winked as she turned to leave, running smack into Nick Barnett, one of the partners in the town's two saloons.

Grasping her arms, he steadied her, seeing a flush creep up her face. They'd been dancing around feelings for each other since he'd first come to town, taking a room in her boardinghouse. Neither had acted on their attraction.

Since then, he'd built the Dixie Saloon, welcomed his business partner, Lena Campanel Evans, to town, and partnered with Lena and Gabe to purchase the existing Wild Rose Saloon. They'd then built an upscale hotel, the St. James, at the other end of town. Their latest project was to buy into Suzanne's boardinghouse and expand the restaurant, as well as the number of rooms she offered. The two of them had been working closely together for weeks, yet neither had acted on the desire whirling around them.

"Steady, sweetheart." Nick's smile triggered an immediate increase in her heart rate, his touch causing heat to flow through her body.

A widow, losing both her husband and young daughter to a blinding snowstorm years before, Suzanne had sealed herself off from the possibility of loving again. Nick's quiet resolve, absolute loyalty to those he cared about, and strong presence continued to chip away at her resistance, making her wonder how much longer she could avoid the truth in her heart.

"Sorry, Nick. We're so busy, I..." Her voice trailed off as she looked up at his face. Tall with broad shoulders and his trademark black attire, he wore a patch over his left eye. She didn't know the history behind it, but it didn't deter from the strength she saw when her gaze met his.

"Why don't you rest for a few minutes? I can ask one of the other servers to handle your tables."

She stepped away, instantly missing his touch when his hands slipped from her arms.

"Who would you ask? We're *all* busy tonight." She bit her lower lip, then drew in a deep breath. "Why don't you join the deputies?" She glanced over her shoulder at the table behind her, noticing Beau's and Cash's attention on her and Nick. "I'd better get back to the kitchen."

A sigh escaped as Nick watched her go, then he turned toward Cash and Beau. "Mind if I join you?"

"Not at all." Cash took a bite of the pan fried steak Suzanne had prepared to celebrate his return. Waiting until Nick took a seat, he cut another bite, holding the steak in the air. "When are you going to claim her?" He narrowed his gaze at Nick before slipping the steak into his mouth.

Leaning back in his chair and crossing his arms, Nick let out a breath. "You know, I could pretend I have no idea what you're talking about."

"But you won't," Cash countered, taking a bite of mashed potatoes.

Nick glanced over his shoulder toward the kitchen, seeing Suzanne emerge juggling three plates piled high with food. "The timing isn't right."

Beau laughed, cutting another piece of his steak. "It's never right. I say state your feelings. If you don't, someone might beat you to it."

Nick tensed at Beau's comment. "Have you heard something?"

"I'm always hearing things, Nick. You know Stan Petermann's wife died last summer. Word is he's got a sweet spot for Suzanne. And Silas Jenks at the lumber mill has been coming in here more often than he used to. Makes me wonder." Beau lifted his brows as he stuck another bite of steak in his mouth.

Mumbling a curse, Nick stood, shoving his hands in his pockets. "I'm headed to the Dixie. Stop by and I'll buy you two miscreants a drink."

Cash shook his head, a grin splitting his otherwise somber face, staring at Beau as Nick walked away. "You may have gone a mite too far."

"It's all truthful. I spoke to Silas yesterday and he asked me about Nick and Suzanne, as if I'd know anything. Told him I didn't know what he was talking about and left." Beau leaned forward, lowering his voice. "Nick needs to make a move or that woman's going to be snatched up by another man."

"You wouldn't be referring to you, right?"

"Suzanne's a good woman, but I've got my sights on someone else." Beau set down his fork, chewing slowly.

"Caroline Iverson."

Beau's eyes widened, but he stayed quiet, a muscle in his jaw twitching.

"She's a wonderful woman. Beautiful, kind. You couldn't do much better." Cash slid his chair back as the front door opened and Alison walked in, slipping out of her coat.

Beau turned, lifting his hand in a welcome gesture, then lowered his voice. "Well now, it's Mrs. Burns. Have you seen each other since having supper together?"

Cash didn't respond. He couldn't stop staring, the attraction he felt for her squeezing his chest. She stood not fifteen feet away, her hair twisted into a loose bun at the nape of her neck, and even from this distance, he could see her radiant brown eyes searching the restaurant. Seeing Beau, she took a hesitant step forward before her gaze locked on

Cash. He could see her suck in a quick breath, knowing she felt the same attraction to him.

Standing, Beau made a slight bow. "Good evening, Mrs. Burns. Won't you join us?"

"Well...I..."

Cash stood, pulling out a chair, encouraging her to sit down.

"Thank you, Mr. Coulter. I don't want to hold either of you up from any plans."

Not glancing at Beau, Cash answered. "I have none."

Beau cleared his throat, already feeling like an outsider. "Cash, I need to start the rounds. I'll see you later." Shifting his attention to Alison, he made another slight blow. "I'll check your shop while I'm out."

"Thank you, Mr. Davis. I appreciate it."

He shot a look at Cash before leaving, his mouth twisting into a knowing smile.

"What would you like tonight, Alison?" Suzanne stood next to them as she set a full cup in front of Alison, refilling Cash's cup with coffee.

She blinked a couple times before forcing her gaze from Cash's. "Whatever your special is would be fine."

Suzanne pursed her lips, eyes sparking. "Anything else for you, Cash?"

"I'll wait to have dessert until Mrs. Burns is ready."

Suzanne nodded before leaving the two alone.

"Thank you for letting me join you, Mr. Coulter."

Cash leaned forward, resting his arms on the table, flashing her one of his rare smiles, transforming his closed features into one of the most handsome faces she'd ever seen. "This is a small town. Would you do me the honor of calling me Cash?"

The deep timber of his voice washed over her, reminding her of what had almost happened in her shop a few days before. "All right, but only if you call me Alison."

"Done. Now, I have a question for you."

"All right." Her voice didn't shake, even as her mind went on alert.

"You said your husband fought and died in the war."

"Yes. Like you, he served the Confederacy." Another lie she'd add to her growing list of deceptions.

"Under whose command?"

Her lips parted as her mind tried to rifle through the names of Confederate commanders. "Um...I'm afraid his name escapes me right now. Who did you serve under?"

"General Hood." Saying the name, remembering the lives lost, caused his chest to tighten. All he wanted was to put the war, the death and destruction, behind him. "You mentioned your mother died not long after your husband. It must have been a hard decision to move across the country and build a new life."

"Um...yes, it was."

"Why Splendor?"

Alison knew her standard response wouldn't quell further questions. Cash was too perceptive. She opened her mouth to speak, saying a silent prayer for the right words, when Suzanne walked up.

"How about some pie?" Suzanne picked up the empty plates and waited.

"One for each of us, Suzanne. And more coffee, please." Cash touched the rim of his empty cup. He looked back at Alison. "You were about to tell me why you picked Splendor."

"It's simple. I saw an ad Mr. Clausen posted about a shop for sale. We came to an agreement and here I am." She took a forkful of the pie Suzanne had set before her. "Oh, this is wonderful. She makes the best pie. Don't you think?"

Cash knew he'd struck a nerve, but decided to let the change of subject pass. He needed to bide his time. Eventually, the truth would surface.

"Yes, she does."

They continued with small talk of inconsequential, impersonal subjects while finishing their dessert and coffee. When Suzanne took the last of the plates away, Cash pulled out some money, laying it on the table.

"I'll escort you home." Standing, he pulled out her chair.

"It's not necessary. You already know I live above the shop."

"Then it won't take long to walk you home." After helping her with her coat, he held out his arm.

They walked in silence, passing several closed stores and the crowded Dixie Saloon before crossing the street and stopping at her shop.

"May I call on you, Alison?" The question sprung from his lips unbidden, surprising Cash. Meeting for supper a couple times, helping her with her shelves, even buying her meal tonight didn't constitute a true courting. His question went beyond being neighborly.

He couldn't remember the last time he'd been attracted enough to a woman to want to court her, knowing it had to be before the war. Even with the secrets he knew she held, he wanted to see her, learn about her past, discover if they could build something together.

Her tongue slid out, moistening her lips. Alison knew she should decline and not become too close to anyone in Splendor. "I'd like that." Her stomach churned the moment the words were out.

His face relaxed, the creases between his brows smoothing. "Would Saturday evening suit you?"

"Yes, it would." A smile tugged at her lips when she saw the relief on his face.

He waited as she unlocked the door and stepped inside.

"I'm glad you were in the restaurant tonight, Cash. I look forward to Saturday."

"Same here, Alison." He lifted his hand, wanting to brush his knuckles along her jaw and down her neck. Instead, he touched the brim of his hat, nodded, then walked away.

She watched him leave, moving a hand to her throat as butterflies stirred in her stomach. For the first time in her life, she began to understand what her mother had said about experiencing an immediate pull to a man. But it couldn't come at a worse time or in a more inappropriate town.

Closing the door, her mind raced ahead to Saturday and what she would wear. Although she came to Splendor with one task in mind, Alison convinced herself having a little fun while sorting out her brother's death couldn't hurt. She'd relax and enjoy herself while beginning to ask the questions she'd been holding back. And she'd start Saturday night with Cash Coulter.

Chapter Six

"Parker believes the men in these posters are related to Chet Penderville, one of the robbers killed during the bank holdup." Cash had waited to show Gabe the posters until he'd gone through the older ones in the desk. He'd found nothing on the men killed in the attempted bank robbery.

Gabe studied the images of Milton and Harrison, noting the resemblance. He, Cash, and Beau sat in the jail, talking as the sun began to set over the nearby mountains. Other than the saloon, hotel, and restaurants, most businesses would be closing within the hour.

"I agree with him." Gabe pointed to the name of their home state of Virginia. "Wasn't Chet from there?"

"Near Lynchburg. From what we learned, he and the others in the gang fought for the South." Beau scratched the stubble on his face. "Parker have any more to go on than the posters and his gut feelings?"

"Nope." Cash returned to his chair, leaning back and crossing his arms. "We could talk to Luke and ask him to use his Pinkerton connections to do more digging."

Luke Pelletier had been a Pinkerton agent for a while before meeting and marrying Ginny. According to Dax, he still had a solid relationship with Allan Pinkerton, the founder of the well-known detective agency.

"I'll ride out to their ranch and talk to him. For now, we need to assume they are related to Chet and planning to avenge his death." Gabe buckled his gun belt around his waist, then checked his revolver. "Cash, notify Horace Clausen about these two and show him and his employees the posters. Did Parker have any idea where they were last seen?"

"I don't believe he's heard any more since his friend in the Dakota Territory sent the telegram. That would be about two weeks ago. I'll send him a message, ask if he's learned more." Cash started to follow Gabe to the door when it flew open, almost slamming into Gabe's face.

"Sheriff, glad I found you. You've got to come right away." Stan Petermann's face glistened with sweat, his voice shaking.

"Calm down and tell me what's happening." Gabe nodded toward a chair.

"There's no time, Gabe. Clay McCord is trying to talk young Ben out of shooting, but the kid has this wild look. You need to come with me." Stan took off with Gabe, Cash, and Beau right behind him.

The general store was on the same side of Main Street, three doors down. As they approached, the sounds of shouting came from inside. Gabe reached out and grabbed Stan by the collar when the man continued to surge ahead.

"Get back behind Beau and stay back. We'll take over from here."

"All right, Sheriff, but I think Ben is serious about shooting Clay if he doesn't get what he wants."

"And what does he want, Stan?" Cash stood beside him, his gun drawn.

"Food."

All three lawmen muttered curses at the same time the shouting from inside stopped.

"No gunfire. Maybe Clay is talking some sense into the kid. Beau, stay out here with Stan. Cash, you come with me."

Staying close to the side of the building, they inched forward until Gabe could see inside the store.

"Who is Clay McCord?" Cash asked as he knelt, Gabe looking through the dirt-encrusted window.

"Stan's employee. Rode into town while you were gone." Gabe moved to get a better view. "Clay is talking to the boy. The kid has a gun, but it's by his side." He motioned to Cash, speaking in a hushed voice. "Let's move to the door. We need to be ready if he lifts the gun." They took positions a few feet away, listening to the conversation.

"What's your name, kid?"

"Benjamin. Most people call me Ben."

"Trust me, Ben. You don't want to use that gun." Clay moved a step closer, holding out his hand. "If you're hungry, I'm certain we can work something out with Mr. Petermann. He's a good man, and—"

"I don't believe you." Ben's voice trembled, his body shaking as he spoke. "My sister came in yesterday, asking for some help until we could get the money for food. He said he didn't provide charity." He swiped a hand across his face to stop the tears. "I got some stuff of my pa's we can sell." Reaching into his pocket, he pulled out a worn pocket watch, an old pair of spectacles, and a ring. "This here's his wedding ring. It ought to be worth something, right, mister?"

Gabe watched as Clay took another step closer, crouching low and looking at what he held out.

"That's a real fine ring. And I'll bet no one in town has a watch like that one." He smiled, seeing him nod. "Tell you what, Ben. I'll take the watch and spectacles, but you keep the ring. You might find you need it one day." Clay stood, taking some coins out of his pocket. "Will this be enough?"

The boy's eyes widened as he counted what Clay held out. "Yes, sir."

Clay slid the money into Ben's outstretched hand, shaking his head when the boy took one last look at the watch and spectacles.

"You could do me a big favor, Ben. I don't have a true home right now and it would be a real shame to lose these fine items. Would you mind keeping them for me until I get a place where I can keep them?"

"Yes, sir. I can do that." His shoulders relaxed as he slid his pa's belongings into a pocket. "Do you think I have enough for flour, sugar, beans, and some bacon?"

"I can guarantee you do." Clay walked around the store, picking up what Ben needed, setting the items on the counter before giving him a price. "Looks like you may have a little left over for the next time."

Ben turned and ran toward the door, picked up a worn war bag, and tossed it on the counter. Clay stuffed the items inside, then handed it back.

"I'll bet your ma and pa will be real proud when you come home with this."

Ben's face went still. "It's just me and my sister."

Clay walked around the counter, looking down at Ben. "You come in here anytime and we'll work something out with Mr. Petermann. If you need anything, my name's Clay McCord and I'm staying at the boardinghouse."

"Yes, sir." Slinging the old war bag over his shoulder, Ben started for the door.

"And Ben?"

"Yes, sir?"

"You be mighty careful with that gun. Most people don't take too kindly to having it pointed at them."

Ben chewed his bottom lip, nodded, then took off outside. Breaking into a run a few yards from the store, he never noticed Gabe and Cash standing a few feet away.

Sliding the gun into his holster, Cash took a breath before he and Gabe stepped into the store.

"Gentlemen. What can I do for you?" Clay folded his arms, resting a hip against the counter. He recognized the sheriff, but not the man with him.

"That was quite a job getting Ben to put away his gun."

"He just needed a push in the right direction, Sheriff."

"Still, it was mighty generous of you. Clay, this is my other deputy, Cash Coulter."

The men shook hands, sizing each other up, as Beau and Stan walked inside.

"Why didn't you arrest that boy, Sheriff?" Stan's face reddened when he saw Clay standing by the counter. "You didn't give him any food, did you?"

"No, sir. Ben paid me for what he needed." Although congenial, Clay's voice held a trace of disgust. "I don't suppose you'd consider giving Ben and his sister a little credit? Seems they could use a little help to get on their feet."

Stan paced to the counter, then turned abruptly toward the front door. "Those two have all the credit I can give them. Their pa ran up a bill of fifteen dollars before he took off without a word to anyone."

Clay cocked his head. "Ben told me his ma and pa are dead."

"Ma's been dead a while. Their pa couldn't deal with losing her and raising two children, so he left about the time you came to town. I feel for them, but I can't provide food to everyone on credit." Stan's arms hung at his sides, his shoulders slumping. "Wish I could, but I have to draw the line somewhere."

"Where do they live? Does the sister work?" Clay understood Stan's situation. Still, he believed there had to be a solution.

Gabe stepped forward. "There's a rundown shack about a mile north of town. Ben and his sister, Rosemary, live there, along with a couple other kids who've lost their parents. We've tried to find places for them, but most families aren't doing well enough to take on extra children. Plus, the sister is a little older."

"Older?" Clay's eyes narrowed.

"Ben is nine. Rosemary is eighteen, maybe nineteen." Gabe scrubbed a hand down his face. "Suzanne Briar has Rosemary help clean the boardinghouse, same as Ginny Pelletier used to do before she married Luke. It's not much, but I know Suzanne gives her leftover food a couple times a week. The reverend and his wife are trying to set up a fund for children who've lost their parents, but it's going slow. Nick is planning to offer her a cleaning job when business picks up at the hotel."

At the sound of shouting from across the street, Cash walked toward the front window, glancing out. "Well, damn." He glanced at Gabe. "Looks like the miners got paid and are already starting a ruckus at the Dixie.”

“I’ll head over there while you and Beau make the rounds. Stop by for a drink when you’re done.” Gabe nodded at Stan and Clay before leaving.

“If all is good here, we’ll take off, Stan. Good to meet you, Clay.”

Clay nodded, his mind focused on Ben, his sister, and the other children who were barely able to survive.

Cash and Beau split up. Cash headed toward the bank at the south end of town, still needing to warn Horace about the gang of robbers who might be headed toward Splendor. Beau took the other side of the street. They’d check the businesses before joining Gabe for a drink, take one more tour around town, then bed down for the night.

The bank had closed by the time Cash arrived. Pulling out his pocket watch, he considered riding to Horace’s place a little ways from town.

“Mr. Coulter. How are you this evening?”

Cash turned at the familiar voice to see Alison locking her shop door, then strolling toward him. The now familiar sense of desire rolled through his body as she stopped next to him.

"Alison, I told you to call me Cash, remember? I'm doing fine. Where are you off to?" His gaze wandered over her before settling on her face.

"Mr. Petermann and I have a deal. If he's had fabric in his store for a few months without selling it, I buy it from him at a fair price, then make it into dresses."

"An enterprising woman. I like that."

She flushed at the compliment, then glanced at the bank. "I saw Mr. Clausen walk past my store to his carriage a little while ago. Did you need to see him?"

"Nothing that can't wait until tomorrow. I'll walk with you to the store."

Although it wasn't far, Alison enjoyed the company, as well as the opportunity to ask some questions.

"I heard there was a bank robbery in town a few months ago. Were you here when it happened?"

"Yes."

"It must have been horrible. I mean, all that bloodshed." She worked to keep her voice calm, anxious to get the answers she needed.

"Dealing with outlaws is never easy. This time was no different."

"I heard several of the robbers were killed."

Cash stopped outside the general store, his lips thinning as he thought of that day. The memory wasn't pleasant.

"Yes, they were." He looked up to see Stan and Clay still inside. "Looks like Petermann is waiting for you. Have a pleasant night, Alison." Taking a few quick strides, he turned back toward her, reining in his irritation. "I'll see you Saturday."

Her heart sank at his abrupt departure and hard voice. She'd pushed too far, too soon, hoping to get some information about that day, how it happened, and the robbers involved. Cash, as a deputy and possible friend, seemed to be the best person to ask. It was clear he didn't wish to speak of the robbers or their deaths.

Before leaving Kentucky, Alison and her mother had argued about what she'd ask once she arrived in Splendor. Her mother urged caution, telling her not to draw too much attention to herself, or mention her connection to Bobby. It would do no good to storm into town and make allegations before getting the facts. Her mother believed the same as Alison—Bobby would never have taken up with a gang of robbers, let alone drawn a gun on innocent people. Somehow, he'd been gunned down by mistake or in anger. Or it was just a cold-blooded killing. Alison took a deep breath, reminding herself to take it slow.

"You have a pleasant night also, Cash." She stepped inside when Stan opened the door, taking one last look over her shoulder as Cash walked away.

"You sure have been staring into your whiskey a long time, Cash. Do you plan on drinking it?" Beau tossed his drink back, then signaled for Paul to pour another. He'd been the bartender at the Dixie since it opened, knowing enough to keep the drinks flowing until Gabe or Nick cut someone off. Paul saw no need to hesitate when the sheriff leaned against the bar on the other side of Beau.

"Got some things on my mind." Cash closed his eyes, remembering a woman from his past. A girl he'd known since childhood and loved as he became a man.

He'd been young and foolish. They'd exchanged promises before he joined the Confederacy. As two years of brutal warfare passed, all that kept him sane were thoughts of her waiting for his return. Then the letter arrived, announcing her plans to marry another. A merchant who'd chosen to sit out the war and grow fat, taking advantage of the profits to be made from supplying armies on both sides. The last Cash heard, he'd been shot by Confederates as a spy, his wife stripped of their home and wealth, the man she'd chosen over him mired in scandal.

Opening his eyes, he picked up the glass, finishing the drink in one swallow.

"Another?" Paul stood on the other side of the bar, the bottle ready.

"Not tonight." Cash turned toward Gabe and Beau. "I'm going to make one more round, then turn in. Guess the last few weeks are catching up with me."

He didn't wait for a response. Pushing open the swinging doors, he stepped into the chilled night air, taking a deep breath, shoving his hands in his coat pockets. Two doors down, the St. James Hotel shown bright in the cloudless sky. Gabe had been smart to partner with Nick and Lena in building the grand structure. They still had a few pictures to hang and furniture to buy, but it had done well since opening a month earlier.

Crossing the street, he headed straight toward Alison's shop. He could see the pale glow of light in the upstairs window where she made her home. Pulling on the front door of the shop to confirm she'd locked it, he stepped back and looked up, hearing the faint sound of someone humming. It tugged at him in a way he didn't expect and didn't want to admit. He had no plans to marry. From his point of view, the world wasn't a place to give your trust to one woman, and it certainly wasn't a safe place to raise children. Besides, he had little to offer, other than a blackened heart.

The smart move would be to stop by tomorrow, cancel their plans for supper on Saturday, and get back to the life he'd started before leaving Splendor for Stephen's ranch. Forming an attachment to any woman would lead to nothing except grief and despair. Learning to trust one was out of the question.

Turning, he walked past the bank, another restaurant, the general store, and a couple other closed shops before entering the jail. He'd down a cup of stale, bitter coffee, then take the short walk home to swallow what remained in his bottle of whiskey, and pray for a night of peace.

Chapter Seven

"It may take some time to find my replacement, Uncle Charles. Don't you think we should start soon?" Rachel paced back and forth in the cramped exam room.

She'd moved to Splendor a few years before to help her uncle in his clinic. As a nurse in Union field camps during the war, she'd seen more death than most nurses saw in a lifetime, treated horrific wounds, and taken care of soldiers with every type of malady. Her marriage to Dax Pelletier, then the birth of their son, Patrick, meant she couldn't devote as much time as needed to patients.

Doc Worthington stepped closer to his niece, placing a hand on her shoulder. "Of course, you are right, Rachel." A deep sigh preceded him lowering himself into a nearby chair, a tired resolve claiming him. "Do you know anyone in Splendor with the experience?"

"I wish I did. Many of the men have dealt with gun or knife wounds and setting broken bones. Some of the women have helped as midwives and nursed family during an illness. Few have dealt with most of the illnesses and injuries we get in the clinic. We'll need to look at Big Pine, or perhaps bring someone out from the east, the same as you did with me."

He chuckled. "You are family and had finished your work for the army. It didn't take a lot to convince you to join me. I'm afraid finding someone to replace you will require much more of an effort."

"Perhaps. We won't know until we start. I can announce it at the church ladies' meeting this week, and ask Suzanne to post a notice at the boardinghouse. I'm certain we can also post notices at the general store, telegraph office, lumber mill, and restaurants. That's how we found our school teacher. The people in Splendor sent letters to their relatives and friends."

"Doc! Doc, are you in there?" Noah Brandt's anxious voice boomed through the front door.

Doc pulled open the exam room door, stepping aside to let Noah carry Abby inside and set her on the table.

"Noah, I'm fine." Abby placed both hands on her stomach, her face wrenching in pain as another spasm ripped through her.

"Her water broke, Doc." Noah held his hands out, palms up, his eyes pleading for support.

"You did right. Why don't you wait out in the front while we get Abby comfortable?" Doc held the door open, signaling for Noah to leave.

"But..."

"Come on, Noah." Rachel slipped her hand into his, tugging him through the door, then closing it. "It could be several hours. Why don't I go get Suzanne or Gabe to keep you company?" Noah and Gabe had grown up together in New York, joined the Union Army at the same time, and traveled west together after the war. They were closer than most brothers.

Noah's hands shook as he scrubbed them down his face. "I, uh..."

The door slammed open as Gabe and Lena rushed inside.

"Is Abby all right?" Gabe placed a hand on Noah's shoulder. "Lena saw you carrying her across the street."

"She's..." Noah's voice faltered.

"Yes. She's having the baby." Rachel touched Noah's arm, waiting until he looked at her. "I'm going to help the doctor. Will you be all right out here?"

"We'll stay with him." Lena tugged at Noah's hand, pulling him toward a chair, as Rachel stepped into the exam room and shut the door.

Noah started to lower himself into a chair before he heard a scream.

"I've got to get in there." He tried to push past Gabe.

Gabe grabbed both of his arms, forcing Noah to look at him, his voice low and commanding. "Let Doc and Rachel do their job. All you'll do is distract them."

"Can't sit right now." Noah glanced between Gabe and Lena.

Lena's expression softened. "Gabe, why don't you take Noah to the Dixie for a couple drinks? I'll come get you once I have news."

"I can't—"

"Lena's right, Noah. No sense in you sitting here stewing. Once you get a couple whiskeys in you, you'll feel a lot better. Come on." Gabe gripped Noah's thick arm, guiding him toward the door.

"You'll come right away and get me?" He glanced over his shoulder at Lena, not wanting to go, yet knowing he might lose his sanity if he stayed and waited.

"Yes, Noah. I will." She held his gaze, giving him what reassurance she could, understanding how difficult this had to be for him.

Cash, Beau, and Nick approached from different directions as Gabe guided Noah toward the Dixie.

Nick reached them first. "Any news?"

Cash and Beau stopped next to them, listening.

"Nothing yet." Gabe moved an unwilling Noah further away from the clinic. "Rachel thinks it could be a long wait. How about you three join us for a whiskey? Lena will come get us when she knows more."

Noah sat at a corner table, his friends close, an untouched shot of whiskey on the table before him. Even though he wanted to down a full bottle, he didn't want to cloud his mind.

It had been three hours since Noah stormed into the clinic with Abby. Gabe had walked back a couple times to speak with Lena. Each time, he cringed as Abby's labor pains continued, her screams piercing the thin wall.

"Noah just sits, Lena. His gaze focused straight ahead, refusing the whiskey sitting in front of him." Gabe sat next to her, leaning forward, cradling his face in his hands. "I'm glad we have Jack. I don't think I could go through this if it were you in there."

"You'd do fine, Gabe, and so will Noah. Every man deals with his wife having a baby in a different way." She turned as another loud moan preceded a scream. A moment later, the unmistakable crying of a baby drew her attention. She gripped Gabe's arm. "It's the baby."

Jumping up, Gabe dashed toward the door. "I'll get Noah." He covered the distance to the Dixie in no more than a minute, shoving open the saloon door, his gaze latching onto Noah's.

"What?" Noah pushed from the table, knocking over his chair, his legs trembling as he walked toward Gabe.

"Come on, Papa." A broad smile split Gabe's face. "Abby's had your baby."

"What will you name him?" Doc Worthington's expression softened as he watched Noah hold the small bundle in his arms.

"What do you think, Abby?" Noah didn't take his eyes off his son.

She let out a tired breath, her face showing her exhaustion as a weak smile tilted the corners of her mouth. "Unless you've changed your mind, I believe we settled on Noah Gabriel Brandt."

"Yes." Noah's eyes clouded as moisture filled them. "We'll call him Gabriel."

"Noah Gabriel Brandt. That's a fine name." Doc finished scrawling in a journal, then turned toward them. "His heart and lungs are strong, color's good, and his size is what I'd expect. Abby will need rest, Noah. Do you have someone to stay with her and Gabriel when you can't be there?"

Noah glanced up in alarm. "I didn't think about that."

"I may have someone for you." Doc thought a moment. "In fact, I believe you already know her. Lydia Rinehart."

"Of course I know Lydia. She's the oldest of the orphans living with Dax and Rachel." Noah thought it an excellent idea.

Rachel walked back in, holding a cup of coffee for her uncle. "Did someone say my name?"

"Don't you think Lydia would be perfect to help Noah and Abby with Gabriel?" The doctor accepted the cup, taking a sip.

"Gabriel? What a wonderful name." She winked at Noah, thinking it quite appropriate he named his son after his closest friend. "I agree. Lydia's been wonderful with Patrick, and I'm certain she'd be excited to help with Gabriel. Would you like me to speak with her?"

"We'd appreciate it, Rachel." Noah shifted the baby to his other side, never losing eye contact with his son. "She's welcome to stay with us in one of the extra bedrooms, if that's all right with you, Abby." He looked down at his wife and smiled. Her closed eyes and easy breaths indicated she'd fallen asleep.

"Sit down, Noah. She'll wake up as soon as Gabriel starts demanding to eat." Rachel pulled a chair closer to the bed. "Fair warning. Life as you know it is officially over."

Bloody Basin, Dakota Territory

"I don't understand why we're hesitating, Milt. We need to hit the bank and get out of this worthless town." Harry Penderville threw back another shot of whiskey, wincing as it burned down his throat. "The boys are restless, and so am I."

Milt Penderville didn't react to his younger brother's frustration. Instead, he kept his focus on the woman standing at the top of the stairs. He didn't care how long they stayed in Bloody Basin, as long as they got two things before they left.

First, he'd bed the woman staring down at him. It had been too long since he'd felt soft, hot skin against his. Milt had watched her for three nights, stunned that she seemed to be saving herself for one man—a rancher who strolled in late each night. It didn't matter to Milt. He'd bide his time and get what he wanted.

Second, the boys would rob the lone bank in town before anyone realized they'd been cleaned out, then they'd ride to the next town on his list. Maybe he'd even take the woman with him.

"Milt, did you hear me?"

"Yeah, I heard you." He reached for the bottle of whiskey, topping off his glass.

"What do you say? Let's get the money and leave. There's no reason to stay another day." Harry's frustration flared as the whiskey took hold. The longer Milt did nothing, the more he and the others drank. The combination was deadly. "And why are we even up here? We could be robbing banks in Arkansas, Kansas, or Missouri where there's more people and more money."

Milt's gaze shifted from the woman leaning against a banister, keeping track of the girls and the action below.

"You know the answer to that. We're getting as much money as we can before riding into Splendor, where we'll take the town apart."

"Hell, Milt. None of us gives a damn about what happened to Chet. Our brother was a worthless, arrogant sonofabitch, who cared nothing about anyone except himself."

Harry's eyes bulged as Milt grabbed him by the collar, pulling him off the chair.

"No one knows better than I do what a bastard he was, but we *will* take care of those who killed him." He let go, pushing Harry back toward his chair.

Harry ran a finger around his collar, not backing down as his voice hardened. "He chose to take some of the men and ride out, Milt. Chet left on his own, paying for it with his life. We don't owe him a thing. You're going to risk hanging to avenge a man you hated? Makes no sense."

Milt's gaze bore into his brother. "Kin is kin. Besides, we've already got someone in Splendor. By the time we get there, he'll have all the information we need to clean out the bank and kill the man who shot Chet. Nothing more to say." Milt tossed back the rest of his whiskey. "Unless you plan to take over." He sneered at his younger brother, knowing

Harry didn't have the guts to confront him, or the desire to lead the others.

Although he believed in going after the man who killed Chet, Milt held no love for his dead older brother. Ten months apart in age, they'd fought since boys, agreeing on little, except the desire to fight for the Confederacy and never return to their poor, dirt farm life in Virginia.

Organizing a gang of thieves and raiders after the war had been easy. Deciding who to rob and when caused great strain within the group until Chet took off with several others after another bitter confrontation with Milt and Harry. News of Chet's death caused relief among the remaining gang members. As the original leader, Chet ruled the men with an iron fist, doling out harsh punishment for botched jobs without a hint of remorse. He cared nothing about loyalty or protecting the men riding with him.

"Hell no, I don't want to take over. I want you to think about what you're asking of men who celebrated Chet's death. Let it go, Milt."

Milt reached across the table, picking up the bottle of whiskey and filling his glass. His gaze wandered back to the woman still standing on the stairs, seeing her eyes widen when the door of the saloon opened. The rancher walked inside, nodding to the bartender, then taking the stairs two at a time.

Wrapping his arm around her waist, they disappeared down a hallway.

Cursing, Milt swallowed the whiskey, then poured another, taking a slow sip. He had to get his mind off the woman and back where it belonged—on the money sitting in the Bloody Basin bank, and where they'd ride after they robbed it.

His musings about the woman were forgotten as his eyes locked on a man standing at the bar, his stern features keeping others at a distance, his narrowed gaze missing nothing as he watched the activity in the saloon. As the man turned to lean a hip against the bar, Milt noticed the star pinned to his chest. A moment later, the deputy straightened, seeming to see Harry and Milt for the first time, and moved toward them.

"Don't believe I know you gentlemen. Are you new in town?" The deputy stood between Harry and Milt, watching each shift in his chair, allowing them better access to the guns at their waists.

"Been here a couple days." Milt set his glass down, resting his arms on the table.

"Passing through or looking for work?"

"Staying a few days to get the road dust out of our bodies and take on supplies. We won't be staying." Milt stood, nodding at Harry. "We were just ready to head back to the hotel." He didn't want any trouble with the law. If all went well, they'd bust into the bank tonight and be gone long before the deputy and his cronies knew what happened.

"Deputy." Harry nodded to the man as he followed Milt outside. It never did them any good to draw the attention of local lawmen.

The deputy watched them leave, then walked outside, seeing them enter the hotel next door, a sense of recognition niggling at him. Crossing the street, he walked into the jail, grabbing a stack of wanted posters from the top drawer. Settling into a chair, he studied each one, certain he'd find the two men. His hand stalled on one about five posters from the top. He sucked in a breath, knowing he stared at an image of the older of the two men in the saloon. Milton Penderville. Setting it aside, he continued through the stack until he found the one showing the younger of the two. Harrison Penderville. Both wanted for bank robbery, rustling, and attempted murder.

Placing the others back in the drawer, he grabbed the two posters and walked outside, heading toward the sheriff's house at the end of the street. He didn't like being interrupted during supper, but this was important. In his gut, the deputy knew something was going to happen in Bloody Basin, and he'd bet a month's wages it had to do with the large amount of money in the bank and the two men he'd seen in the saloon.

"It's time, Milt." Harry checked his guns, spinning the cylinders, confirming a bullet filled each chamber. Satisfied, he slipped them back in the holsters.

"Are the men ready?"

"They're waiting for us behind the livery."

Milt grabbed his rifle and nodded. "Let's go."

They slipped out the back door of the hotel, staying close to the buildings as they walked in quiet strides toward the livery. The men would have their horses ready. They'd gone over each man's job several times, confirming which would be watching for activity on the street, and which would help Milt and Harry in the bank. One had been assigned to watch the sheriff's house, and another would watch the jail. No one believed two lawmen would offer them much resistance.

Going straight to the back door of the bank, Harry pulled out a pouch of tools and worked his magic. The door opened in less than a minute, allowing Milt, Harry, and three others to walk inside. Harry and Milt went straight toward the safe, the others taking positions at windows, helping the men outside keep watch.

Harry pulled out the dynamite. He figured they'd have two minutes to blow the safe, grab the money, and get to their horses before the sheriff and deputy would be able to reach the bank. Assuming they made it past the men watching them. The orders were always the same. Shoot the lawmen in their legs, disable them, then get out of there. So far, the strategy had worked in each job pulled over the last few months.

"All set." Harry and Milt moved several feet away from the safe, squatting behind a counter, plugging their ears. Experience had taught Harry how much dynamite to use and the length of time between lighting the fuse and the explosion.

The detonation set them in motion. Milt and Harry rushed inside the safe, not waiting for the debris in the air to clear. Filling two bags, they dashed out, signaling the other men to get to their horses. That's when the plan went straight to hell.

The first man out screamed as bullets riddled his body. The second took bullets to his shoulder and leg, slumping to the ground. The third backed inside, following Milt and Harry to a window as gunfire continued outside. They were under siege, an occurrence they'd never experienced in the past, yet understood what needed to be done if it ever happened. Whoever survived knew where to meet and how long to hang around for others to join them.

Breaking the glass, the three men scrambled out of the opening, running to their horses without a backward glance at the rest of the gang providing cover. Jumping into the saddles, they turned the horses away from the main street, kicking them into a run.

Three hours later, Milt, Harry, and six of their men huddled together, thinking of those they'd left behind and what all considered a botched job. Milt had opened the bags as soon as he dismounted, dumping the contents on the ground. What they believed would be a big haul had turned into a bust. The bank had been ready for them. The bundles of money were stacks of blank paper with a few bills on each side. Coin bags had been filled with rocks.

"We can't stay here any longer." Milt stood. "A posse is probably tracking us right now. Somehow, they knew about us." Letting out a string of curses, he kicked the contents of the bags aside, then swung into his saddle.

"Where to, Milt?" Harry edged up next to him.

"Out of the Dakotas." Milt looked at the others. "We ride to Montana."

Chapter Eight

Splendor, Montana

Cash smoothed back his thick, blond hair, then grabbed his hat. Letting out a shaky breath, he wondered what had gotten into him. The last time he'd shared a private supper with a woman he courted was before the war, before the fighting had devastated the South, changing everyone's lives.

The thought triggered an image of Stephen, who made his way through each day without a single complaint. He didn't begrudge the fact he'd lost his leg to a cause that ultimately failed. His friend had believed in what the South stood for, giving his service willingly, accepting the consequences.

So had Cash. At least that's what he'd thought.

Then why did he find it so hard to put the carnage behind him and return to the life he'd planned before the war? A life which included a wife, children, and work he enjoyed. A life so far out of reach, he could hardly remember his dreams.

Stephen had returned to the woman he loved, married her, started a family, and built the life he'd always imagined. Cash had never returned to Savannah, his boyhood home, or his uncle's farm in Louisiana. He'd run fast and far, joining up with Beau to become a bounty hunter, focusing their pain on those committing crimes of opportunity. Without an ounce of guilt, they'd taken outlaws out of this world, hauling their bodies to the nearest town to collect the reward.

Then after one particularly treacherous search resulting in the deaths of several outlaws, their hunger for revenge stopped. Staring across the campfire one night, Cash had turned to Beau, shaking his head.

"I'm done."

Beau didn't say a word for several moments, then nodded, knowing what Cash meant. "What now?"

Cash had dragged a hand down his weary face, then rubbed his eyes. "I don't know."

They'd finished one last job, then ridden to Splendor, the home of Cash's boyhood friends and fellow ex-Confederates, Dax and Luke Pelletier. Once they'd settled in, the two agreed to become deputies under Gabe Evans, an ex-Union colonel.

Their plans now included buying some land from the Pelletiers, raising a few head of cattle while continuing to protect the town. They'd once discussed a future of meeting the right woman, falling in love, and having families. Each had dismissed the notion. They were too jaded and long past worn out.

Yet here he stood, clutching his hat with both hands, wearing his best Sunday clothes, a few minutes away from sharing supper with the most intriguing and attractive woman he'd ever met.

Beau came through the back door, slinging his gun belt over a nearby hook before pouring a cup of stale coffee "You going to stand there all night and make that pretty girl wait for you?" Settling into a chair, he placed the cup on the table, then crossed his arms. "Get out of here before she changes her mind."

Cursing, Cash slammed his hat firmly on his head, flung the door open, and stepped into the cooling air. Staring up at a late afternoon sun, he shook his head, then closed his eyes. He'd allow himself one evening with Alison, one supper with a beautiful woman, before returning to the life he'd created, a life he could depend on to get him through each day. The life of a survivor.

"Good evening, Cash." A tentative smile swept across Alison's face before her brows drew together, her face sobering. "I thought you'd changed your mind." She had opened the door after the third knock, a severe case of nerves causing her hands to shake.

Taking off his hat, Cash's face softened. "I'd never do that, Alison." Without stepping inside, he held out his arm. "Shall we?"

They walked in silence, Alison keeping her shawl wrapped tight around her to ward off the chill, wondering if the shivers she felt had more to do with the man next to her than the temperature. As they approached the restaurant, she chastised herself. She'd never learn the truth about her brother's death if she became distracted by anyone in Splendor, especially a much too handsome lawman who set her heart racing with each encounter. She'd agreed to supper to discover what Cash knew about Bobby's death. At least that's what she kept telling herself.

"Good evening, Alison, Cash." Suzanne took Cash's coat, directing them to a table near the front window. "The special tonight is roast beef. Fanny also made some wonderful chicken stew."

"Alison?" Cash asked.

"The chicken, please."

"I'll have the beef, Suzanne. And save a piece of pie for each of us." Settling back in his chair, Cash watched Alison fidget with her shawl, twisting the corners. She didn't look at him. Instead, her gaze darted around the restaurant, never focusing on one spot too long before returning to stare down at her hands.

Leaning forward, he rested his arms on the table, waiting for her to acknowledge him. When a few minutes passed, he cleared his throat, tired of the quiet.

"Tell me about your husband."

Her head snapped up, her eyes wide. "My, uh…"

"Husband? You told me he died in the war."

"Oh, yes." Shifting in her chair, she licked her lips. "There isn't much to tell. He was a few years older than me. A farmer, like my father. We didn't know each other well before we married. He joined the Confederates a few months after our wedding, saying he could no longer watch others die for a cause he believed in." She stopped for a moment, trying to recall what she'd told Rachel and the other women about him. "I got word a few months later he'd been killed."

"No children?"

"Um, no." She glanced toward the kitchen, grateful to see Suzanne carrying plates heaped with food to their table. "Thank you, Suzanne. This smells wonderful." Alison inhaled as the plate was set down, her face flushing pink when her stomach growled.

Smiling, she set Cash's plate in front of him. "You let me know if I can get you anything else." Suzanne filled their coffee cups, then moved on to another table.

Cash tucked into his meal, casting curious glances at Alison, who picked at her food. The evening hadn't gone quite as he expected. Her answers to simple questions seemed stilted, as if she were searching for the right words. Setting down his fork, he picked up his coffee, taking a sip as he considered his next words.

"Do you plan to stay in Splendor?"

"If business continues as it has, then yes, I'll be here for a while. What about you, Cash? Is this now your home?"

"As much of a home as I've had in a long time. Beau and I are talking about buying a small section of land, maybe raising some cattle. It's a ways off yet."

"You'd both stop working for Sheriff Evans?"

"No, ma'am. Gabe and the town have been good to me. Speaking for myself, I'd stay a deputy."

She took a few more bites, then pushed her plate away. The time had come to get some answers. "Do you have many instances of bank robberies?"

Cash's eyes widened at the abrupt change in direction of their conversation. The last topic he wanted to discuss was the robbery and its outcome. His gaze became hooded as he considered his answer. "I suppose no more than any frontier town."

"I see. Were any townspeople shot during the robbery a few months ago?"

Placing the cup back on the table, he crossed his arms and leaned back. "Only the outlaws."

"And they all died?"

"Yes, they did." Although he tried to moderate it, his voice hardened with each answer.

"Did you kill any of them?"

Cash's shoulders tensed, his back straightening. He didn't like talking about the senseless waste of lives. The death of one young gang member in particular still haunted him.

"Why so many questions, Alison? It was their decision to threaten the people of Splendor, and their misfortune to discover how far we'd go to protect the town." Cash stopped when Suzanne replaced their supper plates with servings of pie. He couldn't remember getting so many questions about the outlaws from a woman. Most wanted the slimmest details, enough to know the innocent were safe and the gang had paid. Alison wasn't content with such a small amount of information. "Surely you don't believe what happened was wrong."

The fork slipped from her fingers, clinking against the plate. Fumbling, she picked it up, lowering her voice when she saw other diners watching them.

"No, of course not. It's idle curiosity, nothing more." Taking a regretful look at her pie, she pushed the almost full plate away, attempting a smile. "I'm afraid I can't eat another bite."

He studied her face another moment, his doubts about her increasing when she failed to meet his gaze. Her answers, continued questions, and reasons for traveling across country to buy an almost worthless seamstress shop ate at him. Cash didn't trust actions he couldn't define or understand.

Standing, he walked around the table, pulling out her chair. "I thought we could take a walk."

"That would be lovely." She let out a shaky breath, smiling up at him as he helped straighten her shawl. His fingers lingered on her shoulders a little longer than necessary, his body moving behind her as he inhaled her unique scent of roses and lavender.

The sensations passing through Cash were swift and powerful, causing his chest to tighten and gut to clench. He hadn't felt this amount of desire for a woman in more years than he could remember. The fact he'd felt this way each time he'd been around Alison bothered him more than a little. The belief she hadn't been truthful with him should have caused him to ignore the attraction and walk away. Instead, the allure became more intense, chipping away at his defenses.

Snatching up his coat and hat, he held out his arm, trying to calm the conflicting emotions of attraction and apprehension. He needed to sort out the contradictions before doing something he couldn't undo.

"I thought we'd take the path below Noah and Abby's house. There's a clearing not far up with a beautiful view of town and the mountains. Have you been there?"

Alison thought it sounded perfect. "To be honest, I haven't been outside of town since I arrived. The Pelletiers invited me for supper, but running the store and keeping up with orders has taken all my time." She slipped her arm through his, tightening her grip as they started up the slight incline.

"I'm going to supper at the Pelletier's tomorrow. Why don't you join me?" He winced, wishing he could pull the words back, not understanding what inspired him to extend the invitation. His friends would be fine with Alison coming along. If she said yes, he'd be forced to spend most of his day with her, which wasn't a good idea—not with his misgivings about her past, or the strong desire he felt, which intensified with each minute they shared.

"If you're sure you wouldn't mind, I'd be pleased to accompany you." As they walked into a meadow, she turned her gaze toward the mountains, gasping at the sight. "Oh, Cash. It's incredible." Dropping her arm from his, she stepped closer to the edge of the clearing, looking down on the town, then letting her gaze sweep over the surrounding hills as the sun's rays disappeared to the west. Clasping her hands in front of her, she took a deep breath of clean air, unable to control the smile spreading across her face. "It's simply beautiful."

Watching her face light up and her eyes shine, he allowed himself a moment to be caught up in her unrestrained enthusiasm. For the first time since the war, Cash wished he didn't feel so tired and cynical. Wished he had a life to offer a beautiful woman such as Alison, who seemed to embrace each day, even when faced with loss and hardship.

Flashing him a mischievous grin, she gripped his arm, pulling him forward. "Let's get closer."

Chuckling, Cash let her drag him a few steps closer to the sloping edge of the meadow, getting a better view of Splendor. Candles and lamps were lit as the sun set, allowing a yellow glow to filter onto the street. A few people walked the boardwalk. Some alone, some couples arm-in-arm as they finished their day. A normal evening in a remote, quiet town on the frontier.

"Who would have thought Splendor would be such a beautiful place?" Her eyes sparkled as she looked up at Cash, her face inches from his.

His gaze locked with hers as his hands moved to her waist, turning her toward him. "I've never seen such a gorgeous sight as tonight." Slowly lowering his head, he waited for her to turn, move away, and break the spell. Instead, she settled her hands on his arms, steadying herself, waiting.

Alison's breath hitched when she felt Cash's hands grip her waist, but she couldn't pull away, didn't want to break the contact. His large palms and strong fingers almost spanned her slim body, drawing her closer as his gaze held hers.

She'd been kissed once by a boy from a neighboring farm. It had lasted seconds and made no impression, other than causing her to grimace and swipe an arm across her mouth. He'd wanted to do it again. Instead, she'd pushed him away, turned, and ran as fast as possible back to her home. Her feelings today couldn't be more different.

Although unwise and against all her plans, Alison looked up, her tongue darting out to moisten her lips. She closed her eyes at the feel of his lips brushing hers.

On a low groan, Cash slanted his mouth over hers, ignoring the warnings in his head in favor of the sensations she made him feel. Warmth spread through his body as she allowed him to take control, sweeping his tongue into her mouth when her lips parted on a sigh. She tasted of coffee and pie. He couldn't get enough and deepened the kiss, tightening his hold, aligning his body with hers. She wrapped her arms around his neck, brushing her fingers through his hair.

Her taste, touch, and unique scent messed with his rational thought and common sense. For a man used to dealing with situations in cool, dispassionate logic, Cash felt all control slip away as their embrace and actions became more zealous.

Knowing he had to stop before the passion caused them both to lose all restraint, he broke the kiss, resting his forehead against hers, his breathing unsteady and ragged.

Taking a step back, Alison looked into eyes reflecting the same desire and confusion she felt. When he placed one more kiss on her forehead, she inhaled a deep breath, touching a finger to her still sensitive lips.

Clearing his throat, Cash grasped her hand in his. "We should be going before we lose sight of the path."

Unable to form a coherent thought, Alison nodded, leaving her hand in his as he guided her off the hill and back toward town. Neither of them spoke until they stood outside the door to her shop. At least the time had allowed her to get her breathing and erratic heartbeat under control.

"Thank you for a wonderful evening, Cash. It was...well...unexpected."

Eyes dark and hooded, he pulled her close for one more kiss before setting her aside so as not to draw attention from those few people still on the street. Clearing his throat, he glanced around, searching for control.

"I'll come by at noon tomorrow and we'll head out to the Pelletier's. That is if you're still interested in going with me."

"Yes, I'd like to go if you're certain they won't mind." She sucked in a breath, realizing they'd be alone during the ride, posing a temptation she didn't need. Alison wrapped her arms around her waist to help control the shivers from their brief, intense kiss. "Perhaps it would be best for me to wait. I don't want to impose." She let her gaze slowly move from his chest to the opening at the top of his shirt before traveling to his face, which now held an easy smirk.

"You're not afraid to be alone with me, are you, *Mrs. Burns*?" He leaned forward, his warm breath washing over her cheeks, his lips brushing hers.

Drawing away and straightening her shoulders, she glared at him. "Of course not, *Mr. Coulter*."

Moving close to her ear, he lowered his already husky voice. "You should be, Alison."

Chapter Nine

Big Pine, Montana

"Telegram came for you, Sheriff." The clerk from the Western Union office dropped the message on Parker Sterling's desk.

Opening it, Sterling read through the telegram twice, mumbling a curse before looking back at the clerk. "You go back and send a reply to the sheriff in Bloody Basin. Tell him I want any information he has, including descriptions. And tell him I think this is the Penderville gang." He stood, resting both hands on the desk, considering what he needed to do to protect the town. Looking up, he saw the man hadn't moved. "That's it. Get back to me right away with his reply."

"Yes, sir."

Strapping on his gun belt and grabbing his hat, Sterling dashed outside, running toward the restaurant his deputies favored for lunch. When they saw the look on his face, all three pushed their plates aside and stood.

"We have trouble, Sheriff?" Tall and lanky with skin leathered from years in the sun, the oldest deputy had known Parker for years and could read him as well as anyone.

Parker stepped closer, lowering his voice. "Appears the Penderville gang robbed the bank in Bloody Basin. Thankfully, the sheriff got wind of it beforehand and was prepared. Killed a couple of the outlaws, but the rest got away. Tracks indicate they're riding west."

"Toward Big Pine?"

"Seems likely. Finish your meals, then meet me at the jail. I need to round up the others." Sterling stormed outside, heading toward the end of town where his other deputies would be bunked down after their overnight shift. Pounding on the door of the house provided by the town, he didn't wait for an answer, barging inside. Shaking awake a deputy collapsed on the sofa, he moved to one of the closed doors and threw it open, his jaw going slack as he took in the sight of a naked female straddling his youngest deputy.

"Gall darn, Felix. I told you not to bring your women here." He almost laughed at the panicked scream and terrified expression on the young woman's face as she fell to the floor, scrambling to pick up her clothes. "Sorry, ma'am, but I need Felix at the jail." He didn't recognize her. By her bright red face and tears streaming down her cheeks, he guessed she must be the daughter of one of the ranchers who seldom brought their families to town.

"Yes, sir, Sheriff." Nineteen, good-looking, and cocky, Felix flew off the bed as if it were on fire, fought with his pants until he finally got his legs through the openings, then jammed his arms into his shirt. "Sorry, Sheriff. This won't happen again."

Sterling held up his hand, shaking his head. "I don't want to hear it, boy. One more time and you're out. The town isn't paying for this house so you or the others can bring your women here. You pay for your own place if that's what you want. Do you understand me?"

"Yes, sir. I reckon I do."

"You roust the others. I need you all at the jail in ten minutes." Sterling moved toward the door, then turned around. "No more than ten or don't bother coming, Felix." Slamming the front door behind him, Sterling grumbled to himself about taking on the mayor's youngest son. He should've told the man no, but he'd given Felix a chance. Damn if the boy wasn't messing up this opportunity, just as he had the others his daddy had provided.

"Sheriff!"

Sterling glanced across the street to see the telegraph clerk running toward him.

"I got that reply you expected." He shoved it at the sheriff. "If you don't need me, I should get back to the office."

Sterling nodded, reading the message from the sheriff in Bloody Basin. By the descriptions, he had no doubt the Penderville gang were the robbers and were now riding hard toward Big Pine.

"Alison! What a wonderful surprise." Rachel dashed outside and down the porch steps as Cash helped Alison down from the wagon.

"She almost didn't come, but I assured her you and the others wouldn't mind." Cash let his hands linger on Alison's waist a moment longer than necessary before she stepped away.

The ride to the Pelletier ranch had been uneventful. Cash had been a complete gentleman, even if he did keep his mouth clamped shut most of the trip. She'd been careful to stay clear of any mention of the bank robbery or his part in stopping the outlaws. Instead, she'd focused on the scenery, the weather, and questions about the Pelletiers.

"You're always welcome on Sundays, Alison. Luke and Ginny ride over from their place, and several of the ranch hands usually join us. It's our ritual after church."

Alison's face heated a little at the mention of Sunday services. She couldn't recall the last time she'd set foot in a church. It had to be close to a year.

"Thank you, Rachel. Cash said the same, but I still didn't want to intrude."

"Hey, Cash. Glad you could join us." Dax Pelletier strolled out of the barn, then clasped his friend's hand and slapped him on the back. "Where's Beau?"

A wry grin twisted his lips. "He is taking his meal with Caroline Iverson."

"Caro?" Rachel broke in, her eyes widening.

"Yes, ma'am. He's grown pretty fond of her." Cash stepped closer to Alison, refraining from slipping an arm over her shoulders.

"Well, I'll be. She hasn't said a word to me. Maybe Ginny knows." Rachel turned at the sound of the front door closing.

"Maybe I know what?" Ginny's expression brightened at the sight of Cash and Alison. "Hello, you two. Where's Beau?" She glanced behind them, not seeing Beau's horse.

"He's having Sunday supper with Caro." Rachel crossed her arms, arching a brow at Ginny.

"Well, well..." Ginny's voice trailed off as she thought of Beau and Caro together.

"Now, ladies. Don't go jumping to any conclusions." Dax circled an arm around Rachel's waist, drawing her close. "They've become friends since she moved to Splendor. Everyone knows she plans to move on to San Francisco in a few months. Right, Cash?"

"I haven't heard otherwise."

"All right, everyone. Supper's on the table." Luke stood on the front porch, holding the door open. "Lydia says to come quick or the ranch hands will gobble it all up."

"Is Bull already inside?" Cash asked, feigning concern.

"Sure is. As you know, that boy can eat an entire cow." Luke laughed, slipping his hand into Ginny's when she stepped beside him.

"Bull, how is it going as the new foreman of Redemption's Edge?" Cash forked another piece of roast beef, his gaze focusing on the man across the table. Having muscled arms, molasses-colored hair, kind eyes, and an almost boyish face, Bull already worked at the ranch when Dax and Luke inherited it from a friend they'd served with as Texas Rangers. He'd proven himself over and over, earning the foreman position over men who were older with more experience.

"Good, Cash." Bull cast a furtive glance at Lydia sitting next to him. It was no secret to those at the table that the two were attracted to each other—had been since Lydia and the other orphans were brought to the Pelletier ranch and made part of the *extended* family. Unfortunately, Bull had yet to state his feelings and make his intentions known.

"Any plans for changes?" Cash noticed his questions were drawing the attention of others at the table. Most notably, Dax and Luke.

"I've got some ideas. Need to sort them out before I talk to the bosses."

"Any ideas you have are welcome, Bull. Just let Dax and me know when you're ready to talk." Luke studied his friend, a man he'd grown close to since taking over the ranch. He knew whatever suggestions Bull offered would be worth serious consideration. "Lydia, I hear you're planning to move in with Noah and Abby for a while to help with baby Gabriel."

"Um, yes. I'll be leaving tomorrow." Lydia could feel Bull tense next to her. Glancing at him, her breath hitched, noticing his gaze riveted on her face. She'd spoken to Rachel and Dax about helping out, but had yet to mention it to Bull. Once she'd come to trust him, they'd talked about everything and become friends. She could almost feel the sense of betrayal as he looked at her.

"How long?" Bull asked, his voice low and strained.

She cleared her throat, the anxiety she felt clear to everyone. "Rachel said it could be a few months." Pushing her chair back, she stood, picking up her plate. "I'll get dessert ready."

"I'll help." Standing, Bull grabbed his own plate, following her through the kitchen doorway.

Alison watched the interaction, hearing the anxiety in Bull's voice, and wondered what had just happened.

"Damn fool. He'd better make a move soon or one of the single men in Splendor will snap Lydia up." Luke tossed down his napkin, ready to head into the kitchen until Ginny's hand on his arm stopped him.

"Let them be, Luke. They'll work it out. Lydia isn't going to agree to let anyone court her except Bull, and we all know it." Ginny glanced at Rachel, who nodded.

"So they care about each other, but neither has said anything?" Alison looked around the table, seeing most everyone nod. "Well, that's just plain sad."

"Bull's got his reasons, and I suspect Lydia knows and understands them." Luke crossed his arms, leaning back in his chair.

"Sorry. I didn't mean to insert myself into their business." Alison bit her bottom lip, wishing she'd kept quiet.

"It's fine, Alison." Cash put an arm around the back of her chair, shifting toward her. "This has been going on a while." He glanced at the others. "I agree with Luke. Bull has some good reasons for waiting to state his intentions. I'm thinking becoming a foreman is going to push him a bit."

"I sure hope so." Rachel set down her napkin, glancing at the closed kitchen door. "They've had enough time alone. I'm going to go make fresh coffee."

Lydia and Bull walked back in with Rachel a few minutes later, each carrying a pie, which Ginny quickly sliced and passed out. The mood had sobered since Lydia's announcement, neither she nor Bull showing any indication they'd talked about her decision.

Finishing his pie, Cash pushed his plate away and stood. "Do you all mind if I take Alison for a walk?" He moved behind her chair, resting his hands on the back.

"Not at all," Rachel answered. "You know you're welcome to stay here tonight."

"Thank you, but I need to get into the shop early. I'm finishing some hats for a couple local women." Alison grinned at Rachel and Ginny, causing them both to laugh.

"And I can't wait to see them." Ginny picked up plates, casting a curious look at Rachel as Cash escorted Alison outside. "What do you think is going on with those two?"

Rachel shrugged. "I don't know, but it's good to see him spending an evening with someone other

117

than Beau." They laughed, carrying the empty plates to the sink.

"Dax told me they have a new foal. I thought you might like to see him." Drawing her arm through his as they walked toward the barn, Cash gave in to the desire to pull her close to his side.

"I'd love to see it. We had two horses at our farm. One old, the other ancient." She grinned at his robust chuckle, enjoying the warmth of his body close to hers.

"Am I correct in guessing you didn't ride much?"

She nodded. "Someday, I'd like to have a horse meant for riding."

"If you're interested, I'll take you riding as soon as my horse heals. You can ride Joker, the horse Noah's letting me borrow, and I'll ride Hunter. There are some beautiful places to ride near Splendor."

"I'd love to ride with you, although I don't know if I'll be able to keep up."

Cash's face softened as he looked at her, knowing he wouldn't leave her side. Opening the barn door, he rested a hand on the small of her back, guiding her inside toward a nearby stall.

"There he is."

"Oh my. He *is* new, isn't he?"

"Born just before we arrived today. By tomorrow afternoon, they'll be let out into the field behind the barn." He watched Alison's eyes widen.

"Isn't that a little soon?"

"Not for horses."

Alison climbed onto the last rung of the stall, letting her head rest on her arms as she watched mother and foal. "They're so beautiful."

"Yes. Very," he whispered, never taking his gaze off her face.

She watched a few more minutes before stepping down and wrapping a hand around his arm, staring up at him. "Thank you. I've never seen such a wonderful sight."

Neither looked away, their gazes locking with each other.

Alison's heart strummed, the tempo increasing the longer he stared into her eyes. She couldn't move, didn't want to break the spell. Sucking in a ragged breath, she tilted her head to the side as she caught her bottom lip between her teeth. Lifting her hand, she traced his lower lip with her fingers, having no idea the effect her touch had on him.

"Be careful, Alison." His hoarse voice stopped the movement of her hand, her eyes indicating her lack of understanding. He grasped her wrist with his hand, lowering it to his chest, holding it over his heart. "My control isn't as strong as it should be."

She gasped as his meaning became clear, but she didn't step away.

He lifted her chin with a finger, lowering his head to within an inch of hers. "I want to kiss you."

She couldn't find the words to deny him. "Yes," she breathed out, unable to stop the heat coursing through her body.

Dipping his head, Cash took her mouth with his, moving his arms around her waist to draw her close. He groaned, deepening the kiss when her arms wound around his neck, pulling him to her.

Splaying his hands across her back, he held tight, feeling the heat from her body. He couldn't think, could hardly breathe as her taste and the feel of her played with his senses, his emotions reeling with need. He wanted her with an intensity he didn't understand and didn't want to control.

"Cash, are you out here?"

Luke's question had them stepping back, their breathing labored. Cash scrubbed a hand down his face, turning to shield Alison behind his back. The timing of Luke's intrusion was both a blessing and a curse. It would've taken little encouragement for the rampant desire between them to ignite into unwise actions and possible regret.

"We're by the foal."

When Cash turned, he saw Alison standing on the lowest rung of the stall, the same as before, her attention riveted on the foal and its mother.

"What do you think?" Luke asked as he stepped beside Alison, unaware of what he'd interrupted.

She took another slow breath, getting her heart rate under control. "They're beautiful."

Luke nodded, then turned toward Cash. "Dax said you wanted to talk to us about some outlaws who might be headed our way."

"Yeah." He placed a hand on Alison's shoulder, drawing her attention. "Let's go inside. I need to talk to Dax and Luke before we leave for town."

They shared a look as she stepped to the ground.

Neither of them spoke as they walked to the house, Cash wondering how he was going to keep his distance during the long ride home.

Chapter Ten

"Bernie Griggs just gave me this." Cash handed the telegram to Gabe. "You aren't going to like it."

Cash dropped into a chair, taking off his hat, raking a hand through his hair. Following a challenging ride home from the Pelletier ranch, he had slept little the night before.

It had been a struggle to keep the distance he felt they needed as Alison continued to inch closer. He sat motionless, guessing she sought the warmth and comfort his body provided. About fifteen minutes into the trip, he'd given in, slipping an arm around her and holding her to his side. Her gaze occasionally searched his, yet he'd refused to give into the temptation of her closeness. Lying in bed, staring at the ceiling, he'd mentally thanked Luke's interruption in the barn for saving him from acting on the passion he hadn't been able to resist.

Gabe read the telegram, his jaw clenching. "Appears the Penderville gang is riding toward Big Pine. Unless Sterling is able to stop them, I've no doubt Splendor will be their next stop."

"How do you want to handle it?"

"There isn't much to do now except wait for another telegram from Sterling. Moosejaw is the only town between Bloody Basin and Big Pine, and there isn't enough there for the outlaws to risk getting caught or killed." Gabe set the telegram down and leaned back, stretching his arms behind his head. "You've told Dax and Luke about the Pendervilles?"

"They know and are ready if we need them. I still need to talk to Horace at the bank."

"I hate to stir this up before we have more information, but I'd better talk to the town leaders." Gabe stood, picking up his hat and gun belt.

"You know, Gabe, since King Tolbert was murdered and Amos left town, the leadership has changed an awful lot. Seems to me it's Horace, the Pelletiers, Nick Barnett, Stan Petermann, Noah, and you." Cash stood. "Does Nick know what's going on?"

"He and Noah both know about what Sterling told you. That leaves Stan and Horace. Stan's the only one who might panic and spread the word around town, alarming others. Can't leave him out, though. You go to the bank. I'll deal with Stan."

Before they could reach the door, it burst open, Monty from the lumber mill rushing inside, panting, his eyes wild.

"Silas told me to come fetch you, Sheriff. We've got some miners causing a commotion 'cause their order isn't ready." Gunfire sounded as Monty got out the last words. "That's those miners, Sheriff."

"Let's go find out what those fellas want and stop them from doing something foolish, Cash."

Gabe and Cash rushed out, leaving Monty alone in the jail, pacing back and forth.

Cash stuck his head back inside. "You coming?" He signaled the boy to get moving, then closed the door as Monty took off toward the lumber mill.

They dashed past the Wild Rose Saloon and Western Union office before coming to a stop near Noah's livery. Gabe almost laughed at the sight of his closest friend holding his Spencer repeating rifle, pointing it at the unruly miners. Although it wasn't the Sharps rifle he used as a sharpshooter during the war, he was still deadly accurate with it.

"You boys listen to me." Noah's voice boomed above the shouts and gunfire. When one of the miners pointed his revolver at him, Noah squeezed the trigger of his Spencer, the bullet knocking the gun right out of the man's hand. Not lowering the rifle, he took a step closer. "Now, I mean business. You fellas drop your guns and step away from Silas."

Not one argued as they tossed their weapons away.

"I wish you'd reconsider and become one of my deputies, Noah. I could use another good man." Gabe chuckled, his gun drawn and pointed toward the miners. Cash stood next to him, ready to shoot the next man who moved.

"You've been trying to boss me around all our lives, Gabe. I'm not likely to let you do it officially."

"Didn't think so." His attention swung back to the men, who were none too pleased to be without their weapons. "Cash and I have this now."

Noah lowered the rifle. "You need me to stay back while you gather their guns?"

"Looks like Beau is on his way from the boardinghouse." Gabe tilted his head toward the opposite side of the street, seeing his other deputy running towards them, his gun drawn. "We're fine. Besides, if anything happened to you, I'd have to answer to Abby—and that's too scary a thought to consider."

Noah laughed as he stepped aside, letting Gabe and the others take over. No one noticed the lone man standing behind the Western Union office, his gun ready, eyes scanning the crowd. Seeing the sheriff and deputies taking control, he holstered his gun, taking the path behind the building toward the other end of town.

Alison's head jerked up at the sound of gunfire. Dropping the hat she'd been working on, she dashed to the front door, opening it a crack to peer outside. A few townspeople stood on the boardwalk, all facing the other end of town, but no one moved. She opened the door wider, taking a few steps outside, calling after a man she didn't recognize as he hurried toward the commotion.

"What's going on?"

He never stopped, yelling over his shoulder. "I heard the sheriff and his deputies are having a shootout with a group of miners."

Closing the door behind her, she crossed the street, stopping in front of the St. James Hotel, then moving along the boardwalk until she could get a clear view. The sight jolted her. One of the miners was holding his bleeding hand as Gabe, Beau, and Cash approached, all brandishing guns. She moved until she got a clear view of their faces. All were intense, focused, and watching for any movement from the miners. As if he sensed her, Cash's gaze shifted toward her for a brief instant, a scowl appearing, his eyes flashing before he returned his attention to the crowd.

"Come on, Alison. Let's get you out of danger. You never know when those miners might do something stupid and try to grab for their guns."

Alison turned to see Gabe's wife, Lena, grasping her arm, gently guiding her away from the danger.

"The lawmen might do something just as stupid and shoot for no reason," Alison protested, her features drawn. When she saw the stunned look on Lena's face, she realized what she'd said. "Sorry. I know Gabe's your husband, and I'm sure he's a fine man. Lots of lawmen aren't like him, though. They'll kill as easily as most outlaws." Alison didn't recognize the cold tone or disdain in her voice, or feel the way her body began to tremble.

"I know some lawmen go bad. Those three aren't anything like the men you're thinking of. They don't kill for pleasure, but they *will* shoot someone if he's threatening others." Lena wrapped an arm around Alison's shoulders, steering her toward the Dixie. "How about some coffee while we wait for the men to clear this up?"

Alison glanced over her shoulder one more time, deciding she could wait no longer to find out the identity of the man who killed her brother. A shiver ran through her at the thought one of the men a few feet away—Gabe, Beau, or Cash—might be the person she sought. Swallowing the bile in her throat, she allowed Lena to lead her away.

"Coffee sounds good," she lied, knowing nothing sounded good right now.

"Who wants to tell me what this is all about?" Gabe's voice held a hard edge, although the sight before them almost made him laugh. Several miners stood around, glaring between him, Silas—the owner of the lumber mill—and a short, lone figure hunching in the background, trying not to catch anyone's attention.

Silas pointed to the miners. "These men threatened me and my new man. Said they'd burn the mill down if I didn't replace him with one of our own."

Cash moved closer, not sure about what he'd heard. "Our own?" he murmured to Gabe, who shrugged, then turned to the group of men, holding the gaze of the one who'd been the most belligerent.

"You want to explain this to me?"

Stepping forward, the man planted his feet, crossing his arms. "He's the problem." He uncrossed his arms, pointing toward the man trying to hide in the shadows of the mill.

Gabe recognized him as a man known as John. He'd come into town after the gold mine in Cave Gulch was abandoned. He'd been emaciated and sick from exposure. Doc Worthington treated him, then marched John down to the lumber mill to meet Silas. From what Gabe knew, he was a quiet, hard worker who hadn't caused a single problem.

"Exactly what is your problem with him?" Gabe slid his gun into the holster, nodding to Cash and Beau to do the same.

"It's *him*," the miner ground out, as if those words should be explanation enough. When Gabe's brows rose, the man huffed out a frustrated breath. "He's a Chinaman, Sheriff, and we don't want their kind here." He looked around at his fellow miners, who mumbled their agreement. Emboldened, the man took a step toward Gabe, who stood his ground. "We don't want to do business with the likes of him."

"What mine do you men work for?" Cash asked. There were only a few near Splendor, and only one that employed more than a handful of miners.

"Devil Dancer," one called out, stating the largest mine, which employed a couple dozen men.

Cash grinned at Gabe, who shook his head.

"Well now, I believe we can work this out. You see, my wife, Magdelena Evans, controls that mine. I know for a fact she has no issues with John." Gabe smirked at the shocked looks on the miners' faces.

"That ain't right," one of the men yelled. "We was told Jackson Campanel owns the mine with his partner, Thomas Pennington."

"You've got your facts wrong, mister. Jackson Campanel is my stepson. He inherited half the mine when his father died."

"You see there. I'm right," the same man called back.

"Not quite. Jackson is seven years old. As his guardian, Magdalena controls the mine."

The miners shot surprised glances at each other, mumbling amongst themselves.

"What about that Pennington fella. Don't he have a say in this?"

"He's in prison. Magdalena bought him out. Jackson, who now owns a hundred percent of the Devil Dancer, is your employer." Gabe took a couple steps closer, his face hardening. "I suggest you get done with any business you have in town, including picking up supplies from John over there, then get back to the mine. I'll be sure to let Lena know how you feel."

"Hell, there's no call for that, Sheriff." An older miner, tall and rail thin with a shaggy, graying beard, stepped forward. "She don't need to know about any of this. We'll get the supplies and head out. We won't cause no more trouble."

"Just get the supplies and go. And I don't want to hear you've created any problems for John." Gabe glanced at Cash and Beau. "You two stay here and make sure they do as this man says." He didn't add that he'd be talking with Lena.

"You go ahead and take care of business, Gabe. Beau and I have this." Cash turned to the miners. "You heard the sheriff. Get moving." Shifting his gaze, he scanned the area for Alison, wondering where'd she'd gone. It didn't matter. He'd already made up his mind what he needed to do. As soon as the miners rode out, he'd get to work on it.

"I need to send a telegram, Bernie."

"Sure, Cash." The clerk slid a piece of paper across the counter, then handed Cash a pencil. "Write it all down and I'll get it out right away."

A couple minutes passed while he composed his message, then handed the paper to Bernie. He pushed his glasses further up on the bridge of his nose and read it a couple times, his brows furrowing. Glancing up, he started to speak, but Cash stopped him.

"Not a word of this to anyone, Bernie. Not even Gabe. This is between you, me, and the man at the other end of the telegraph line. Understand?"

Bernie looked offended as he set the paper down and crossed his arms. "I'd never say a word and you darn well know it. I'm just a little surprised, that's all. Thought you two had a spark going."

Cash's jaw tightened. "Well, you're wrong." Shoving a hand in his pocket, he pulled out some cash. "Get to me right away when you hear back." Stalking outside, he drew in a deep breath, making his way back to the sheriff's office. He'd put off dealing with his questions long enough, and the warnings in his gut continued to get stronger. The answer would come back confirming what she'd told him or it wouldn't. Either way, he'd deal with it.

Alison's frustration had risen several levels after three days without learning anything about the day her brother was shot. She'd asked subtle questions of Bernie Griggs, Stan Petermann, and Silas Jenks. All longtime residents. They'd all told her the same. The robbers were gunned down as they tried to get away, using innocent people as shields. Several townspeople, as well as the sheriff and his men, were involved, but no one saw who fired the shots killing each outlaw.

By the way each man had avoided looking her in the eyes, she knew they were either protecting her from the gruesome details or hiding a killer. The idea of Bobby getting involved with a band of outlaws simply couldn't have happened.

He'd always been quiet and gentle, with a sweet nature. Picking up a rifle and joining the Confederate States of America had been an act prompted by anger and loss. The war had lasted a few short months after he enlisted, not nearly enough time to turn a kind young man, with a love of animals and children, into a ruthless outlaw. Alison couldn't accept it, knowing there had to be more to what happened.

"Good evening, Mrs. Burns." Clay McCord removed his hat as he walked into her shop, looking around at the fabric, dresses, and hats displayed throughout.

"Mr. McCord." Her voice caught as she took in the sight of the lean, muscled clerk from the general store. Close to six feet tall with thick, light brown hair, olive skin, and gray eyes rimmed in a deep brown, he seemed more suited for working outside with his hands, possibly giving orders, than standing behind a counter selling flour and sugar. They'd spoken a few times, leaving her with the impression there was much more to the man than he wanted anyone to know. "I was about to close up. What may I do for you?"

"I know this may come across as being presumptuous, but I wondered if you would have supper with me tonight."

The request caught her by surprise, washing the easy smile from her face. She knew rumors were circulating about her and Cash, and as much as she'd hoped they were true, he hadn't tried to talk to her for almost a week. She'd walked by the sheriff's office a few times and once by the house he shared with Beau, hoping to catch a glimpse of him. Although embarrassed, she'd left a message with Gabe, asking Cash to stop by when he had time. He never appeared.

Each night, she'd drawn up the covers, then stared at the ceiling, wondering what she'd said or done to keep him away, deciding he'd simply lost interest. Given her quest to find out the truth about Bobby, becoming close to Cash wouldn't be smart. Still, she missed him more than she cared to admit.

"What a lovely offer, Mr. McCord. Of course I'll have supper with you. It will take me a few minutes to finish and lock up. Would you like me to meet you?"

"No, ma'am. I'll wait if that's all right." He fingered the brim of his hat, shifting his feet.

"Of course. I'll just be a minute."

Putting away the hat she'd been creating, she grabbed her shawl, then turned off the lamps before joining him near the door. Locking up, she walked alongside him to the restaurant she'd visited with Cash. Betts sent them a broad smile, nodding toward a table near the front as she finished taking orders from a couple in an alcove close to the kitchen.

As Alison took her seat, she glanced toward the couple and smiled, raising her hand when she recognized Caroline and Beau. Both returned her greeting before resuming what appeared to be an intense conversation, Beau's voice rising before Caro placed a hand on his arm.

"Doesn't look good."

Alison's attention moved to Clay, who still watched the now animated conversation across the room. "What doesn't look good?"

"Beau and Mrs. Iverson."

"It's probably nothing more than friends disagreeing." Alison had heard the rumors of the two being more than friends, but she'd never seen them together until today.

"I heard she's decided to continue on to San Francisco as soon as the snow clears between Montana and Idaho. I'm guessing she'll be here no more than another month, six weeks at the most."

Seeing Betts approach, he glanced up at a board hanging on the wall where the menu had been listed.

"That's a shame. I'm sure Mr. Davis won't be happy with her decision."

Alison knew Caroline Iverson had made the decision to travel west after the death of her husband. She'd run into her childhood friend, Gabe Evans, in Big Pine, making the decision to winter in Splendor before resuming her trip to San Francisco. Alison was certain neither Caro nor Beau had ever expected to form an attachment.

"What would you like, Mrs. Burns?" Betts asked, smiling.

Alison hastily read the menu, deciding on the chicken.

"And you, Mr. McCord?"

"I believe I'll have the stew tonight. And coffee."

"I'll get coffee for both of you and bring your food right out."

As Betts hurried away, Alison heard the bell on the front door chime, sucking in a breath as Cash entered, walking straight toward Beau's table. He hadn't noticed her, didn't even look at the other diners as he stopped at their table. Removing his hat and nodding at Caro, he leaned down to speak with Beau, whose face turned grim at whatever Cash said.

Alison stared, unable to turn her gaze away from him. Dressed all in black, his broad shoulders squared, light stubble on his face, he presented a striking presence, making her chest tighten and mouth go dry. Before she could turn her head, he whipped around, his gaze locking with hers, then moving to Clay, eyes narrowed. In an instant, he'd closed the space between Beau's table and theirs, staring down at her.

"Good evening, Cash. Would you care to join us?" Clay couldn't miss the tension between Cash and Alison. He'd already heard the deputy might be courting the young widow, but he'd never seen them together, and he'd been watching. When Clay believed the rumors were untrue, he'd decided to take a chance and invite her to supper. Amusement tilted his mouth up, even as he held his tongue. He surely didn't want to get on the bad side of Cash Coulter.

"Not tonight." The reply held no warmth as he continued to watch Alison. "How are you, Mrs. Burns?"

Her heart pounding in her chest, she cleared her throat, taken aback at the formality. "I'm wonderful, Mr. Coulter. It's a beautiful evening, don't you think?"

Hell no, he thought before ripping his gaze from hers, ignoring her question. "Thanks for the offer, Clay, but I've had my supper. You two enjoy yourselves." Smashing his hat down on his head, he stalked out, letting the door slam behind him.

"What do you think that was about?" Clay sipped his coffee, a slight gleam in his eyes.

Unfolding her napkin, she played with the edges, unsure of what to make of Cash's response. She'd accepted Clay's offer after not hearing from or seeing Cash for almost a week, even though the jail stood a hundred feet from her shop. The man had her in knots and it was all his fault. Frustration gripped her. Here she sat with a handsome man, about to enjoy a good meal. Instead of letting herself appreciate the evening, Alison found herself fighting down growing anger.

"I'm sure I don't know." She picked up her coffee, taking a healthy swallow as Betts set down their plates. Breathing in the wonderful aroma, she grabbed her fork. "This is such a wonderful treat, Mr. McCord. Thank you for inviting me."

A smile spread across Clay's face. "Believe me, Mrs. Burns. It's my pleasure."

Chapter Eleven

Cash slammed open the door and stalked into the sheriff's office, startling Gabe into reaching for his gun, then pulling his hand back.

"Something bothering you?"

Cash shot him an evil glare, tossing his hat on the desk. "You're supposed to be at the Dixie with your wife. What are you doing here?" He'd hoped to have some time alone to calm down after seeing Alison with Clay. His reaction made no sense. After his decision to send a telegram to a friend in Kentucky, he'd decided to let their friendship cool off until he figured out what bothered him about her. But when he saw her tonight, the reality of how he felt slammed into his stomach like a mule's kick. Walking to a cabinet, he opened the door, pulling out a bottle of whiskey and a glass. "You want one?"

"No, thanks." Gabe watched his friend toss back a shot, then pour another, wondering what had happened. "You want to talk about it?"

"Hell no. I'd rather drink it away."

Gabe chuckled. "Must be about Alison Burns."

Cash almost choked on his next swallow. "Who says it has to be about anybody?"

"The way you're acting, it sure better be." Gabe sat back, interlacing his hands behind his head.

Mumbling a curse, Cash plopped into a nearby chair. "She's having supper with Clay McCord."

Gabe thought about the information for a moment, his mouth twisting into a wry grin. "And?"

"And what? She's letting Clay court her."

"You remember me giving you a message from her?"

Cash's lips thinned as he nodded.

"Did you ever go see her like she requested?"

"I've been busy." Cash set down his glass and crossed his arms.

"Yeah. Playing cards at the Dixie or Rose, having supper with Noah and Abby, and taking extra rounds around the town at night. Seems like your plan to avoid her worked." Gabe stood, grabbing his hat. "Guess I'll head over to the Dixie, see if I can convince Lena to come home early." He walked toward the door, turning back toward Cash. "Did you ever hear back from Kentucky?"

Cash's head snapped up. "What do you know about that?"

Gabe held his hands up. "Wasn't Bernie's fault. The new kid he hired mistook me for you. Bernie told him to tell you he hadn't gotten a reply from Kentucky. Poor boy turned beet red when he realized he'd given the message to me and not you." Gabe's face sobered. "You don't believe her story about being a widow and moving to Montana, do you?"

Cash picked up his glass, rolling it between his fingers, not looking at Gabe. "No."

He took a couple steps forward, clasping Cash's shoulder. "Then it's best you stay away from her until you get the answers you need. Your instincts have saved you more than once."

"And if what she told me is true?" Cash squeezed the bridge of his nose.

"Then you take her away from Clay."

"Simple as that?"

"The way she looks at you, Cash? Yes, it could be as simple as that."

"Thank you for supper, Mr. McCord. I had a wonderful time." *Until Cash arrived, spoiling what had been a pleasant evening,* she thought. "Perhaps you'd like to come for supper one night."

Clay shifted from one foot to the other as he stood outside her shop. He respected Cash, knew his reputation as an honest man, and didn't want to cause trouble between him and Alison. Still, Alison was a widow, and quite an attractive one.

"I didn't believe the rumors about you and the deputy were true. After his appearance at supper, I'm beginning to think there's truth to them after all."

Her eyes widened at his words. She knew of the rumors, and Cash had been open about wanting to see her. Did that mean he'd been courting her? He'd kissed her more than once, sparking unexpected desire she'd thoroughly enjoyed. After returning from the Pelletier ranch, she'd expected him to visit, invite her to supper or to join him on a walk. Instead, he'd kept his distance, not even stopping in to say good evening.

The worst had been when he'd sent her what could best be described as a menacing glare when he'd spotted her watching the commotion with the miners. She'd hoped he'd seek her out afterwards, explain what caused the incident, assure her all was well. He hadn't.

Clay watched as her expression changed, as if she were struggling with different answers to a difficult decision. He didn't need someone to spell it out for him. "It may be best to keep our distance until you know your feelings for Cash." Clay had no intention of causing her added anxiety or stepping between her and Cash.

"You may be right. It's just..." She caught her bottom lip between her teeth, keeping her eyes focused on the floor.

"Just?" Clay quirked a brow, waiting.

Raising her gaze to his, she studied his face, deciding she could confide in him. "Until seeing me with you at supper, he hadn't spoken to me in almost a week. I don't know what he's thinking, except he's changed his mind and has lost interest."

Clay let loose with a robust laugh, his eyes shining. "Believe me, Cash Coulter hasn't lost interest. If he's who you want, wait him out. I don't know him well, but he seems the kind of man who keeps his feelings under tight control, sharing with a few people he trusts."

She thought of who he seemed to be close to, coming up with Beau, Dax and Luke Pelletier, and possibly Gabe. Charming and smart, he could hold a conversation with anyone. Opening up about how he felt, though? She doubted that came as easily. Then again, she'd kept her reason for living in Splendor to herself, sharing nothing of her true beliefs with anyone. When he discovered why she'd traveled across country, Alison had no doubt he'd push her out of his life.

"Such as Beau?"

"That's my guess." Clay set his hat atop his head. "Goodnight, Mrs. Burns. It was a pleasure."

"Mr. McCord, may I ask you a question?"

"Of course."

She braced herself, hoping he might have some answers. "Do you know who killed the men involved in the bank robbery last year?"

Of all the questions he would've guessed she'd ask, this one wasn't even on his list. He narrowed his gaze, wondering why a robbery months in the past would draw her interest.

"Why would such an unsavory event hold any interest for you?"

Crossing her arms, she worked to control the frustration bubbling inside. Not one person would give her a straight answer, even though she felt certain they had them.

"I'm curious, nothing more. It's a simple question, Mr. McCord."

His lips thinned. "Sorry, but I arrived in town after the robbery, so I don't have any answers for you. Why don't you ask the sheriff? From what I've heard, he and his men were there, along with several others." He shot her one last look. "I'd best be leaving."

"I don't even know why I'm so curious." Another lie added to all the others. "It's not important. Goodnight again, Mr. McCord."

Tipping his hat, Clay strolled away, chewing on the possibility there was much more to Alison's question than simple curiosity.

Cash saddled Hunter, ready to get out of town on a long ride, ending at the Pelletier ranch. Noah told him his horse had healed enough to ride, as long as Cash didn't push him too hard—whatever that was supposed to mean. Horses were always pushed hard, but he'd be careful. He and Hunter had been partners a long time, and he trusted the horse more than most people.

He'd received a short telegram the morning after seeing Alison with Clay. Although there were a number of people named Burns in the area, his contact had found nothing so far about a marriage involving an Alison Burns near Richmond, Kentucky. He needed her maiden name and the first name of the groom. Cash had crumpled up the piece of paper, swearing under his breath, wondering how he'd get those pieces of information.

Then he had a thought. Rachel and Ginny Pelletier had used her services and became friends with Alison. They might have the answers.

"Thanks for letting me use Joker." Cash swung up on Hunter, looking over at Noah standing a few feet away, holding baby Gabriel in his arms. "Isn't he a little young for you to be wandering around town with him?"

The grin splitting Noah's face forced a smile out of Cash. "Abby and Lydia are having lunch at Suzanne's. I thought little Gabe and I could use some time alone..." As his voice trailed off, he spotted his wife stepping outside, searching for him. "There's your mama now," he whispered to Gabriel.

"You're a lucky man, Noah." Cash couldn't help the slight pang of jealousy, although he didn't begrudge Abby and Noah a moment of their happiness. They deserved every bit of it after the ordeals they'd endured before marrying.

"How well I know it. I'd best give him back to his mama before he starts fretting."

Cash turned Hunter north, toward the Pelletier ranch. First, he'd ride by the house Noah was helping Gabe build a few miles from town on a hill overlooking a spectacular waterfall.

Taking a path off the main road, he meandered up a winding trail until he came to a meadow dotted with stands of pine and fir. At least a foot of snow still covered the ground, and if Cash had to guess, he believed more snow would come before they moved into summer.

In the center of the meadow, a large, four-walled structured had taken shape over the last few weeks. Gabe had spent whatever time he could spare from his duties as sheriff and co-owner of the hotel to get the house ready to move into by July. He'd moved Lena out of Suzanne's boardinghouse and into his small structure behind the jail. Now he was anxious to give his bride a real home.

Hearing the sound of hammering, Cash nudged Hunter forward.

"Thought I'd find you here." Cash slid to the ground as Gabe tossed the hammer aside.

"Been here since dawn and I can't tell a lick of difference." Even with the chill of the snow, he wiped a sleeve across his brow. "Is there trouble in town?"

"Not at all. Thought I'd come by to see your progress before riding out to see the Pelletiers. Beau's on duty today. At least until I get back." He skimmed his hand over the wooden frame, appreciating the level of detail. "I'd be happy to help out for a while."

"I heard you're pretty good with wood." Gabe handed Cash a ladle full of water. The creek a few yards away would supply them with what they needed.

"Where'd you hear that?" Cash took a swallow, then gave it back.

"Monty at the lumber mill said you built shelves for Alison's shop. Said you did a real good job." Gabe chuckled at the disgruntled look on Cash's face.

"How the hell would a kid like Monty know good from bad? He can't be more than fifteen."

"Seventeen, according to Silas. Anyway, you're welcome to work here anytime, although your services would be most useful inside where you wouldn't have to deal with the melting snow."

"Cabinets and doors?" Cash perked up at the thought of working with his hands again, creating something useful.

"And bookcases. Lena and Jack love to read. There must be six boxes full of books in the office at the Dixie, and I think they've both read every one." Gabe's features softened as he talked about his wife and stepson.

Another twinge of envy washed over Cash. Besides himself, Beau, Bull, Nick, and Travis were still single, although each seemed to have their sights set on someone. Travis had a fondness for Lena's lifelong friend, Isabella. Bull couldn't keep his eyes off Lydia whenever she was around. Nick's feelings for Suzanne were clear, although neither would admit it. And Beau had been smitten with Caro since the first day she rode into town with Gabe. Her announcement she'd be moving on to San Francisco in early summer had struck Beau hard. There wasn't much his friend could do or say about it. She'd told everyone of her plan to winter in Splendor, then head west to see the Pacific Ocean. A rich widow, she had the means and strength of character to do whatever she wanted, including leaving Beau behind.

"Any word on Alison?"

Gabe's question pulled Cash from his musings. "Not much. So far, there's nothing about a marriage involving the name Burns near her home in Kentucky." He told Gabe of his plan to speak with Rachel and Ginny.

"Some weddings weren't recorded properly during the war, and a good number of records were lost or destroyed. You know, Cash, there's a chance you won't find answers. What will you do if your friend comes back with nothing?" Gabe leaned against the side of his unfinished house, hoping whatever Cash learned would validate Alison's story.

Cash picked up Hunter's reins, swinging into the saddle in one smooth movement. He looked at Gabe, his face intense. "I don't know."

"Sorry, Cash. I wish we knew more." Rachel refilled his coffee cup, then sat down next to Ginny. "We probably know less about her than you do."

"She's not too open about her past." Ginny slid forward on the sofa. "You don't believe her story about being a widow?"

He didn't want to cause problems between Alison and the people of Splendor. If his suspicions were groundless, she'd hate him for digging into her past and sharing his doubts with women she thought of as friends.

"I'm not certain what to think."

"About what?" Cash turned to see Dax walk in, heading straight for him and extending his hand.

"He's looking for information about Alison," Rachel offered. "Why don't you sit down and I'll get you some coffee."

Dax kissed her on the cheek, taking her place on the sofa, then sent a questioning look at Cash. "What are you looking for, and why?"

He walked to the window, watching a wind funnel kick up dirt in the pasture by the barn. Turning back to Dax, Cash expelled a deep breath. "It's a gut feeling. Her past doesn't make sense to me. Neither does her traveling across country to start a new life."

"Caro did the same, as did Isabella." Dax took the cup Rachel handed him, then tugged her down next to him.

"Caro is financially secure with the desire to travel, see the west. Besides, Gabe grew up with her. Isabella came out to bring Jackson home to Lena. She's Lena's closest friend. Alison knew no one in Splendor before getting off the stage. She has little money and no friends or relatives west of Kentucky—at least none that she's mentioned." Cash thought a moment about another inconsistency. "Besides, she's a widow, but her kisses..." He looked at Rachel and Ginny, both with eyes wide, holding back smiles. "Sorry, ladies. I shouldn't have mentioned—"

"Just say it, Cash. Nothing will leave this room." Rachel patted Dax on the thigh before glancing up at him. "Right?"

Dax scrubbed a hand over his face, his lips tipping up in amusement. "No, Rach. Nothing leaves this room."

"So?" Ginny prompted.

"Ah, hell,'" Cash mumbled before deciding to say it out load. Maybe it would sound ridiculous when he presented his biggest doubt to his friends. "She doesn't kiss like a woman who's a widow."

"Without experience," Rachel said, more to herself than the others. "Maybe she wasn't married long before he went to war."

"I don't think so. The woman is as green as they come." Cash wished he hadn't said anything.

"I wondered why she doesn't wear a ring. Most widows wear their wedding band for months or years after their husband's death." Ginny stood, pacing toward the dining room. Everyone sat in silence for a few moments until she turned back to them. "I have a friend in Richmond, Kentucky. Would it help if I sent her a telegram and asked if she ever knew Alison or a man named Burns?"

"That's right. You're from Kentucky. I had no idea you lived in Richmond." Rachel turned her head at the sound of Patrick's voice as he awakened from his nap. "I'd better go grab him before he starts pounding on the wall by his bed."

Cash heard little of what Rachel said, still focused on Ginny's offer. "I'd appreciate it if you'd get a message to your friend."

"I'll ride into town tomorrow." She walked up to him, settling a hand on his shoulder. "And don't worry. None of us will say a word to Alison or anyone else."

Chapter Twelve

Cash sat outside the sheriff's office the following morning, watching farmers and ranchers come in for supplies or visit the bank. By late Friday afternoon, the town would be busy with miners and cowboys collecting their pay and celebrating at either the Dixie or the Rose. Gabe, Beau, and he stayed alert Friday afternoon through Saturday night. He doubted it would change when Gabe and Lena moved into their new home in a few months. Unless he quit his job as sheriff to focus on helping with the hotel and its growing business.

"Deputy." Silas tipped his hat, stopping in front of Cash's chair. "I wanted to thank you and the others again for helping with the situation with John. I don't know what would've happened if you three weren't in town."

Just then, the door opened and Beau stepped outside, a cup of coffee in his hand. "Good morning, Silas."

"Beau."

"Silas stopped by to thank us for helping him with John." It always surprised Cash the way people thanked them for doing their job.

"No need for thanks, Silas. That's what we're here for. Do you want some coffee?" Beau asked, grabbing a nearby chair, the legs scraping against the boardwalk as he pulled it forward.

"Not this morning. John asked me to meet him at the other end of town and I'm already late. I'll see you boys around." Silas took off, leaving Cash and Beau to stare after him.

"What do you think that's about?" Beau sipped his coffee, his gaze following Silas.

"I've no idea."

A few minutes later, they had their answer. John and Silas sat atop a wagon filled with Chinese men and at least one woman, passing in front of them as it headed toward the lumber mill.

"What the..." Cash's voice trailed off as he and Beau stood, following the wagon to the end of the street.

"What's going on here, Silas?" Beau asked.

"Seems John sent word to some of his friends up north at Cave Gulch. With the closing of the mine, they had no way to make a living." Silas waved his arms in the air. "I don't know what he expects me to do with them. I've got all the help I need."

"Looks to be five men and one woman." Beau noted how they all huddled together in the wagon, talking amongst themselves, John sitting in a prominent place in the middle of the group.

"You may have yourself a problem, Silas. Did you say anything to John about hiring more people?" Cash rubbed the short stubble on his jaw and chin.

"Guess we could ask around, see if anyone needs help."

"What's going on?"

The men turned to see Gabe ride up behind them on Blackheart, the stallion he'd owned since he joined the Union Army. Dismounting, he walked closer, noticing the people in the wagon.

"Seems like Silas's helper, John, told his friends in Cave Gulch there were jobs in Splendor. So..." Cash nodded toward the six newcomers.

"So they decided to come." Gabe would've laughed if the situation weren't so precarious. Tension against the Chinese ran high in many towns. The fact they took jobs at far reduced wages, worked long hours in dismal conditions, never complained, and lived on little food and less sleep prompted many mine owners and those funding the railroads to hire them over immigrants from Europe, the traditional workers in these industries.

"Silas doesn't have any jobs. Noah's decided to hire help, but he needs someone with experience in a livery, working a forge, and doctoring horses. I doubt any of the people in the wagon could handle it." Reluctantly, Cash strolled over to the wagon. "John, do any of them speak English?"

"No one here speaks English but me, Mr. Cash." John stood, gesturing toward his friends. "But they work hard. You know of jobs?"

"Sorry, John. I only know of one, and that's with Noah Brandt at the livery. He's going to be real picky about who uses his equipment and tends the horses he takes in. I can ask around, but you'll need to find them a place to live. And they'll need to find work soon."

"What kind of work do they want?" Gabe strolled up behind Cash, Beau standing a couple feet away.

"They are miners, Sheriff. This man, Zhao, is good with animals. This man, Wu, is a cook."

"And the woman?" Gabe stared at the woman cowering behind the men.

"Li is a serving girl." John's gaze darted away from Gabe, telling the sheriff what he suspected.

"We'll ask around, but you need to find them a place to stay. I'm warning you. There will be some people in town who aren't going to like the fact you brought them here." Gabe turned toward Cash and Beau. "Cash, check with Stan. See if he needs any help at his store. And you might as well check with Alison. She seems to be getting pretty busy."

"Gabe, I don't think—"

"Just ask her, Cash. You don't have to stick around afterwards. Beau, you ask around with the other merchants. I'll talk to Nick and Lena and the local ranchers. Spring is almost here so they may need some help."

Cash turned abruptly, heading toward the general store, muttering words Gabe was certain he didn't want to hear.

"You know, I can talk to Alison instead of Cash." Beau glanced over his shoulder at his friend, knowing the last person Cash wanted to see was Alison.

"You could, but that wouldn't get them together, would it?"

"Anyone ever call you an evil man, Colonel Evans?" Beau joked, although he struggled to find any humor in Cash's situation.

"Only those who reported to me during the war, Captain." Gabe still found it surprising how men who fought for the South, such as the Pelletiers, Cash, and Beau, could become such close friends of an ex-Union colonel. Maybe it was their way of putting the destruction behind them. Or perhaps it was their desire to start a new life and forget the prejudices and hatred of the past. Either way, he felt fortunate to live in a town where men from both sides could work together.

Cash's exasperation with Gabe built the closer he got to the general store. He didn't mind talking to Stan, letting him know about the people John brought into town. The same request to speak to

Alison caused a different reaction and had him seething. His friend, and boss, knew what he asked of Cash, knew he could have sent Beau instead, yet still went ahead and ordered him to face her.

The problem wasn't that he didn't like her. The problem was he liked her *too* much—to a point he couldn't sleep at night without dreaming of her and wanting her. He'd woken up more than once with his bed soaked from vivid images of them together. Being around her made the desire worse, threatening the tenuous control he forced himself to maintain. And the reasons for such tight restraint centered on the suspicions he held about her past. He'd almost thrown those suspicions away when he'd seen her and Clay at supper. Anger and jealousy had flared fast and intense until he'd wanted to pull the man out of his chair and toss him out the door. Not that he could. Clay stood about as tall and weighed as much as Cash. At best, it might be an even match.

Stomping his feet on the boardwalk to rid his boots of dirt, he pushed the door open and stepped inside the general store, coming face-to-face with the man he'd been cursing—Clay McCord.

"What can I do for you, Deputy?" Clay stepped away from a table where he'd been rearranging items, and faced Cash, his features watchful and wary.

"Is Stan around?"

"He left to take care of something at home. I'll be glad to give him a message, or you can come back in about an hour."

"Giving you the message will do." Cash explained about the Chinese workers, asking Clay to pass the information along to Stan.

"I'll be glad to tell him. I doubt he'll hire anyone right now, but I've been wrong before."

Seemed like a good time to bring up the fact Clay had been wrong to step between Alison and him. He'd stepped over a line most men wouldn't when it came Cash. Yet, in a way, he couldn't blame Clay. Cash hadn't expressed his feelings to Alison, and he didn't know how she felt about him. The fact she'd let Clay escort her to supper didn't bode well for them continuing to see each other. And Cash had no one to blame but himself. His actions had said as much as any words, pushing her away, causing her to believe he held no feelings for her. Nothing could be further from the truth. The problem didn't lie with Alison herself. His instincts were the culprit, ripping him apart as he searched for answers he could accept. Answers that may not surface for weeks or months.

"Fair enough. Have him talk to Silas or John at the lumber mill if he does need help. They'll know where the men are staying." Turning, he grabbed the door handle, halting at Clay's words.

"She's a real nice lady, Cash. Any man would be honored to court her."

"Are *you* courting her?" Cash ground out, not turning to look at Clay.

"No. I made it clear that as long as she has feelings for you, I'd stay away." Clay walked up next to him, pinning him with a look Cash couldn't quite decipher. "But if you decide to back off, I'll be at her door before you have a chance to change your mind." He stepped away, never taking his gaze off Cash.

Cash nodded once, then left, closing the door behind him.

"Thank you, Mrs. Burns. This is just what I wanted."

"You're quite welcome, Mrs. Ivie. I hope your daughter likes it, as well." Alison followed her to the front door, holding it open as she left. When she tried to push the door closed again, a hand stopped her. Looking up, her breath hitched. Cash stood on the boardwalk, his arm extended, keeping the door open.

"Good morning, Alison."

Her heart beat a fast rhythm as her gaze wandered from his hat to the star on his chest. A thrill passed through her, the beginnings of a smile forming...until she remembered he hadn't been to visit her in a week. The joy at seeing him faded.

"Cash. What are you doing here?" She didn't step aside to allow him entry. Instead, she moved forward, blocking his path.

He let out a deep sigh, not moving his hand from the door. "May I come inside?"

"There's no need. Say what you came to say, then leave."

"I came for two reasons, Alison. This will only take a couple minutes." His gaze settled on the wary expression in her eyes, then wandered down to her full, red lips. The lump in his throat increased as he waited for her response.

"I'll give you two minutes." Yanking the door open, she moved aside, letting him pass. Closing the door, letting her back rest against it, she worked to keep her breathing normal and even. It wouldn't do her any good for him to see how much his presence affected her. How much she'd missed him.

Taking several paces away, he leaned his hip against a table, setting his hat aside.

"Gabe asked me to stop by to see if you might need any help."

Her brows crunched together. "Help?"

"A group of Chinese workers came to town and are looking for work. They've been working the mines up north at Cave Gulch. It closed down, so they moved south. We're spreading the word in case anyone needs some help."

Her heart sank. She'd thought he'd come by to see her, explain why he hadn't sought her company, maybe even ask her to supper. Instead, he'd come at the order of the sheriff.

"You can thank Gabe for thinking of me, but I don't need any help. If that's all..." She pushed from the door, ready to open it.

"There's something else."

"And what would that be?"

Cash dropped his gaze from hers, focusing on a gouge in the wooden floor, wondering why this was so hard. He'd rather face a bank robber than expose his feelings to a woman. And Alison wasn't just any woman. The desire drawing him to her wouldn't subside, no matter how hard he set his mind to it. Each day he missed her more, needing to see her smile, hear her laugh. Pushing her away hadn't helped at all.

"I've missed you," he breathed out, looking up, watching her eyes widen.

"I don't know why. I've been right here every day, a few doors away from the jail." Even as she spoke the words, her feet carried her toward him.

"True."

She shook her head, confusion taking over the irritation she'd felt at his arrival. "I don't understand."

He reached out, waiting until she took the last few steps to stand in front of him, touching her fingers to his. Threading his fingers through hers, he tugged her closer.

"I'm not an easy person, Allie. I've never believed in happy endings or felt the desire to settle down." He closed his eyes, searching for the words, allowing her time to stop his confession.

Her chest tightened at his use of her nickname. The one her family and friends in Kentucky used. Odd, but the sound of it from his lips made her feel as if she were home.

Opening his eyes, his gaze locked on hers. "Trouble is, I can't stop thinking about you. I want you more than I've ever wanted any woman. Staying away hasn't helped. The more I try, the more I need to be near you. Does that make any sense? Or have I completely lost my mind?"

A shaky laugh escaped as she tightened her grip. "You may have lost your mind, but that's not for me to decide. However, you *do* make sense." Her lips curved upward as her face softened.

Moving his other hand behind her back, he drew her closer until they were a breath apart.

She tensed at the intimacy. Even though they'd shared several kisses, this felt more personal, more familiar. The passion she felt for Cash thrilled and scared her. He thought she was a widow, experienced. It couldn't be further from the truth.

Feeling her stiffen, he loosened his hold, allowing her to step away. She didn't. Instead, she settled her hands on his arms and waited.

"Unless you say different, I'm still courting you, Allie. I've been a fool, trying to ignore my feelings for you. No longer." Tilting her chin up with a finger, he studied her face. "All right?"

Words wouldn't come, as if some magical force had claimed her, rendering her speechless. Instead, she nodded, watching as he drew her closer.

"I'm going to kiss you."

Again, all she could do was nod, closing her eyes. A moment later, his warm lips brushed across hers, igniting a heat she didn't know how to control. Her body began to tremble, her heart pounding as he traced her lips with his tongue, seeking entry. Opening for him, her mind began to spin when he delved inside. A voice in her head warned her to back away, break the kiss. Ignoring it, she moved her hands to the back of his head, threading her fingers through his hair, drawing him down.

A deep groan signaled his approval. His arms became a band of steel around her, tightening, as if he planned to never let her go. Splaying his hands on her back, he pressed their bodies closer, feeling the fire from her flow into him. He couldn't get close enough, and this wasn't the time or place to take it further. Breaking the kiss, he sucked in a ragged breath, setting her a few inches away.

"What I want to do to you can't be done in the middle of your shop." He grinned, watching her glazed expression take in his meaning.

Stepping away, she touched a finger to her lips, certain she could still feel the vibrations from their kiss. "I, um... That was..."

He almost chuckled at the stunned look on her face. "Yes, it was, and we aren't done, Allie." Straightening, he picked up his hat, touching his lips to her forehead. "I'm taking you to supper tonight." Watching her expression, he waited.

Finding her voice, her lips parted. "I'd like that."

Chapter Thirteen

"Mind if I join you?" Cash settled against the bar, signaling Paul for a whiskey.

"Doesn't seem I have a choice." Nick Barnett stared down into his own glass, not looking over at Cash.

Taking the glass from Paul, he raised his eyebrows at the bartender, who glanced at Nick, then shrugged. Nick seldom had what most people would consider a bad day. He took good and bad news with the same even temper, showing little emotion except when someone he cared about was threatened.

"Everyone all right, Nick?"

Shifting, he glanced at Cash. "Yes. Why do you ask?"

"Curious is all. You seem to be wrestling with something, so I wondered if Lena or Jack were sick, or..."

Nick let the silence stretch out between them. The only other person who knew what troubled him was Gabe, his friend and business partner. Not even Lena, whom he had known since they were children in New Orleans, trying to pull themselves out of the lives they'd been dealt by having prostitutes as mothers, knew what bothered him.

"As far as I know, both are fine. Gabe would be the one to ask." He picked up his glass, started to take a sip, then set it back down.

"And Suzanne?"

Nick's head snapped toward Cash, his eyes narrowing. "What about Suzanne?"

"Nothing. Just wondered if she was doing all right." Cash took another swallow of whiskey. He'd allow himself one drink before making his last tour of the town, then he'd clean up to escort Alison to supper. A slight grin formed at the thought.

"How should I know what's going on with Suzanne? She doesn't answer to me." Nick's hardened voice might dissuade most people. Too bad Cash wasn't most people.

Turning to face the bar, he lowered his voice. "Hell, Nick. That woman can't buy a new dress without you knowing about it. From what I can see, you won't even let her go into the general store alone. Don't tell me whatever's going on with you has nothing to do with Suzanne because that would be plain hogwash."

Nick picked up his glass, glaring at Cash before he tossed it back in one gulp. "I'm tired of waiting."

"For what?"

"For that skittish woman to give me some indication she wants more from me than friendship."

Cash's bark of laughter had heads turning in their direction. Ignoring them, he lowered his voice.

"When did you start backing down from a challenge? Seems to me you're the one who ought to make it clear how you feel. You know her story as well as anyone."

Nick sighed. He did know her story. How her husband and daughter were killed in a freak blizzard years before, leaving her more broken than living. It had taken time, but she'd moved past the pain, opening the boardinghouse and building a solitary life by putting all she had into her work. With a heart as big as Montana, she looked out for everyone except herself, rarely taking a day off and eschewing any thought of finding love a second time.

"And her story is why I've been so patient. Look around, Cash. Not a person in this town is immune to heartbreak. All of us have faced loss." He nodded at Paul to fill his glass a second time.

"Some people take longer to heal. Truth is, some never do, accepting whatever is left of their life." Cash finished the last of his whiskey, leaning his arms on the bar. "I think Suzanne has gotten into a routine she understands. Unless someone gives her a reason to change, she'll keep getting up each day, doing what she did the day before. *You're* the one who has to change it."

"What would you suggest?" Sarcasm seeped from Nick as a scowl crossed his face.

"Court her. Take her to supper or for a ride in the country. Get her out of the boardinghouse."

"I've tried. Every day, she gets up before dawn, works her fingers to the bone, then falls into bed about midnight." Nick rubbed his temple, feeling his head throb.

"As I recall, you, Gabe, and Lena own half the boardinghouse and are paying to expand the restaurant. Can't you get someone to take her place for a day or evening?"

Nick thought a moment, his eyes taking on a familiar glint. "Mondays are slow. That's one of the days Suzanne has that orphan girl, Rosemary, come in to help clean. Sometimes her brother, Ben, joins her. She's been talking to Rosemary about working in the dining room..." His voice drifted off as he seemed to be working through the idea. "I might be able to arrange something."

Cash clasped him on the shoulder. "No time like now." Straightening, he turned toward the door.

"How do you know so much about this?"

"Plain ol' experience," Cash muttered under his breath, wishing it were true.

Alison closed the shop, locking the front door at least an hour before she expected Cash. Her stomach, and thoughts, had been in turmoil since he'd left, leaving her body tingling with a need she had no idea how to soothe.

Dashing upstairs, she slipped out of her clothes, then grabbed the sponge, washing her chest, neck, and arms. Taking a seat at the table she used as a vanity, Alison let down her hair, brushing it until it shown, then re-pinned it in a loose bun. A bottle of rose water caught her attention. Her parents had given it to her before her father joined the Union Army. She hadn't used it since his funeral, and had never intended to wear it again. On impulse, she opened it, using a small amount on her neck, behind her ears, and on her wrists.

The final touch was the new dress she'd finished a week before, hanging on a hook behind her. When Alison saw it on a woman during the trip west, she vowed to make a pattern, then showcase the completed dress in her shop. Instead, when the last stitch was in place, she took it upstairs.

Slipping it on, she fastened the buttons. Standing in front of the mirror, she rotated in a circle twice, inspecting each detail. Seeing nothing amiss, she picked up her reticule and a shawl, took a deep breath, and headed down the stairs.

As she walked around the shop, adjusting hats and rearranging fabric, she heard a hearty knock. Sucking in a breath, she straightened her shoulders and unlocked the door. The look on his face pushed away the apprehension she'd been trying to ignore.

Until she saw him slowly shift his gaze from her face to her shoes, Alison hadn't realized how much she wanted Cash's approval. When he looked back into her eyes, she could've launched herself into his arms. Approval, clear as any spring day, shown on his face.

"You look stunning." The huskiness in his voice told her how much he meant his words.

"Thank you, Cash. You look very handsome." She smiled as she let her gaze drift over him. To her, he always looked magnificent, with his striking green eyes and blond hair. Tonight, he looked beyond handsome in a black shirt with a green ribbon tie and matching black slacks. The black coat hung to his thighs, and his boots had been polished until they gleamed.

Remembering his manners, he removed his hat and made a slight bow. "Are you ready?"

She nodded, locking the door to the shop, then slipping her arm through his.

They strolled down the boardwalk. When they passed Bett's restaurant, she believed they'd be eating at the boardinghouse. As they crossed the street, she looked up at him in surprise when he continued past Suzanne's and headed back toward the other end of town.

"Where—"

Cash placed a finger over her lips, silencing her question. "It's a surprise."

As they approached the end of the boardwalk, she glanced around, wondering where he was taking her, then looked up at him. His grin told her how much he was enjoying her curiosity.

Coming to a halt in front of the St. James Hotel, he hesitated a moment before opening the door.

"But Cash, they have no restaurant..." Alison's brows arched as her voice drifted off.

Without saying a word, he nodded at the clerk behind the front desk, then made a slight turn. In an alcove to the left stood a single table with a white tablecloth, a stunning silver candelabra, and the most elegant silver tableware she'd ever seen, adorned with intricate engravings. Her gaze settled on the lustrous china decorated with a fine pattern of leaves and flowers in greens and blues. In all her life, Alison had never seen anything so stunning.

"Do you like it?" The apprehension in his voice warmed her. It was obvious her answer meant a great deal to him.

"I love it, Cash." Her eyes sparkled as she looked up, seeing his features relax.

"Good evening, Mr. Coulter." A young waiter took the back of Alison's chair, pulling it out for her.

"Good evening, Bradley. I didn't know Nick and Gabe had hired you." Cash waited a moment while Alison adjusted her dress before taking his seat.

"I spoke with Mr. Barnett about a job once the restaurant opened. Sheriff Evans rode out to the ranch a few days ago and said they were ready for me. You are, well, my first customers since the full dining room doesn't open until next week." He blushed, his enthusiasm for his new job obvious. Handing them each a handwritten menu, he walked to a nearby serving cart, picking up a bottle. "May I offer each of you a glass of our Isabella wine?"

Cash glanced at Alison, whose blank face almost made him chuckle. "Thank you, Bradley. A small amount for the lady."

Pouring a half glass for Cash and a quarter glass for Alison, he set the bottle aside. "I'll give you a few minutes to read the menu and decide."

They picked up their glasses, Cash tilting his toward her. "To a memorable evening."

A smile tugged at her lips. "A memorable evening." Taking a sip, her eyes danced at the taste.

"Have you had wine before?" Cash rolled the dark red liquid around to coat the sides of the glass, then took a sip.

"Only what I've made."

He almost choked at her declaration. "You make wine?"

"Not anything as elegant as this, of course. My mother taught me how to make it. I use apples, cherries, or elderberries. Whatever is available. I have a bottle of apple wine at home if you'd like to try a glass sometime."

"Mrs. Burns, you are full of surprises."

This time, it was Alison who almost choked on her wine, thinking of the other surprises Cash knew nothing about.

Supper continued, each contributing small talk about their lives before moving west. Alison knew Cash left out much of what he saw during the war, the same as she did since her brother died. She longed to ask him more about the robbery and what happened that day.

The change in her thoughts about Splendor and the shootings unsettled her. Anger and the need for retribution controlled Alison from the moment she'd learned of Bobby's death. She still believed he never would have been willingly involved with a gang of outlaws. The thought of him pulling a gun on innocent people sent a chill through her, as questions about his innocence mounted.

"May I get you anything else?" Bradley filled their coffee cups once more, then picked up the empty dessert plates.

"I don't believe so." Cash reached into his pocket, pulling out a worn leather wallet.

"Mr. Barnett told me your supper has been taken care of, Mr. Coulter." When he saw the dark look passing over Cash's face, Bradley cleared his throat, his discomfort obvious. "He said if you have any problem with it, you need to see him."

Before Cash could react, Alison reached across the table, placing her hand over his. "Please tell Mr. Barnett thank you for us and that the evening couldn't have been better."

"Thank you. I'll certainly tell him." Flashing Alison a look of gratitude, Bradley pulled out her chair. "I hope you'll come back when the main dining room opens. It will be quite the sight."

"Oh, you can bet your horse on it, Bradley." Cash moved next to Alison, placing a hand on her lower back as he guided her outside.

"It was quite nice of Nick to treat us to supper."

Cash's scowl indicated he didn't feel the same. "I'll talk to him. Give him your regards."

He knew the irritation he felt was unreasonable. If Nick wanted to pay for their supper, so be it. Yet a part of him wanted to play a little bit the hero with Alison, which included handing over the money himself.

Ignoring his change in mood, she slid her arm through his as they crossed the street, walking toward her shop.

"I've watched them move furniture into the hotel over the last few months. Tonight is the first time I've been inside. It's magnificent. More than I would have expected for a town the size of Splendor."

"It's what Gabe, Lena, and Nick wanted. They believe Splendor's growth will continue, bringing in people with money. It will attract different kinds of people than the boardinghouse. You know they own part of Suzanne's boardinghouse, too, right?" When she nodded, Cash went on. "Gabe grew up in the hotel business in New York, so he's the intellect behind it. Nick's real sharp at business, so he runs the daily operations."

"And Lena?"

"She helps hire, although she says there isn't a lot to choose from around here for a hotel such as the St. James. They have four or five people now. Pretty soon, if no one around here is interested, they'll be looking to hire from Big Pine."

"What about the Chinese workers who came to town?" They stopped in front of the shop door, neither in a hurry to end their conversation.

"The Pelletiers hired Wu as a cook for the ranch. Lena already promised a cleaning job to a girl named Rosemary or she might have hired Sun Li." He turned her toward him, resting his hands on her shoulders, feeling a spark pass though him.

"Is Rosemary the girl who helps Suzanne now?" she asked, her voice breathless.

"Yep. She'll work both jobs." His voice became heated as he gently rubbed his hands up and down her arms.

Turning, she opened the door, gesturing inside. "Would you like to come in for a few minutes? I can make coffee."

The last thing on his mind was coffee. He should've been thinking about her reputation, what the people in town would say if someone spotted him going inside at this time of night. It seemed unlikely. Her store stood at the far southern end of town. The bank was on one side, nothing except vacant land on the other, the church and hotel across the street. Looking around, he didn't see a single person, even though the sounds of tinny piano music spilled from each of the saloons.

"Are you sure, Allie?"

Shivers washed over her again when he used her nickname. It sounded so right coming from his lips. "Well, it *is* a lot of work to make coffee, but I suppose you're worth the effort."

He chuckled. "Then yes, I'll come in for coffee."

Picking up an already lit lantern, she moved to the back of the store and upstairs to her living quarters. Until she walked through her door, it hadn't occurred to her the two of them alone might not be such a good idea. All she'd thought about was how much she didn't want him to leave, wasn't ready to end their evening together.

"You can put your hat there." She pointed to a row of hooks near the door, then moved into the kitchen. "Would you mind stoking the fire? I filled it before leaving for supper, but it's probably burned down by now." Moving to the counter, she picked up a tin of coffee, filling the empty pot from a nearby barrel.

Stoking the fire, Cash watched her, his brows knitting together. "How do you get the water up here?"

"Oh, I bring it up in a bucket. There's a well behind the building."

Her words stalled his casual efforts at bringing the fire back to life. Cash thought about her living alone and all the chores that fell to her, along with the work in her shop. Most people brought water into their home in a similar way. Same with firewood. Why did it bother him so much that Alison hauled hers upstairs by herself? Especially when he'd done the same most of his life.

She set the coffee pot on the stove, then wiped her hands. "It will be a few minutes. Do you want to have a seat?" Glancing toward the only two chairs in her home, she selected one and sat down, threading her fingers together in her lap. Instead of joining her, Cash looked around, his gaze landing on a few framed pictures. Walking to them, he bent down to get a better look at one with a young girl and boy.

"This looks like you. Who's the boy?"

Her fingers tightened as her chest constricted. There was a good reason why she never mentioned her brother.

"A neighbor boy. Very sweet. He loved animals, and would've daydreamed away most days if moth...um...his mother hadn't kept after him." She winced at the slight mistake, although Cash didn't seem to notice. Standing, Alison pointed to the picture of her mother and father, then a single one of her father in uniform. The last picture showed all four of them. "Guess he snuck into this one, too."

He heard a small catch in her voice. Sweeping his gaze across each picture once more, he looked at her, sensing a significant clue to Allie's past lay in front of him, yet he couldn't see it. "Whatever happened to him?"

"I honestly don't know. People move about, life changes. You know how it is." She didn't wait for him to answer as she walked back to the stove, picking up two cups from a nearby shelf. "I have sugar and milk if you'd like."

"No. Black is fine." Even though she'd invited him upstairs, a chill had settled over them. His asking about the pictures made it worse. When she'd handed him the cup, her hand had shaken enough for him to notice. "Is there anything wrong, Allie?"

"No. Why would you think so?" She added sugar and milk to her coffee, stirring much longer than needed to blend them.

He walked toward her, setting his cup on a nearby table. "Maybe it isn't a good idea for me to be here. I should go."

Reaching out, she touched his arm. "There are some days I miss my family more than others. They called me Allie. Did you know that?"

His eyes widened at her admission. Shortening her name had seemed natural, the same as shortening Abigail to Abby.

"I'm sorry. I shouldn't have taken the liberty, especially if it brings back bad memories."

"No. I like it when you call me Allie. It makes me feel, well...like I'm back home."

Stepping close, Cash took the cup from her hand and set it aside, then slipped his arms around her. "I like the way it sounds. You seem more of an Allie than an Alison." His warm breath washed over her face, causing her to lean further into him.

"And why is that?"

"Don't know. It's carefree, less formal. Allie is how I see you in my dreams." He touched his lips to her forehead, then tucked her head against his chest.

"You dream about me?"

"Darn near every night." His deep chuckle made her smile as her heartbeat quickened.

"I dream about you, too."

"That so?"

"Almost every night." Her breath had become ragged. She felt certain he couldn't miss the thundering of her heart against him. Shifting, she looked up into his face, eyes dark with passion.

On a groan, Cash covered her mouth with his, tightening his hold as she snuggled into him. A flash of heat so strong, so powerful jolted through him. Lifting her into his arms, he moved to the bed, then sat down, settling her on his lap, never breaking contact. His hands moved up and down her back, skimming to her slim waist, resting on the flare of her hips. She tightened her hold, as if she never planned to let go.

A firestorm of passion ripped through her as he continued to stroke her back. She squirmed against him, unable to satisfy her need to get close. Her body demanded more, even as her mind raced to understand how to sate her growing desire. When a loud moan escaped, it took a moment for her to realize it came from her.

If it had been any other woman, any other night, Cash would've continued, uncaring as to the consequences. As a widow, Allie knew what to expect and would accept the outcome of her actions. Yet something seemed amiss. No matter how much he tried to make sense of it, she didn't come across as woman of experience. He had his share of women, some being widows, and nothing about Allie spoke of an understanding of what happened between a man and a woman when passion took over.

When another moan passed from her lips to his, the reality they had to stop gripped him. Breaking the kiss, he let his lips drift from the corner of her eye, down her cheek, and along the curve of her jaw before he shifted her off his lap and onto the bed. Drawing in a shaky breath, he winced at the confusion on her face.

"Did I do something wrong?" The pain in her voice tore at his heart.

"No, sweetheart. You didn't do anything wrong." Wrapping an arm around her shoulders, he tugged Allie to his side, brushing a kiss across her temple. "You did everything right, and that is why I have to leave."

"But—"

He touched a finger to her lips. "It's late, and you consumed a good deal of wine tonight. When we make love, which I hope we will, I want you to be clear-headed, remembering every detail. You're too special to do this any other way." And he needed time to sort out his feelings, understand how a widow could be such an innocent. "If you can close the shop early on Saturday, we'll take a ride. All right?"

Swallowing the lump in her throat, she nodded, wishing he could at least hold her a little longer.

"You get some rest." Touching his lips once more to hers, he stood, walking to the door. Grabbing his hat, he glanced at her once more, a hesitant smile on his face, then closed the door behind him.

Chapter Fourteen

Big Pine, Montana

"What do you think?" Harry Penderville slid off his horse, huddling next to his brother near a dwindling campfire. Two of their men had ridden into Big Pine on several nights over the last week, getting to know the town, learning about the sheriff and his deputies, and identifying the largest bank. Harry and Milt continued to talk about the best scheme for hitting the bank and when.

"We've got to make our move before the local mine manager withdraws the payroll money on Friday." Milt sat on his haunches, using a stick to trace lazy patterns in the dirt. "Best time will be right after the bank reopens after lunch. They won't be expecting us in broad daylight. According to the boys, that's when the deputies make their afternoon rounds."

Harry straightened and paced in circles, not fond of the idea of a robbery in the middle of the day. Their older brother, Chet, had tried the same in Splendor and ended up dead, along with the others who rode with him. Harry also knew they had few options. While in Big Pine, the boys had heard Milt and his name mentioned, knowing the sheriff in Bloody Basin had sent word the gang might be on their way. Until now, all their raids had been at night. The lawmen wouldn't expect a raid in the middle of the afternoon.

"We'll post men across the street. You and I will go inside, get what we can, and get out." He watched Milt continue to draw meaningless circles in the dirt, knowing it was his brother's way of releasing stress. "Or we skip Big Pine and ride straight for Splendor."

Milt's surprised gaze locked with Harry's, his mind working as he thought about passing up a small fortune in payroll. "The money could set us up for months."

"And warn the people of Splendor we're on our way. If we take the payroll, I say we ride south, out of Montana and into Idaho, then on to California as we planned. Forget about Splendor and avenging Chet." Harry crossed his arms as he planted his feet shoulder width apart. "We'd be fools to do both."

Milt tossed down the stick and pushed to his feet, considering what Harry had said. His brother came up with a good idea once in a while, and this one made sense.

"They won't have any idea where we are if we don't ride into Big Pine. May even think we rode out of the territory." Milt glanced at the men as they sat playing cards several feet away. "We could ride on to Splendor, get our business done, then come right back here before word has spread."

"It would be a hard day's ride, but it could be done. The mine pays every two weeks. We could plan it so we find the men who killed Chet and the boys, then ride back to Big Pine before they withdraw the money." Harry drew a hand down his face, massaging his stubbled chin. Milt wouldn't give up on avenging Chet, yet the gang needed the money before riding out of Montana on their way to California. "It could work."

"Luke and I are riding into Splendor for the town meeting. Why don't you come with us, Bull?" After a day chasing cattle, Dax tried to brush off the dirt before stepping into the house.

"I've never been to a town meeting. Is something going on I haven't heard about?" Unless his bosses needed something, Bull rode into town for two reasons—to drink and play cards, or to see Lydia. Ever since she'd taken the position to help Abby Brandt with Gabriel, they'd seen little of each other. The separation wore on him, and from what he'd seen, it bothered Lydia about as much.

"They're talking about forming a town council with a mayor. It's been informal up until now. Maybe putting it down and having elections is a better way to go. Think about it. You know Noah will be there, which means Abby and Lydia will be taking care of Gabriel." Dax saw the moment Bull understood his meaning. "We leave in an hour."

"I'll be ready." Bull nodded, picking up his pace as he walked to the small house the Pelletiers provided him. He hadn't seen Lydia in over a week, and the hole in his heart got bigger each day. Dax and Luke had changed his circumstances with the offer of becoming their foreman.

He had his own place. The same house Hank and Bernice Wilson, an older couple who had worked for Dax and Luke since they arrived, had called home until they moved to California due to her health. Although small, it came furnished and included a living room, kitchen, one bedroom, a large pantry, and wood room. He took many of his meals with the Pelletiers, meaning he saved a large portion of his monthly wage, which he'd asked Noah to help him invest. Life was the best it had ever been, then Lydia agreed to work in town.

Bull didn't begrudge Noah and Abby drawing her away. They needed help with Gabriel, and Lydia loved children. The remaining orphans were older, able to do chores and pay for their keep. They no longer needed Lydia to watch over them. He couldn't believe how much the young runaways had changed since a group of men, including himself, discovered them hiding in a cave above Luke's original house near Wildfire Creek.

While washing off the day's dirt and donning clean clothes, Bull considered his future. Growing up in Ohio, he'd worked alongside his father in the family construction business. Then he'd joined the war, fighting for the North. After his service, he needed space, distance from his past, a place to start over. He'd ended up in Splendor and started working for deceased Texas Ranger, Patrick Hanes, whose will bequeathed the ranch to his two Ranger friends—Dax and Luke. They'd convinced Bull to stay on and work with them. It had been the right decision. They weren't only his bosses, they were good friends. Finances, though, continued to be tight, to the point he didn't see a way to support a wife and family. With the promotion, his future had turned.

Bull never thought his situation would change enough to state his feelings to Lydia, ask her to marry him. Now she'd left the ranch. From what he knew, she spent a good deal of time in town with Abby and the baby. A town full of single men looking for a woman like Lydia to claim. *Well*, he thought, *they'd do it over my dead body.*

"Bull, you ready?" Luke shoved open the door, as was his custom when visiting Bull. "Lordy! Is there a special occasion I don't know about?"

Bull scowled as he finished buckling his gun belt. "Let's go." He glanced at Luke, challenging him to say more. Over six foot four with broad shoulders that didn't clear some doorways, few people ever pushed him too far. They were lucky his temper burned at a slow pace.

Luke's smirk fell as he shook his head, heading outside. It didn't take a genius to guess what Bull planned. Grabbing the reins of two horses, Luke swung up on Prince, tossing Abe's reins to Bull. Dax joined them on Hannibal a moment later.

"You two ready?" Dax looked between Luke and Bull.

Luke let out a loud whoop. "Race you to the rock." He kicked Prince into a run, laughing as he headed toward the huge bolder marking the entrance to Redemption's Edge.

Dax cast a furtive look at Bull. "We going to let him win?"

"Hell no." A broad smile flashed across Bull's face a moment before he took off after Luke.

"The vote carries. We will be forming a town council and electing a mayor." Gabe stood at the front of the room in the crowded schoolhouse. He'd been pressured into leading the meeting the moment he'd walked in the door. "Now, we need the names of six people to be voted onto the town council. Yes, Reverend Paige. Who do you nominate?"

The meeting continued until the town ended up with a full council, which included Stan Petermann, Nick Barnett, Noah Brandt, Silas Jenks, Horace Clausen, and Dax. Luke and Gabe had both been nominated, each begging off for different reasons.

"All right. There are two more items, then you can all go home." Gabe glanced down at the list, glad his work was almost over.

Bull leaned toward Luke, his voice low. "I'm going to ride up to Noah's and visit with Abby and Gabriel."

Luke's raised brows got the reaction intended.

"All right. I'm going to see Lydia. Satisfied?" Bull rose as quietly as a man his size could and walked out, wasting no time riding up the hill above town to the Brandt's home. Reining Abe to a stop, he sat a moment, breathing in deep, letting it out in a slow whoosh, then slid to the ground. The sounds of laughter reached him as he stopped at the front door, helping him relax. Raising his hand, he knocked, then stepped back. A moment later, the door swung open.

"Good evening, Bull. It's so good to see you. Please, come in." Abby gave him a brief hug, then slipped her arm through his. "How did you get away from the meeting so early? I've been expecting Noah any time now." They walked through the entry and into the parlor where Lydia sat in a chair, rocking a wide awake Gabriel.

Tearing his gaze from Lydia, he looked over at Abby. "I'm sure he'll be along shortly. The meeting was still going when I left."

Walking over to Lydia, Abby held out her arms. "I'll put him to bed. Why don't you get Bull some coffee and a slice of that wonderful spice cake you made?"

Bull waited, watching as Lydia disappeared into the kitchen, returning moments later with a cup of coffee and thick slice of cake.

"I hope you like it." Her eyes lit up when she looked at him.

"If you made it, I know I'll like it." He waited until she took a seat, then selected one next to her. Taking a sip of coffee, he smiled. "You made it the way I like it."

A slight blush colored her face. "A half teaspoon of sugar."

Bull asked a few questions in between bites of cake. He'd never finished dessert so fast, but his need to be alone with her overruled any restraint. Setting down the plate and finishing his coffee, he stood, holding out his hand.

"Would you go for a walk with me?"

"I'd love to. Let me take these dishes—"

"I'll get those, Lydia. You and Bull go ahead." Abby picked up the dishes and disappeared into the kitchen, humming as she waited for them to leave.

As they stepped outside, the wind rustled through the trees, blowing strands of hair across Lydia's face. Placing a hand on the small of her back, Bull guided her down the stairs toward the barn and adjoining pasture. Neither Noah nor Abby had intended to run cattle or have more than a few horses on their land. They had a couple cows, a few pigs, and a dozen chickens—enough for their own use. Noah had also prepared a section of land near the house for a garden. Their friends teased him about trading in his spurs for a plow.

"How do you like working for Abby?"

Pulling the shawl tighter, she shrugged. "Abby and Noah are wonderful, and Gabriel is such a sweet baby. I wouldn't be surprised if he and baby Patrick become good friends. Still..."

"Still?" Bull prompted when she didn't continue, noting the wistful tone of her voice.

"I do miss the ranch and all the activity."

"And baby Patrick?"

"Of course. He's walking. Soon, he'll be talking and getting into more mischief than Rachel can imagine." She looked up at him. "I feel like a spinster aunt, living through my friends' families."

Bull laughed at the comparison. "Trust me, Lydia. You are nothing close to a spinster aunt. You have a gift with children. Our friends recognize it, and believe me, are grateful for your help."

"I'm almost twenty-one, Bull."

His eyes narrowed. "And?"

"*Twenty-one*," she emphasized. "Most of my friends back home would be married with their own family by now." She didn't want to say more, making him think she was pushing for marriage. Stepping up to the fence, she placed her feet on the bottom rung, resting her arms on the top. "I haven't said anything to Abby or Rachel, but I'm thinking of returning home."

"*What?*" Bull couldn't contain his shock or the harsh tone in his voice. He wrapped his arms around her waist, pulling her off the fence and setting her in front of him. "You can't leave, Lydia. I won't let you."

Shrugging out of his grasp, she stepped back. "This isn't your decision, Bull. It's mine."

Taking off his hat, he shredded his fingers through his short hair, face twisting in disbelief. He turned his back to her, taking a few steps away, then stopping to stare up at the sky. A moment later, he felt her arms wrap around him from behind. Placing his hands on hers, he let out a shaky breath.

"I love you, Lydia. I don't know what I'll do if you leave." Pain ripped through him at the thought of losing the woman he'd loved since finding her sick and frail in a damp cave where the orphans had been hiding.

Dropping her arms, she moved to stand in front of him, placing her hands on his chest, her eyes searching his. "You love me?"

"Of course I love you." He choked out the declaration, wanting nothing more than to wrap her in his arms, not knowing if he had the right. Clearing his throat, searching for control, he focused his gaze on hers. "I want to marry you, Lydia. Have children. Build a life here in Splendor."

Her gaze dropped from his, her heart throbbing almost painfully. She'd wanted to hear him say the words, confess his feelings for so long that the reality of hearing it rendered her speechless. After all this time without an indication of his love, she'd been forced to think of a future without Bull. Although it had been difficult to even consider such a life.

Settling his hands on her shoulders, he searched her face, the pain in his eyes more than she could bear.

"If you don't love me, just say so. It isn't what I want to hear, but I'll understand. I know I'm not the man of your dreams. I don't have land, or much money, or—"

She stopped him with a hand over his mouth. "Stop. You *are* the man of my dreams, Bull. Until tonight, I believed you didn't feel the same and only wanted to be my friend." She let her hands settle on his chest, lowering her gaze to the ground as her eyes grew damp.

"Friend? Of course I'm your friend. I'm also in love with you." Tipping her chin up, he used his thumb to wipe away the tears streaming down her cheeks. "I know I've surprised you."

Her ragged laugh accompanied an unsteady smile. In that moment, she knew there'd never be another man for her. Bull was everything she wanted and needed.

"You have surprised me, but in a good way. I love you, too, Bull. If you're asking if I'll marry you, the answer is yes." She laughed at the sight of his jaw dropping, his eyes widening to the size of saucers.

Recovering in seconds, he picked her up and swung her around, letting out a loud yell. It was then he saw Noah riding up, reining Tempest to a stop.

"You two all right?" Noah tipped his hat back, then rested his arms on the horn of his saddle.

"Yes," Lydia laughed, swiping at the dampness on her face.

"You're the first to know. Lydia's agreed to marry me."

"Well, I'll be. That's wonderful news." He dismounted, giving Bull a slap on the back, then hugging Lydia. "Congratulations. I wondered when he'd come to his senses."

"What's going on?" Abby came running outside, concern etched on her face.

Noah settled an arm around her shoulders, pulling her close. "Bull finally asked Lydia to marry him."

"And?" Abby raised a brow, looking at Lydia.

"I said yes." She raised up on her toes to place a kiss on Bull's cheek.

A smile lit Abby's face. "It's about time, Bull Mason." She drew Lydia into a hug, kissing her cheek.

"Come inside and we'll toast to your engagement." Noah took Abby's hand, turning toward the house.

"We'll be right in." Bull waited until they'd disappeared inside, then pulled Lydia into his arms. "Are you certain? It's forever, Lydia."

"I'm completely certain, Bull." Wrapping her arms around his neck, she stared into his eyes, a shiver running through her as he lowered his lips to hers.

Minutes later, they were still locked together, their breathing erratic when the sound of a door opening and Noah's shout pulled them apart.

"There'll be plenty of time for that later, Bull. Now's the time to celebrate."

Bull smiled at Lydia before his expression sobered.

"I don't have a ring for you yet."

"I don't need one. Your wedding ring is all I want." She reached up and kissed him once more before clasping her hand in his, pulling him up the steps and into the house.

Chapter Fifteen

"Where's Gabe?" Lena pushed through the door of the sheriff's office, her breath coming in gasps.

"He rode out to one of the southern ranches an hour ago. What is it? Are you all right?" Cash grabbed a chair. "Sit and tell me what happened." He walked over to the stove and poured her a cup of coffee. "Here." Handing her the cup, he leaned against the desk.

She wanted her husband, not coffee, but she wouldn't refuse Cash's gesture. Taking a sip, she sat back, thinking through what she'd seen at the mine.

"I just got back from the Devil Dancer. I wanted to check on the Chinese men I sent there a few days ago. This morning, the manager found all four beaten and tossed into one of the wagons. My God, Cash. They were bruised and bloody, hardly able to move. The problem is they don't speak English. Even if they could, they don't seem interested in helping us learn who hurt them. I need Gabe to help make them understand we need to know who did this."

Reaching out, Cash rested a hand on her shoulder. "Gabe may not be back for hours. I'll get John and ride out to the mine."

"All right. Let's go." She stood, setting the cup down.

"Not you. Just John and me."

"I'm responsible for what happens there. Of course I'm going." She placed fisted hands on her hips, glaring at him.

"Lord... Are you this obstinate with Gabe?"

"Of course. I'll get my horse and let Nick know what's happening."

Cash followed her outside, dashing toward the lumber mill. "Silas! Where's John?"

"In the back. Why?" Silas trailed after Cash as he moved past him. "What's going on?"

He stopped and looked around, not seeing John until Silas pointed to him.

"John, the deputy needs to talk to you."

Cash saw a look of fear cross John's face before he walked around several stacks of wood to join them.

"There's been some trouble at the Devil Dancer. I need you to come with me to translate so I can find out what's going on."

John's gaze shifted to Silas before returning to Cash. "Yes, I can translate."

"Do you have a horse?"

"No horse." John shook his head.

"Do you know how to ride?" Cash tilted his head, already thinking about where he could get a wagon.

"Take my wagon," Silas offered. "It's already loaded with a shipment for the mine. I can send Monty along to help unload."

"Great. Let's get going." Cash hurried to the livery, saddled Hunter, then rode out onto the street to see Lena waiting for him. "John and Monty will be coming on the wagon. They have a load to deliver to the mine." The words had just left his mouth when Monty, John sitting next to him, drove the wagon out of the lumber mill side yard and came to a stop.

"We're ready, Deputy."

Monty slapped the reins as Cash and Lena took the lead.

"I told Nick what's going on. He's going to find Beau and let him know."

"Thanks, Lena. Don't worry. We'll find out what happened and arrest those responsible." Cash felt his gut tighten. He had a bad feeling, believing the beatings would involve some or all of the miners who'd caused the disturbance at the lumber mill. The last thing the mine, or Lena, needed was a revolt over the hiring of Chinese workers.

The trip took almost two hours, the wagon lumbering along at a frustrating pace. At one point, Cash almost pulled John up behind him on Hunter so they could ride ahead, but he didn't want to leave Monty to finish the journey alone.

They rode into the mining camp in early afternoon. A group of miners milled around near the office…some grumbling, others listening. No one seemed happy. Dismounting, Lena and Cash walked up to the group.

"Where is Reuben?" Lena stood, hands on hips, waiting for a response. "Well?" She glared at the man who'd been the leader of the miners who caused the problems at the lumber mill.

"Answer the lady." Cash moved to within a foot of the man, his eyes cold, features hard.

Anger flashed in the man's eyes before he turned, jerking his thumb toward a tent a hundred feet away. "He's with those Chinamen he hired."

"Come with me, John." Cash signaled for him to follow, Lena keeping pace alongside.

"I don't like any of this," she whispered as they approached the tent Reuben used as a makeshift clinic.

Pulling back the flap, Cash looked inside, seeing the four men sitting near each other, Reuben doing his best to patch up their injuries. Their eyes widened when they saw John follow Cash into the tent, followed by Lena.

"Reuben, I'd appreciate it if you and Lena would wait outside."

"No, I need—"

Cash fixed a hard stare on Lena when she began to protest. "You'll wait outside, Lena. I'm here to get answers. They will talk more freely if neither of you are present."

"He's right, Mrs. Evans. If they decide to talk, we'll find out what happened soon enough." Reuben held the flap open for Lena to precede him out, not missing the scowl she aimed at Cash.

"All right, but I want you to tell me everything you learn."

Cash nodded, watching her storm outside, then turned his attention to John.

"I need to know who did this and if they can identify them."

John spoke in rapid Chinese, pointing to Cash a couple times. One of the men responded, the others shrinking into themselves, shaking their heads. After a few minutes, John nodded, then looked at Cash.

"Zhao says they can't tell us. It was dark and the men wore hoods."

The information didn't surprise Cash. Cowards generally struck in the middle of the night and hid their identity. "Did something happen since they've been here? Threats or arguments?"

John spoke to Zhao again, listening to his response. "I am sorry, Deputy Cash. Zhao will say no more. They do not want to cause trouble."

"These men would rather be beaten again, or killed, than tell you what is going on?"

John lowered his gaze to the ground, shaking his head. "They need to work."

"I know they need to work, John, but I can't help them if they don't tell me what they know." Cash's voice dripped with frustration. Scrubbing a hand down his face, he tried to think of something, anything that might encourage them to help. "If we let the miners get away with this, it could make it harder for other Chinese to work for the mines."

"Yes," John muttered.

"Tell them what I said," Cash growled, muttering a curse when John hesitated. "These could be the same men who threatened you at the lumber mill. It will keep happening if we don't stop it. Now, tell them."

John shrugged, his face somber as he turned back to Zhao. This time, his voice was stronger, holding a trace of rebuke. When Zhao shook his head, John's voice grew louder until he stood, glaring down at the others. The four turned their backs on John, talking in whispers. Finally, Zhao looked back at John and spoke.

Nodding, John turned to Cash. "There is one man who threatens them. They don't know what he is saying, but he shoves them, pushes them aside, and takes their tools when Boss is not looking."

Cash considered this a moment before walking to the entrance to the tent, sneaking a quick look outside. Closing the opening, he thought a moment, then looked at John.

"Can Zhao point out the man who has threatened them if he looks through this opening?"

He indicated the flap of the tent. "No one should be able to see him."

John spoke to Zhao, who glanced at the others. No one moved for a moment, then one of the men nodded. Zhao's grim face turned back to John. They exchanged a few words before Zhao stood, joining Cash.

"John, come over here. I want Zhao to look at the men. If he sees him, he needs to tell you which man." Cash stepped to the side, then drew the flap open a couple inches.

Zhao bent low, squinting as he looked outside into the afternoon sun. After a moment, his eyes adjusted and Cash could see him scanning the group of men milling about. Then his gaze lit on someone or something, causing him to jerk away. He spoke to John in a quiet, yet excited voice, his eyes widening and narrowing as he continued talking.

John straightened, meeting Cash's gaze. "The tall, slender man with dirty black hat and red suspenders. He is the man."

Cash motioned for the two to move away from the tent opening. Taking their place, he pulled back the flap and stepped outside, stretching his arms over his head as he casually scanned the crowd. Twenty feet away stood the man Zhao described. The same man who'd led the disturbance at the lumber mill. The same man whose confrontational attitude sparked others to action. The same man who'd reluctantly pointed them toward the medical tent today. The knowledge didn't surprise him.

Lena came up beside him, her hand resting on his arm. Reuben was nowhere in sight. "Did the men identify who beat them?"

Cash turned her away from the crowd, toward the tent, then lowered his voice. "Zhao spoke for the group. They didn't see who beat them. The men came in the middle of the night and wore hoods. Zhao was able to point out one man who has harassed them since they started."

"Who?"

"First, Lena, you need to understand the men are fearful for their jobs and of further retaliation. Plus, we have no proof this man was involved in the beatings last night. All we know is he's been hassling them since they arrived."

"Then we have to get him to talk." She started to turn away, stopping when Cash grabbed her wrist.

"Not yet. He'll deny it, and my guess is enough of the other miners will back him up. The result will increase their anger and put the Chinese workers in more danger."

Lena pulled her arm free, letting out a breath. "What do you suggest?"

"You need to hire a few men you can trust to guard all the miners, keep watch on what's going on, especially at night. Right now, you have Reuben. Do you trust him?" Cash noticed the mine manager approaching from the office, stopping to speak with some of the men, glancing toward Lena and him.

Her eyes widened. "Of course."

"Anyone else?"

"There are two men who guard the shipments to town. Gabe sometimes accompanies them. We take small loads and make the trip twice a week, mixing up the days. The schedule doesn't attract as much attention as large loads once a week. I've never seen a need to hire more guards."

"Seems there's a need now. Unless you want to fire the Chinese men."

"No. If I let them go, I'd be making them victims twice." She fell quiet as Reuben stopped beside them.

"Any progress?" Reuben shot a quick look at the tent, a scowl crossing his face.

Lena answered. "They can't identify who beat them, but did point out one man who's been harassing them since they started."

"Who?"

Cash nodded toward the men who'd begun to disperse, returning to their work. "The tall one with black hat and red suspenders."

"Galt. The man's been a pain in my side since he started. Problem is, he's a good worker. Starts early, works late, and does about twice the work of most men." Reuben whipped off his hat, scratching the thin patch of hair on top of his head. "He's also got strong opinions and a loud mouth. I've told him if he has a complaint to come to me, but he'd rather stir up trouble with the men than find any solutions. If I didn't need him so much, I'd have fired him months ago. What do you suggest, Cash?"

"I've suggested Lena hire some extra men to patrol the mines day and night."

"Can you afford extra men, Mrs. Evans? They'd have to be people you trust. I can't watch over them twenty-four hours a day. I suppose we could let the Chinese workers go. That would stop the problems without hiring more men."

"For how long, Reuben? No matter how much I pay them or the improvements to their living conditions, it seems the men always find something to complain about. Besides, it wouldn't be right to punish the Chinese men more than they've already endured." She let out a breath, thinking of the cost of adding guards. "Four men is the most I can add right now."

Cash nodded. "Two men for each twelve hours should be enough. Their main job will be to keep watch on the Chinese men and make sure Galt, or any of the other miners, don't cause trouble. Do you have any idea who you'd hire?"

"No, Cash. I plan to talk to Gabe and Nick. Do you have any suggestions?"

"Wish I did. I'm happy to pass the word, though. The sooner they're out here, the sooner you can put this behind you and get back to the business of mining." He looked up at the sky, noting the position of the sun. "We'd better start back. I'll get John."

"I had some men help Monty unload the wagon, Cash. He's waiting for you on the other side of the office."

"Thanks, Reuben. With luck, there'll be some men out here to help you before too long. In the meantime, I'd appreciate it if you'd send word if there's another attack...on anyone."

Big Pine

"Ready?" Milt Penderville swung his horse in a circle as the sun began to drift behind the hills to the west. They'd waited long enough. It had been weeks since the failed bank robbery in Bloody Basin and their funds were getting low. Besides, Harry and he were tired of hiding out while their men went into town to gamble and carouse. They were the only two on wanted posters. The chance of getting recognized and arrested wasn't worth a few hours of fun in one of several saloons in the territorial capital. They might be able to get away with it where they were headed.

Harry reined up alongside him. "Let's go." They'd decided to make a wide arc north, avoiding

Big Pine to camp a few hours west. They'd camp overnight, then head out for Splendor early the next morning.

According to what their men had learned, the major threat of riding north was the potential of running afoul of a group of renegade Crow who populated the hill country beyond where the mines were located. The small band of young bucks concentrated their raids on ill-prepared and unsuspecting travelers. They'd swoop down from the hills, steal food supplies and cattle, take an occasional hostage, then storm back into the protection of the dense forest with hundreds of trails coming in and going out. Seldom did they kill. Still, they were a dangerous threat. Once the trail turned south, joining the main road out of Big Pine, the danger would lessen.

"The men heard they have a boardinghouse run by a pretty widow woman in Splendor. I say we stay there, clean up, and visit the local saloons. We should have a little fun before taking care of our business."

A frustrated sigh and muttered curse was Milt's reaction. "We stick with the plan, Harry, the same as we did in Big Pine. Showing our faces is too risky."

"It's been weeks since I had a hot bath and decent meal. You can stay at camp, but I'm riding into town with the men. You're the one with a two thousand dollar bounty on your head. I'm worth no more than five hundred."

Milt held his anger, knowing to show it would ignite a confrontation neither needed until they were well beyond Crow territory. Then he'd lay into his brother, put him in his place, and if necessary, pound some reason into him.

Milt had barely finished the thought when an ear-piercing yell split the night air. On their right, he could see a group of riders coming straight at them.

"Ride!" Milt kicked his horse into a run, bending low while reaching for his gun. He knew who was bearing down on them, and had been warned of the danger of traveling this trail.

The youngest son of the Crow chief had refused to participate in the annuity payments the United States government began disbursing to the tribe in 1868. His pride and arrogance led him and his followers—young men who believed the white men had taken what had been their birthright—to split from their tribe. Attacking white settlers was their way of recapturing some of what had been stolen from them.

The Penderville gang rode hard, putting little distance between them and skilled Crow riders. They couldn't take time to glance over their shoulders for fear the effort would slow them down. Seconds felt like hours as they pushed their horses south toward the main road, the high-pitched cries from their painted enemies sending terror through each man.

Without warning, as if they'd passed through some kind of unseen barrier, the cries diminished. When all they heard was the pounding hooves of their own horses, Milt held up a hand, signaling them to stop. Counting, he breathed out a relieved sigh. All the men were alive.

"What was that about?" The fear in Harry's voice mirrored the terror on the men's faces.

"Hell if I know and I don't care. We'll rest our horses for a bit, then ride on to Splendor. I want to get out of this area before they change their minds and come after us." Milt slid to the ground, bending at the waist, sucking in gulps of air. During all their months moving from town to town, robbing banks and the occasional train, they'd never been attacked by Indians. Perhaps that's why he'd felt so cocky. He wouldn't make the same mistake again.

Chapter Sixteen

Gabe set his hat on the bar, glanced around, then sent a sharp look at the bartender. "Paul, have you seen Lena or Nick?"

"Lena hasn't come back from the Devil Dancer. Don't know where Nick is." He set a whiskey in front of Gabe, cringing at the way his jaw tensed.

Ignoring the drink, Gabe stalked to the office in back, pushing the door open. "Nick?" Getting no answer, he returned to the bar, picked up the glass, and finished his whiskey in one gulp. "Are you sure Lena hasn't come back? She left when I did early this morning."

Paul explained what he'd heard about the trouble at the mine. "It'd be best to find Beau. He might know more about what happened. When Nick comes back, I'll let him know you're looking for him."

Walking out and searching the street, Gabe saw Noah's livery closed tight. He hadn't noticed Lena's horse when he put his own away, but he'd been anxious to see her after a long day and hadn't really looked. Opening the gate, he checked the stables. An odd trickle of fear shot through him when he saw her horse was missing. Paul was right. She hadn't returned.

Slamming the gate closed, he dashed to his office, almost knocking Beau down as he walked outside. Gabe grabbed his arm to steady them both.

"Have you seen Lena?"

"She and Cash left for the Devil Dancer before noon. They also took John from the lumber mill. The four Chinese miners were beaten, Gabe, and they wouldn't talk to Reuben or Lena about what happened." Beau turned back inside. They both took seats, Gabe sagging into a chair from weariness and worry. He dragged a hand down his face, then set his gaze on Beau.

"They hope John can persuade them to talk, identify the men who beat them?"

"That's my understanding. Nick found me after speaking to Lena before she and Cash left. I'm guessing it took them close to two hours to get there with the wagon, and another two to return." Beau saw Gabe's brows knit together. "Monty needed to take a load of lumber to the mine, so John rode with him in the wagon. I'd expect them back at any time now, but if you think something is wrong, I'll ride out with you."

Boots stomping on the boardwalk sounded a moment before the jail door swung open. Cash stepped inside, shrugging out of his coat, a weary smile crossing his face when he saw Gabe. He didn't have to wonder at the question on his mind.

"She went to the Dixie, looking for you."

Gabe dashed outside before Cash could finish.

"And she's fine," he chuckled to himself.

Alison had closed her shop for the entire day, putting a sign on the door and not feeling an ounce of guilt.

"It's been a long time since I've ridden, Cash." Alison stood next to Joker, the horse Noah had saddled for her. He'd told her the horse belonged to Abby, an accomplished rider.

"Joker is a good ride, sweetheart. Abby rode him until a couple weeks before Gabriel was born." Cash stroked a finger down her cheek, seeing her face color. "I'll be right with you the whole time."

The heated look in his eyes sent shivers shooting through her, making her wonder who the greatest threat was...Joker or Cash. She'd thought of little except Cash ever since their time together after supper at the St. James. If she had to do it again, Allie might not have invited him upstairs. It had been an impulsive gesture, one quite out of character for her. After he left, it had taken hours for her to fall asleep. Even then, she'd woken repeatedly, tangled in the bedcovers. Worse, she'd suffered the same scenario each of the following nights, waking early this morning, her body aching with a need she didn't understand.

"If you're certain..." The words had barely left her mouth when Cash settled his hands on her waist and lifted her into the saddle.

"Are you comfortable?" Cash handed the reins to her, stroking a hand down Joker's neck.

Following his lead, she leaned forward and did the same, calming the horse, as well as herself.

"Why yes, I'm quite comfortable." A smile lit her face when Joker shook his head.

"You're going to do fine." He mounted Hunter, glancing over his shoulder at Allie as he started out of the livery and onto the street. "It's going to be a long ride. Suzanne packed a lunch for us." Cash looked up at the clear sky, then glanced at the coat tied to the back of her saddle. "Is your bonnet on tight?"

Lifting a hand, she checked it as Joker took off on his own, following Hunter.

"Oh!" Nervous laughter filled the air as Allie bobbed up and down in the saddle, coming up alongside Cash. "Riding our plough horse wasn't anything like this. He was old, heavy, and very slow." As they left the outskirts of town, she let out a yelp as Joker broke into a gallop ahead of Cash.

"Rein him in a little, Allie. He'll respond." He pushed Hunter forward, coming up next to her to help pull back on her reins. "Like this. Easy," he coached. She licked her lips, concentrating on controlling the horse. "That's it, Allie. Perfect." He let go, letting her take over.

"I can do this." She spoke more to herself than Cash, although he glanced at her as if he'd heard. Which he had.

"No doubt you can do this." He kept a close watch on her, surprised how little experience she had. Most kids who grew up on farms could ride pretty well.

"Besides the old gelding we used in the fields, we only had one horse. He was a beast. Big and mean. My father was the only one allowed to ride him." Her chest constricted on a memory of Bobby pleading with their father to let him ride *a real horse*. He'd refused, telling Bobby when he grew to be a man, he'd have his chance. It never happened. They'd sold the horse upon learning of their father's death, their mother unable to look at him without thinking of her husband.

"You're doing fine, and you'll do better as we keep going. By the time we return, you'll be an expert."

More than an hour later, Cash led them onto an overgrown trail. Covered with a layer of snow and ice, it meandered back and forth, climbing several hundred feet before coming to a clearing not more than a hundred feet wide. Although spring, almost a foot of snow still covered much of the area. He slid to the ground, then grabbed Joker's reins, helped Allie down, and untied her coat from the back of her saddle. Without thought, her hands went to her sore backside, rubbing to ease the aching muscles.

"Why don't we walk so you can stretch your legs?"

She winced as her fingers stroked one particular spot. "I think that would be best."

Holding up the coat, he helped her slip it on, then took her hand. Cash cut a path through the snow encrusted ground and spindly shrub, making his way to the edge of the clearing. There didn't appear to be much to see. The meadow ended and the forest began once more, an endless parade of pine and fir.

"Look." Cash's gaze sliced through the trees to a spot far in the distance.

"What? I don't see anything but trees."

"You aren't looking close enough. Come on." He walked forward another ten feet, stopping again. "Now, look again."

Squinting, she moved her head a few inches back and forth, trying to see what held Cash's attention. "I'm sorry. I just don't..." Her words trailed off as a flash of light reflected off an object yards in front of them. Taking a couple steps forward, she saw the flash again. "There it is." Her eyes sparkled as a brilliant smile lit her face. Letting go of his hand, she took off, leaving him behind.

"Allie, hold up." Cash chuckled, moving to follow her.

She stopped briefly in front of a dilapidated log structure, checking it over for no more than a few seconds before stepping up to a door falling off its hinges, shoving it open. The force of the thrust broke its tenuous hold and it collapsed inside with a thunderous crash.

Jumping back, she whirled around a moment before Cash stopped next to her. Looking at the door, then back at her, his eyes narrowed.

"I've been coming here for almost two years and never had a lick of trouble with that door." Shaking his head, he stepped over the threshold to study the damage. "Yep. It's pretty well gone."

Biting her lower lip, Allie took a few tentative steps, surveying the twisted metal. "I'm sorry, Cash. I didn't mean to destroy it."

Seeing her dismal expression, he couldn't hold back his bark of laughter.

"What's so funny?" Her face turned a heated shade of red as her hands fisted on her hips.

Wrapping his arms around her, Cash pulled her to his chest, resting his chin on her head.

Relaxing, Allie slipped her arms around his waist.

"One sizable thunderstorm and this entire shack might collapse. It's a miracle any of it is still standing." Breathing in the clean scent of her hair, he let out a deep sigh. "You just helped it along a bit." Drawing back, he kissed her forehead.

"What is this place?" Dropping her arms, she took in the tiny interior, noting an old table, two chairs, shelves on one wall with a counter below, and an old stove—all in various stages of disintegration from lack of use. The one contradictory item was a wooden bed frame topped with a thin, surprisingly clean mattress and wool blanket. Sliding out of her coat, she placed it across the bed.

"The locals call the area Survivor Pass. The way I understand the story, a group of settlers tried to make it over the mountains before the first snow. A devastating storm hit, forcing them to stop their journey here. They built this cabin, and through some kind of miracle, survived the harsh winter."

"They survived?"

"According to the legend. When the snows melted, they continued on, becoming some of the first white settlers in Idaho. The shack remained. For years, people stopped here, hoping to survive their own journey west." He picked up a rusted tin, pulled off the top, and looked inside. Tipping it upside down, he watched as a small amount of powder drifted to the floor. "Probably sugar."

"People no longer come here?" Allie's gaze took in everything, trying to imagine spending an entire winter sheltered in the walls of this small sanctuary. Remarkably, the floor was clean, as if someone had taken the time to sweep it. Her gaze shot to him, realizing Cash kept this piece of history from crumbling into a forgotten mess.

"I've never seen anyone in all the times I've stopped. Mostly, I ride up for two or three days and make camp. Get away from the people and chaos of Splendor."

Allie couldn't contain her laughter. "Chaos in Splendor? It's undoubtedly the most peaceful town I've ever seen. A few drunks, some crazy miners, and the town gossips." Placing a hand over her mouth, she forced herself to stop laughing.

Crossing his arms, he leveled a stern gaze at her. "You aren't the one who has to control those few drunks or crazy miners."

Stepping closer, she placed a hand on his shoulder. "You're right, Cash. Still, it's a sweet, peaceful town."

A split second was too long to describe how quick the flash of desire ripped through him. Lifting his hand, he touched her cheek, then cupped the back of her neck, drawing her closer. She didn't try to break his hold or step away. Instead, she leaned into him, glazed eyes searching his.

Neither spoke. The air around them stilled, sounds from the outside fading away as their gazes locked.

Neither moved for several seconds until Cash began to lower his head hesitantly, unsure if he should do what his desire demanded. A desire urging him forward in opposition to his better judgment—judgment he'd always heeded and which had always served him well.

"Tell me to stop," he whispered, his lips a breath away from capturing her mouth.

"I can't," she answered, a moment before their lips touched.

The thundering in his ears increased as the kiss continued, their bodies fused until he could feel the heat from her stab through his clothing. Movements became frantic, their hands traveling over each other, igniting an overwhelming passion neither tried to control.

Holding her tight, his hand drifted to the curve of her waist, moving lower to gather the hem of her dress. Gripping it, hesitating as he wrestled with what to do next, he broke their kiss on a deep groan.

Resting his forehead against hers, he sucked in a deep breath, letting it out in an almost painful hiss.

"Why did you stop?" Allie's voice shook as she tried to calm her racing heart, as well as the fear he'd changed his mind and didn't want her.

Closing his eyes, he loosened his grip on her dress, letting the material fall back into place.

"You know what comes next, Allie. We're in a dilapidated cabin in the middle of nowhere. Is this truly where you want to make love?" He let his hands move up and down her back in a motion intended to soothe them both.

She blinked at his straightforward question. He assumed she understood what would follow their passionate embraces and heated kisses. Other than a vague knowledge from listening to others discussing how a man and woman joined, she didn't know. All she understood was her body's aching need for this man. She wanted him with a desire frightening in its intensity.

"Yes, Cash. I want you here...now. Unless you've changed your mind."

His answer came in a fast motion as he scooped her into his arms, carrying her to the narrow bed and setting her down. Stretching out next to her, his hand cupping the back of her head, he drew her to him.

"I've wanted you since the moment we met." His ragged breath warmed her face.

"Now you have me."

"Yes, sweetheart. Now I have you."

Cash paced back and forth across the width of the cabin, stopping at times to stare at her. His mind whirled at what he'd learned, questions building on each other as her unsteady gaze caught his, then flashed away.

She sat on the bed, the wool blanket wrapped around her, knees drawn to her chest, back against the wall. Swiping at the tears moistening her face, she sucked in a breath, trying to calm the hurtful pounding in her chest.

The shock at discovering she'd never made love before, was a virgin, came too late for him to reverse his actions. It had been the sweetest love he'd ever made—until his shocked mind registered the deceit.

A heartbeat later, Cash lifted his body off hers. Fastening his pants, he slipped into his shirt and boots, needing to get as far away from her as possible in the small space.

Walking to the open doorway, he stared at the trees, branches wavering in the early afternoon breeze. His gaze focused on two pairs of footprints, each creating a path through the snow to the cabin door. Whipping around to face her, he saw her start at his angry gaze.

"Were you ever married?"

Staring at him, her face a picture of misery, she shook her head in a quick jerk.

"Are your parents both dead?"

Swallowing, she glanced down at her clasped hands, knuckles white from the tight grip.

"My father is dead."

"Not your mother?"

"No." Her whispered response was almost lost as the wind flowed through the open doorway.

Muttering a curse, Cash turned back around. Scrubbing a hand down his face, he settled his fists on his hips, unsure of what to say or do. In his heart, he'd known her story held little truth, yet he'd pursued her, ignoring the warnings pulsing through his body. The desire he felt overcame all the caution he should've heeded. Now he had to make some decisions.

"Get dressed. We need to start back."

"Cash, please. Won't you listen to me?"

Turning, his features hard, jaw pulsing, he took a step forward. "So you can tell me more lies?"

"No. I—"

"Was anything you told me the truth, Allie? Is your last name Burns?"

Her face melted in misery. Lowering her gaze, she shook her head. "No. My last name isn't Burns."

"Is Alison even your first name or did you lie about that, too?"

Lifting her head, she glared at him. "Yes. My name is Alison and my family called me Allie."

Throwing his hands in the air, he let out a sarcastic whoop of victory.

"And I am from Kentucky."

"Wonderful. Two truths in a forest of lies." Cash fell quiet as another thought wormed its way into the mess he saw before him. He wouldn't voice it, didn't want to hear the truth from her lips. Perhaps someday when he didn't feel so raw, so betrayed. "Get dressed. I'll get the horses."

"Cash, wait." Jumping from the bed, almost tripping on the blanket around her ankles, she stumbled to the door. "Please. Let me explain."

Stopping a few yards from the cabin, he spun around, his bright green eyes cold, distant. "It's too late. You never should've lied to me."

Chapter Seventeen

Alison dressed in silence, slipping into her shoes and coat before taking one last look around the cabin. She doubted he'd ever bring her here again. Didn't even know if he'd allow her to stay in Splendor. A few words from him could change the course of her hard work since she arrived. In many ways, the real purpose of her trip had been pushed aside, replaced by the sheer joy of finding success in her business. Along with success, she'd gained new friends—a commodity in short supply back home in Kentucky.

The man standing a few yards ahead of her had the means to change it all.

Alison tried to talk to him several times during the ride back, but he silenced her with a hard stare, one indicating he had no desire to hear anything she had to say. By the time they stopped in front of her store, she was tired and heartsick, ready to crawl into bed and never leave.

"I'll take Joker back to Noah." Cash dismounted, reaching up to help her down and take the reins.

"There's no reason I can't—"

"Go inside, Alison. I'll take care of the horses."

Staring at his back as he made an abrupt turn and began to walk away, she stepped onto the boardwalk, then halted.

"I want a chance to explain."

She didn't think he'd heard until she saw the slight stiffening of his back. Glancing over his shoulder, he made a slight turn, shaking his head.

"Leave it be for now. We will talk...just not today."

It wasn't much, a mere thread of hope, yet she clung to it. She'd never intended to care about Cash, to fall in love with him. The thought of tying herself to anyone in Splendor gained her nothing. Her intent had been to discover the truth of her brother's death, deal with the killer, and ride out, leaving all she'd built behind in her quest for revenge. Meeting Cash and developing feelings for the taciturn lawman had never been part of her plan. Now she had to deal with the consequences of her deceit.

She'd been so swept up in her own desire, the building passion, and her body's awakening need, she'd never thought of how her lie had no chance to stay hidden. Now the man she dreamed of, woke each morning thinking about, wanted nothing to do with her, might never allow her a chance to explain.

And truly, what would I say? Alison thought as she walked through the shop and up the stairs. Catching sight of her kitchen, the rumble of her stomach reminded her they'd never eaten. Her stomach had growled before they'd set foot in the cabin. Afterwards, all thoughts of food vanished as fast as Cash had.

Grabbing a tin from the cabinet over her sink, she pulled out a biscuit. It tasted dry and stale, even though she'd purchased them a few days ago. Setting it on the counter, she took a seat at the small table and clasped her hands, working to control the tremor which haunted her since he'd discovered her lies.

Her first thought had been to explain her true reasons for being in Splendor. Considering her choices now, hours later and sitting alone in her room, Alison knew he'd done her a favor by closing himself off. Telling Cash the truth would only push them further apart—if that were even possible. As a deputy, he might have arrested her for voicing her desire to find Bobby's killer and make him pay.

Standing, she took the few steps to her bed, slipped out of her dress and shoes, then drew back the covers. The sun had finished its descent behind the Redemption Mountain Range, yet her body didn't want to do anything except rest. Heeding the deep weariness, she remained under the covers to stare at the ceiling. Maybe when she woke, Alison would be able to better deal with what had happened, maybe devise an explanation Cash would accept, maybe salvage whatever friendship they'd started. *And maybe bulls can give milk*, she thought, shutting her eyes and drifting off to sleep.

"Where've you been all day?" Gabe leaned his back against the bar at the Rose, a cup of coffee in his hand, as he scanned the early evening crowd.

Cash nodded to the bartender when he held up a bottle of whiskey. Pushing his hat off his forehead, he thought of the day which had started with such promise and ended with a bitter taste.

"Took a ride up to Survivor Pass." Accepting the glass of whiskey, he took a sip, tempted to consume it in one gulp. Getting drunk wouldn't change the reality of what had happened. Besides, if he had too much to drink, he'd be tempted to storm back to Alison's and demand the truth. Fact was, he didn't know if he'd be able to handle her version of it. Cash had no doubt she'd try to cover up the truth until no other possibilities remained except her real reasons for being in Splendor.

"Didn't I see you ride out with Alison Burns?" Gabe studied him, aware something plagued his friend.

"Yes." He took another swallow of whiskey, letting it coat his throat, trying to decide how much to say. As his boss, Cash believed he owed Gabe a warning about Alison and the fact she'd been feeding the town a load of lies. Her deception could be nothing, or she could be hiding a past more sinister than he wanted to consider. Perhaps she had her reasons, and they might be innocent. His instincts said otherwise.

"You going to share what's going on with you and the young widow?" Gabe turned toward him, resting his elbow on the bar.

"Not much to share, except she isn't a widow."

Gabe's brows knit together as he considered this new information. "Did she say why she's been saying otherwise?"

"Nope, and I didn't ask."

"Might be a good idea to find out. There could be a valid reason she's letting people believe she's a widow."

Cash emptied his glass, seeing the doors to the Rose push open as four men he'd never seen walked inside. Ignoring Gabe's comments, he nodded toward the table where the men gathered.

"Do you know them?"

Gabe had been watching them, the same as Cash. On any given night, they'd often get one or two strangers passing through or looking for work on one of the local ranches. From the guns strapped around their waists, these men didn't appear to be cowhands.

"Never seen them before." His words were calm, although warnings buzzed in his head at the way the men looked around, as if gauging the others in the saloon.

"Could be part of the Penderville gang. I'd need to look at the wanted posters again, but none of these men look like Milton or Harrison."

When he walked into the saloon, Cash had decided he would leave after one drink. He'd changed his mind once the strangers arrived. Holding his glass toward the bartender, he nodded for a refill.

"I agree. That doesn't mean these men don't work for them. I'm going to find Beau and have him join you here. I'll head back to the jail to take another look at the wanted posters." The knot in Gabe's stomach tightened as he walked outside, a sure sign something was amiss. His instincts seldom failed him and he'd bet money the men who sat inside the Rose didn't come to Splendor to attend Sunday church.

"Don't look like we got much to worry about, Clem. The men in here wouldn't lift a hand to stop us from taking what we want." Louis grabbed the bottle they'd ordered and filled his glass.

"Didn't you see the sheriff and a deputy at the bar when we walked in? That's two who'll try to stop us, and there could be more. Don't forget this is where Chet and the rest of them lost their lives." Clem watched as the sheriff stepped outside, hoping his departure meant the man had looked them over and decided they didn't pose a threat. "Remember, we're here to avenge Chet, not rob their bank."

"Milt's getting weak. We got almost nothing in Bloody Basin, then we skipped Big Pine, even though they have two of the largest banks in the territory. Now he has us sitting in a bar in a town so small you could spit at one end and have it end up at the other." Louis leaned closer, glancing at the other men who'd ridden in with them. "I'm telling you, Clem. This ain't right. And I don't think Harry's none too happy about our little detour, either."

Clem kept his voice low, although the menace in it couldn't be missed. "You keep your head about you, Louis. Milt's done us good so far. It's normal a man wants to avenge the death of his brother. If that's what he wants, I say we get it done and get out of here." He stopped, looking up as a shadow passed over the table.

"Good evening, gentlemen. I don't believe I've seen you in Splendor before."

Louis licked his lips, sending a warning look to the other three men. "Evening, Deputy. Me and the boys are passing through. May spend a few nights playing cards and drinking. Any problem with that?"

"Not as long as you don't cause any trouble. If you abide by the laws and respect the townsfolk, we're a pretty welcoming town." He speared a look at each man, holding his gaze until all but Louis broke his stare. "What's your name?"

"Friends call me Louis." He kept his hands in clear view on top of the table.

"Your last name?"

"Well now, Deputy, I don't recall ever having a real one. My daddy was a real sonofabitch. Never married my ma and took off when I was a young'un. Ma went by Jones, so I guess it's as close as I ever got to a last name."

Cash glanced toward the front to see Beau standing there, an amused expression on his face. Instead of joining them, he leaned against a post, arms crossed. The room had grown silent, and even from his spot several feet away, Cash knew Beau had heard at least some of the conversation. He turned his attention back to the visitors.

"Well, Louis Jones, you make certain you and your friends are out of town and on your way in three days. That gives you plenty of time to fill up on whatever it is you need. See the man over there?" He nodded toward Beau. "He's another deputy. Truth is, he hasn't seen much action in a while and is getting real fidgety. War kind of made him crazy, but it sure as hell didn't hurt his aim. You understand me, Louis?"

"I understand you fine."

"Three days, then I don't want to see your faces around here again." Cash placed a hand on the back of Louis's chair and leaned down. "Just so we're clear."

Louis's dark look lasted only a moment before he glanced away and nodded. "We're clear, Deputy."

Joining Beau near the front, Cash kept his back to the men as he spoke. "They are up to no good. I've given them three days to show their hand. We need to find out where they're staying and alert some of the men in town. Feels dangerously like what happened last summer with the Penderville gang."

"Gabe's checking the posters now. I'll stick around until they leave, then follow them to where they're staying."

"I'm not going anywhere, Beau, if that's what you're thinking," Cash ground out before turning and taking his spot back at the bar.

Following him, Beau took a place beside him. "I didn't mean anything by it. Just thought you'd want to go visit your lady friend tonight."

"Well, you were wrong. I don't have a lady friend. At least not anymore."

Beau's expression changed from good-humored taunting to concern. "So that's how it is?"

"Afraid so. And don't think we're going to talk about it here. Tonight's about those four men and working to not let this whiskey go to my head." He took a slim sip, then set the glass down. "And all I wanted to do tonight was get drunk and fall into bed."

Beau's gaze swept over Cash's face, seeing the drawn lines around his eyes, the pursed lips, and hard set of his jaw. He'd never known his friend to fall for a woman, so he had no real words of encouragement. All Beau knew was that he was about to lose the first woman he'd cared about in a long time, and he felt bad for any man going through the same pain.

"Looks like we're both a couple of old fools. As soon as whatever these men have planned plays out, we're going to go on one long binge and get female yearnings out of our system." Beau picked up his glass, tilting it toward Cash. "I'm tired of fickle women who can't make up their minds."

"And those who lie," Cash added.

Beau's eyes widened a little before his face became a mask. "That, too."

They each took a swallow, then settled back for a long night of watching the four newcomers play cards and drink.

"Alison, it's Rachel and Ginny. Are you here?"

Hearing voices, Alison lifted her head from searching the thread box in her storage room. "I'm in the back. I'll be right out." She continued to look for the spool of a particular color of blue needed for Abby Brandt's new dress. "Got you," she muttered, picking up the spool and holding it to check the color. Slipping it into her sewing apron, she closed the curtain and walked to the front. "Sorry. I've been searching for something and finally found it. How are you ladies?"

She did her best to sound light, as if nothing weighed on her. In truth, each day without seeing or hearing from Cash caused her spirits to sink a little more. The fact she'd been the cause of his rejection made it all worse, and she had no idea how to turn her bad judgment around.

"We're doing wonderfully. Getting ready for a party at the ranch tomorrow and we'd love to have you join us." Rachel fingered a particularly beautiful bolt of fabric, wondering what she could have Alison make with it. "This is lovely."

"I thought the same when I picked it out before leaving Kentucky. It may be a little too much for what most women need in Splendor, though." Alison let out a deep sigh. She'd thought of making a dress from it for display in her window, yet she couldn't bring herself to cut into it. The embroidered green silk needed to be saved for a special occasion.

"About tomorrow. Guests are coming out after church. You'll know most everyone, and it will be a good chance for you to meet any you haven't already." Ginny considered Alison a moment, seeing none of the usual spark in her eyes. "Tell me if it's none of my business, but are you feeling all right? You seem a little, well...down."

"Do I?" She lowered her gaze, surprised Ginny had been able to detect her mood. "It may be because the shop has been quite busy, and I haven't been sleeping well. Other than that, I'm feeling fine." She hoped neither Ginny nor Rachel caught the slight tremor in her voice. It wouldn't do to confide in these women. She wouldn't know what to say, and the thought of lying made her stomach roil. "I'm not complaining. The shop is doing much better than I'd ever imagined. Losing a little sleep is a small price to pay, don't you think?"

"You deserve every bit of success." Rachel smiled at her. "I can't imagine traveling out here alone to start a business. When I came, I already had a position waiting for me in my uncle's clinic. Honestly, I don't know if I would've made the trip otherwise."

"And then you wouldn't have meet Dax or had Patrick, Rachel. I've come to believe everything works out in time." Ginny leaned against Alison's cutting table, looking at her. "So tell us you'll be coming to the party tomorrow."

"I'd love to come, but I have no way to get there."

"There will be plenty of people coming from church who'll have room for you in their wagon," Rachel said. "Or you can ride out with Cash. I'm sure he'd be pleased to accompany you."

"Oh, no." Alison's eyes sparked at the thought of approaching Cash. "I wouldn't want to impose on the deputy. I'll find a ride with someone after church."

Rachel glanced at Ginny, neither voicing what they thought.

"If you have any trouble, you'll ride out with Luke and me. We'll find someone to bring you home afterwards."

"Thank you, Ginny." She glanced at the door as the overhead bell chimed. "I suppose it's time I got back to work."

"We'll see you tomorrow," Rachel called as they walked past the new arrival and opened the door.

"Wait." Alison ran up to them, nodding at a woman with flaming red hair as she passed. "Are we celebrating something special tomorrow?"

"We certainly are." Rachel's eyes lit up, her mouth curving into a smile. "Bull asked Lydia to marry him."

Chapter Eighteen

The Penderville gang sat around the campfire, sharing a bottle of whiskey as they waited for another man to join them. He'd been sent to Splendor a few months before to learn which locals had been involved in killing Chet and the rest of his men. Milt wanted to send a message, even if they couldn't kill every man involved. Rustling in the bushes had the men standing, drawing their guns.

"Who's out there?" Milt held his gun toward the sound, then relaxed as a lone figure stepped forward, hands in the air.

"It's just me, big brother." Monty Penderville lowered his hands, flashing the cocky grin he had used to get out of trouble since he was a boy. Slapping Milt's back, then Harry's, he glanced at the others. "About time you all showed up." He grabbed the bottle Louis held out and took a long swallow.

"Sit down and tell us what you've learned." Milt lowered himself onto a nearby log, leaned forward, and rested his arms on his knees.

"It was a smart move having me get a job at the lumber mill. Silas Jenks knows details about everyone in town."

"And he was there the day of the bank robbery?" Harry asked, his gaze narrowing on his younger brother.

"Yes." Monty took another pull from the bottle, then handed it off. "He didn't participate, but saw most of it."

"What happened? How did Chet die?"

"From what I learned, Chet was the second to die. They rode into town using wagons as cover. He took up a position behind the third one. When shots came from the bank, one of our men inside a wagon was shot first. Silas told me one of the local men, a former sharpshooter in the Union Army, picked off Chet next. The others died in the bank or as they left. Bobby was the last to die at the hand of one of the deputies. It happened fast."

All the men had liked Bobby. The youngest in the gang, he'd been the quietest and most hesitant to use his gun. Naïve in most ways, none of them ever understood why he'd joined them, except to follow a man he'd fought with during the war. The man had grown up with the Pendervilles, understood their anger when General Lee surrendered, and wanted revenge as much as anyone. Bobby had followed him into the gang.

"The sharpshooter. Who is he?" Milt asked.

"Noah Brandt. He runs the livery."

Milt repeated the name, committing it to memory. "And the deputy who shot Bobby?"

"Cash Coulter."

Cash sat at the back of the church. Unlike Gabe and Beau, he didn't attend every Sunday, preferring to keep watch on the town. This morning, he'd woken up, made coffee, and carried a cup to the jail. Stepping onto the boardwalk, he glanced up to see Alison walking toward him, a bible in her hand. She came to an abrupt halt when she saw him.

"Mrs. Burns." He touched the brim of his hat, his greeting mocking her.

Stepping closer, she clutched the bible to her chest, not breaking eye contact. "Deputy."

He knew he should keep quiet. Instead, the insult poured from his lips. "Going to church? Trying to find forgiveness for your transgressions?"

She stepped closer, trying to control the anger his words caused. The effort failed.

"Who are you to judge me, Cash Coulter? You refused to listen, hear my reasons for having people believe I'd been married." Her chest heaved as the anger took hold. "I came hundreds of miles for a reason, and it's a dang good one. One I believe you'd understand."

"If it's such a good reason, why didn't you say something before we..." His voice trailed off as a vision of them together flashed through his mind. "You should have warned me, Allie. It could've been so much different if I'd known."

Her blank expression told him how much she didn't know about being with a man, making love.

"Tell me now. What was your reason?"

Shaking her head, she stepped away. "It's too late now, Cash. You've lost your chance to learn the truth." Turning her back to him, she dashed away, as if she couldn't put him behind her fast enough.

Alison's brisk dismissal didn't surprise him, although it created a profound ache deep in his chest. He'd been wrong to walk away from the cabin, leaving her the way he did, refusing to listen to her explanations. Cash would have never imagined learning about her deceit the way he did, during what he'd expected to be one of many times making love to her. The knowledge stunned and angered him. It might have been different if he hadn't allowed Alison to work her way past his defenses and carve a place in his heart.

As if pulled by an unexpected force, his feet moved toward the church. She'd been wrong to lie, but he'd been wrong to shut her out. Cash had intended to return to Alison's shop, learn the reasons why she felt it necessary to lie to him and all her friends. Instead, he'd busied himself with work at the jail, took on some of Beau's rounds at night, and offered to ride to outlying ranches to check on distant families. Before he knew it, a week had gone by.

Now he sat in the back of the church at the end of a pew across the aisle, a few rows behind her. She'd taken a seat next to Noah and Abby, who held Gabriel in her arms, rocking him back and forth as Reverend Paige spoke. Today's message was about redemption and atoning for one's misdeeds.

Staring straight ahead, Cash thought of his own actions during and after the war, knowing Alison wasn't the only one with secrets. His might be discreetly tucked away so he could deal with them alone and in his own way, but they did exist.

Losing track of time, Cash startled at the sound of the choir singing the closing hymn. The people around him exited the pews and began to file past. He stood a moment, watching as Alison spoke to Noah and Abby. Shoving his hands in his coat pockets, he forced himself to leave, knowing he had unfinished business.

First, he'd send one more telegram to his source back east. And second, he'd find a way to get Alison to tell him what he'd refused to hear at the cabin. After all, he reasoned, there had to be a good reason for her to build a tale of deception. Once he learned it, perhaps they'd be able to put all the poor choices behind them...maybe finding a way to move forward.

"I'm so glad you could come, Alison." Ginny hugged her, then turned to Noah and Abby to do the same. "May I hold him?" Nodding toward Gabriel, she reached her arms out.

Abby tucked the blanket closer around him, then slid the baby into Ginny's arms. She and Luke had been wanting to start a family. Each month, Abby watched Ginny try to hide her disappointment. Then she'd push it aside and draw upon the hope she'd learned to lean upon since arriving in Splendor.

"Did you ride out with Noah and Abby?" Ginny asked Alison as she rocked Gabriel in her arms.

"Yes. They offered when I sat next to them in church." Looking around, Alison recognized most of the people, relaxing when she failed to see one specific face. She didn't believe he'd seen her taking quick glances at him over her shoulder during the service.

The brief triumph she felt at displaying her anger didn't last long before being replaced by guilt. Lashing out at Cash would achieve nothing. It had been her deception that caused his ire and hurtful words.

"There they are now." Rachel dashed outside as Bull pulled the wagon to a stop, then helped Lydia down. She'd never seen such bright smiles on either of their faces, feeling a spear of warmth rush through her. "It's good to have you back here, Lydia, if only for one day." Hugging her, then Bull, she grabbed Lydia's hand, leading her up the steps.

With the arrival of the guests of honor, the noise level increased as the men slapped Bull's back, offering their congratulations, and the women broke into groups to discuss the upcoming wedding.

"She'll need a dress, Alison." Abby's enthusiasm showed, even though it meant she and Noah would need to find someone new to help with Gabriel.

"What a wonderful idea," Caro agreed.

"Oh, I don't know," Lydia interjected. "Bull may not have the money for such an extravagance."

Abby shot a quick look at Rachel, Ginny, and Caro, all smiling. "Then it will be our wedding present to you."

"And I'd be glad to donate my time." Alison couldn't think of a better gift than designing a dress guaranteed to take Bull's breath away.

"Oh, you don't have to—"

"I want to, Lydia. Please. Let me do this for you." Alison's eyes glowed with satisfaction when Lydia nodded, then began to fade when she heard a familiar voice coming from behind her. Her stomach plummeted when the ladies turned to greet Cash, who walked in with Gabe and Lena.

"Good to see you." Dax shook hands with Gabe and Cash. "Beau stay behind?"

Gabe glanced at the group of women who stood together across the room. "We needed to leave someone in town and he volunteered. I don't think he wanted to take a chance of seeing Caro. He's not taking her leaving too well." Gabe had known Caroline since they were children and understood her need to pursue her dreams. As a widow, she had the means. She also had the temperament and sense of adventure to travel alone.

"What man would?" Luke asked as he and Bull joined them.

"How are you doing? Changed your mind yet?" Gabe asked, clasping Bull on the shoulder.

"Never. I finally have all I want." He shifted his gaze to Lydia, whose face lit up when she saw him watching her.

Cash watched the two of them, an odd sense of longing passing through him. Then he saw Allie standing next to Caro at one end of the dining room. Caro's hands flashed in an animated fashion as she spoke to Alison, who kept glancing toward him, then looking away.

Forgetting their earlier encounter, Cash excused himself from the group of men and walked toward her. Ignoring the warning in her eyes, he continued forward.

"Hello, Cash." When Caro looked behind him, he wondered if she had hoped Beau had come along.

"Caro," he greeted before turning his gaze on Alison. "Good afternoon, Mrs. Burns." His voice lacked the smug tone of earlier.

"Deputy Coulter."

Cash watched as Caro glanced between the two of them. Most of the town knew they'd been seeing each other, and he was certain their cool tone had her confused.

"Doesn't Lydia look happy?" Caro gestured toward the living room where Lydia had joined Bull, her hand clutching his. "It's so good to see them together."

A sadness tugged at Alison's heart as she watched the two of them laughing at something Luke said. She didn't know them well. She'd helped Lydia only once, with a dress she'd purchased at the general store, yet felt more of a connection with them and the people in this house, than she had with anyone in Kentucky. The anger and need for revenge, which had brought her to Splendor, no longer held her captive as they once did.

"I have the perfect fabric for her dress. It is embroidered silk..." Alison's voice trailed off when she saw Cash watching her. Thankfully, Rachel chose that moment to join them.

"What color is it?" Caro asked.

"What color is what?" Rachel glanced at Alison.

"I thought the fabric you liked so much in my shop, the green silk, would be perfect for Lydia's dress."

"Oh my, yes. It's perfect for her. Do you have a design?" Rachel asked, glancing at Cash, who didn't seem to be put off by their conversation.

"Yes. It's in my head." Alison looked at her empty punch glass and shrugged. "I believe I'll get some more."

Without a word, Cash left with her, taking the glass from her hand and filling it.

"Is it good?"

"The punch?" Alison asked. "I'm guessing you wouldn't find it as satisfying as the whiskey you prefer." She held the glass up. "Try it and tell me what you think."

Reaching out, he clasped his hand around hers on the glass, feeling the same surge of sensations he did each time they touched. His eyes didn't waver as he brought the glass to his lips and took a sip, grimacing at the taste.

"I concede. The punch does seem more suitable for the ladies."

Tugging slightly, she drew her hand away, her expression resigned. "Then I'll let you join the men and pour yourself a more suitable men's drink." As she began to turn away, Cash's hand settled on her arm, stilling her retreat.

"Walk with me, Allie."

Her brows knit together as her head tilted to one side. "Why? I don't believe we have anything to talk about."

He leaned toward her, lowering his voice as he spoke in her ear. "I need to know why. You had reasons for pretending to be a widow, for traveling so far from your home. I want to know those reasons."

Alison's lips drew into a thin line. She'd offered to explain, almost begged him to listen to her. He'd chosen to walk away. Afterwards, her relief had been great. She had no idea how she could have explained the true reasons for being in Splendor without creating a new circle of lies.

Something inside nagged at her to come up with a confession he could accept without giving away the truth or making the situation worse. She needed time.

"All right, but not here at Bull and Lydia's party. I'll be working long days to finish some orders. After I close the shop on Thursday is the earliest I could meet you."

As much as he wanted to learn the truth today, he didn't want to push. She'd agreed to give him answers, which was more than she'd offered that morning.

"I'll come to the shop on Thursday."

"All right, everyone." Dax stood in the center of the room, a glass in his hand. "Whatever you're drinking, it's time to make a toast to Bull and Lydia."

Dax's voice faded into the background. Agreeing to meet with Cash had only increased Alison's anxiety. She needed to come up with a story he'd believe, one close to the truth that didn't paint her as a woman out for revenge...and she had four days to do it.

Chapter Nineteen

"Get your horse, Cash. I need you to ride with me to the Devil Dancer." Gabe rushed through the door of the jail, grabbing extra ammunition.

"What's going on?"

"Reuben Krause sent word that two of the Chinese workers are missing. The other two were left for dead a mile from the mine." Opening the desk drawer, pulling out a piece of paper and pencil, Gabe scribbled a quick note to Beau. "I've already asked Noah to saddle a horse for John. This time, I want him to get those Chinese men to talk."

"Have you told Doc Worthington?" Cash strapped on his gun belt and picked up his hat.

"He's getting ready and will follow us out. Nick and Lena are riding out, too."

"Do you think that's wise, Gabe?"

Gabe stared at Cash as if the man were insane. "You want to be the one to tell her she can't go to her own mine? If she'll listen to you, I'll be in your debt."

Holding up his hands, Cash chuckled. "I tried to stop her from going the last time. Nothing I could say changed her mind. I thought you'd have better luck."

"Well, you thought wrong. You ready?"

Nodding, Cash opened the door, hurrying toward the livery. Within minutes, he and Gabe joined Nick, Lena, and Doc Worthington, then they took the trail to the Devil Dancer, John bouncing along behind them on the easiest horse in Noah's stable.

Leaving Splendor behind, Cash thought of the men they'd seen in the Rose a few nights before. From what he'd heard, they'd never returned. Gabe assumed they'd ridden out, heeding his warning about not staying around. Cash didn't believe it. He couldn't shake the feeling they were somehow tied to the Penderville gang, which didn't bode well for Splendor.

The situation at the mine had escalated by the time they arrived. Men held picks and shovels before them, squaring off into two groups in front of the mine office, Galt standing in front of one.

"You need to back off, Galt, before someone gets hurt." Reuben held a shotgun in his hands, ready to bring it up at the hint of any violence. In his late fifties, with short gray hair and sparse stubble on his jaw, the man stood five foot eight, yet his thick neck, muscular arms, and thick fingers spoke of physical strength most men didn't want to test. Slow to anger, he had a reputation for managing men without the need of threats.

"You ask me, we're better off without those Chinamen. They've been nothing but trouble since they got here." Galt looked over his shoulder at the men standing behind him. Cash noticed many were the same ones who'd caused the trouble at the lumber mill.

"It isn't the Chinese men causing the trouble. They didn't beat each other up and almost kill Zhao and Wang." Reuben took a step forward, his hard gaze moving from man to man until they fell silent. "The trouble as I see it is you and those who stand with you. You see Sheriff Evans and his deputy over there?" Galt and the others turned, most noticing the riders for the first time. "They're here to get this figured out, arrest those who beat Zhao and Wang, and find Zheng and Qian. Anyone who doesn't cooperate will find himself without a job." Reuben glanced at the riders. "We've got two men in the tent over there, Doc. They're in a bad way."

Doc slid to the ground and untied his medical bag from the back of the saddle. Uncaring of the hateful stares from some of the men, he pushed through the crowd, then disappeared inside the tent.

Dismounting, Lena and Nick joined Reuben outside the office while Gabe and Cash approached the group led by Galt, hands resting on the grips of their revolvers. Gabe didn't waste any words.

"I want to know who's responsible for this. If no one comes forward, I'll arrest every single one of you and put you up for trial as a group." He looked at Cash. "When's the judge due back in town?"

"Two weeks."

The response got the men talking. "You can't arrest us. We ain't done nothing wrong." Galt stepped forward, his words hissing out, his face coloring a blotchy red.

Ignoring him, Gabe turned toward the other group. "You men agree with Galt?"

The men looked at each other, talking in whispers until one man broke from the middle to approach Gabe and Cash.

"We're here to work, Sheriff. We know nothing about what happened to those Chinamen, but I can tell you Galt and a number of those men have been making life hard for them."

"Shut up, Wiggins." Galt took several menacing steps forward, bringing his shovel up.

Drawing his gun, leveling it at Galt, Cash moved to cut him off. "Get back with the others."

"He's lying." Galt pointed an accusatory finger toward the man talking to Gabe.

"That's why we're here. To find out who's lying and who's telling the truth. Now, get back." Cash moved until he was almost chest to chest with Galt, his gun between them. When Galt tried to take a step closer, Cash raised the gun, whipping it across Galt's face before anyone knew what happened. The man fell to the ground, unconscious. "Is anyone else having a problem understanding what's going on here? The sheriff and I are here to find a potential killer. This is not a game, and the consequences will be severe."

Grabbing Galt by his collar, Cash dragged him closer to Gabe and dropped him with a thud, never lowering his weapon from the group of men. "They may be ready to talk now, Sheriff."

Gabe looked down at a bleeding Galt. "Guess you'd better have Doc check him over when he's done with Zheng and Qian. Then start talking to the men in Galt's group. I'll continue with Wiggins and the others. By the end of the day, I expect we'll have the truth, or as close as we're going to be able to get until John is able to get his friends to talk."

Three hours later, Gabe and Cash had all they needed to arrest several miners, including Galt, for beating Zhao and Wang. No one knew what happened to Zheng and Qian. Reuben suspected they'd run, trying to get away from the men who'd descended upon them while they slept. Lena and Nick believed the same, as did Gabe and Cash.

It didn't take long to organize Wiggins and several other miners into a search party, Cash and Gabe taking the lead. John had agreed to go with them, help persuade his friends to return.

"You know this area better than anyone, Reuben. Where would they go?" Cash walked alongside several others as they combed the area, calling out the names as they searched.

"Up, most likely. Going down the hill would take them to the main trails, which they'd want to avoid. There are some old caves a couple hundred yards up. Zheng and Qian probably heard the men talking about them. Trust me," Reuben smirked. "They understand a lot more than you think."

All Cash wanted to do was fall onto his bed and sleep, but he couldn't. They'd spent over twenty-four hours searching the hills, finally finding Zheng and Qian huddled in one of the caves.

Zhao and Wang recovered from their beatings faster than anyone expected. This time, they identified Galt and the men they'd already arrested as the ones who'd beaten them. Reuben had been right. The Chinese men spoke and understood English much better than they let on.

Hauling the prisoners back to town, while listening to them rant about being arrested, had taken over two hours.

The entire time he'd been away, Cash couldn't escape the uneasy feeling about leaving Beau alone to protect the town. He couldn't shake the idea the men who'd been warned out of Splendor were part of the Penderville gang and meant to return.

Beau and he had always believed they hadn't gotten all of the men associated with the bank robbery. The appearance of the Penderville brothers in Wyoming, then in Bloody Basin confirmed what they suspected. The remaining members of the gang were in Montana, possibly camped near Splendor.

Thankfully, his worry over Beau had amounted to nothing. Before they'd dismounted, he'd come walking out of the jail, flashing his customary smile.

"I see we have some new residents for the jail." Bounding down the steps, he helped unload the five prisoners, escorting them inside to their cells. "John's friends decided to talk?"

"They did, as did a few of the other miners. I don't believe the judge or jury will have any doubts about their guilt." Cash ran a hand down his face, then pinched the bridge of his nose. He picked up a telegram he saw on the desk. "This is good news. The circuit judge will be here early next week."

"It is. Means we won't be responsible for those men for too long." Tossing the cell keys down, Beau settled into a chair next to Cash.

"Have the men we ran out of town shown up again?"

Beau shook his head. "Not that I've seen. I asked Al at the Rose and Paul at the Dixie to let me know right away if they see them."

The door slammed open, Gabe not sparing them a glance as he walked straight to the coffee pot. Pouring the warm liquid into a cup, he took a sip, grimacing at the stale taste.

"You ever thought of making a fresh pot, Beau?"

"Figured it would take too much time away from my responsibilities." Beau grinned, linking his hands behind his head.

"I'm too tired to appreciate your humor today." Gabe took one more swallow of coffee, then set it down, pushing the palms of his hands into his eyes. "Why don't you get some sleep, Cash? Beau and I can watch the prisoners."

"You go ahead, Gabe. I'm too restless to sleep." Cash needed to walk the town, satisfy himself none of the men they'd run off were around. Plus, he wanted to check on Alison, make sure she was all right. There were still two more days before they'd agreed to talk. In his mind, that was two days too long.

Pushing from his chair, Gabe nodded at Cash. "I'll be back in a few hours."

"Heard you arrested the men who beat up John's friends." Silas extended his hand to Cash. "Good job."

"I'm glad to get those men where they belong." Cash looked around. "Where's Monty?"

"Boy up and disappeared almost a week ago. Left one night and never came back."

"Did you check his room?"

"Sure did. It's cleaned out. He didn't have much, but it's all gone." Silas scratched his jaw. "Can't understand it. He was one of the best workers I've ever had."

"Did he have a horse?"

"Stabled it at Noah's livery. Hardly ever rode it, but it's gone, too. Noah said Monty never told him he'd be leaving."

Monty disappearing made no sense to Cash. "Do you mind showing me his room?"

Silas shrugged, then walked outside. "He stayed in a room built into the back of the extra storage shed." Unlocking the door, he pushed it open, gesturing for Cash to go inside.

Small and cramped, the room held a narrow bed, worn dresser with a chipped wash basin and pitcher on top, one chair, and a wood stove. Silas had been right. Monty left nothing behind.

"Where did he take his meals?"

"With me most days. Sometimes he'd go over to Suzanne's for supper. That boy could eat more than most two men I know."

Cash took a few minutes to look around, checking under the bed, pulling out dresser drawers, finding nothing. Opening the stove, he spotted a charred piece of paper and pulled it out.

"What you got there, Cash?" Silas stepped forward. "Looks like a wanted poster."

"It was. It's too scorched to make out much besides the five hundred dollar reward. Mind if I keep this?"

"Won't bother me." Silas pulled the key out of his pocket. "If you're finished, I need to get back to work."

Folding what was left of the poster, Cash tucked it into his shirt pocket, chafing at the familiar prickling sensation he'd get when things didn't make sense. Young and eager to please, Monty got along with everyone. He didn't seem the type of person to leave a good job behind.

"Silas, does Monty have any family around here?"

"Nope. He may have brothers somewhere. Mentioned them once or twice, then shut his mouth, like he hadn't meant to bring them up."

"Did he ever mention where he was from?"

"Somewhere back east. That's all I know."

Silas walked into the lumber mill, leaving Cash to ponder what he'd learned. If nothing else were going on, none of this might bother him. Between the issues at the mine, the growing sense the Pendervilles might show up at any time, and his feelings for Alison, coupled with the lies she'd told, he wondered what else was about to crash down on them. Because he knew, as sure as he knew the sun would rise tomorrow, the surprises were far from over.

"Cash. I saw you talking to Silas and didn't want you to walk past." Bernie Griggs held out a telegram. "I believe it's important. Let me know if you want to send a reply."

Unfolding the message, Cash read through it, his jaw tightening. Murmuring a curse, he slapped the paper against his leg, then read it again. Anger surged through him. It all made sense, but he'd never suspected a thing. Cash needed time to consider what he'd learned and what he should do next. Two days remained before his meeting with Alison. Two days to make decisions that would define his future.

"Noah Brandt stays in town most of the time, so he won't be hard to find. Deputy Coulter might be harder to get alone." Monty watched the town below through his telescope. He and his brothers had ridden out after breakfast to get a better view of the town and make plans for going after the men who killed Chet and Bobby.

"Do either of them have a wife or woman friend?" Milt asked.

"Brandt has a wife and baby. Coulter doesn't have a wife, but he does seem partial to Mrs. Burns, who owns a shop next to the bank."

"Burns?" Milt's eyes widened at the mention of Bobby's middle name.

"Yes. Why?"

"Bobby's full name was Robert Burns McGrath. He told me Burns was his mother's maiden name." Milt looked at Harry. "Bobby didn't leave a wife behind, did he?"

"Hell if I know. He did have a sister. He called her Allie."

"I'll be," Monty mumbled. "Mrs. Burns' first name is Alison and she's from Kentucky, same as Bobby."

"Seems we have a woman looking to do the same as us. Find Bobby's killer." Satisfaction rippled through Milt. "We might have ourselves a partner, boys. Where does Coulter live?"

"In a house behind the jail. But he likes to ride out on weekends to this old shack on Survivor Pass. I followed him up there one day. He usually goes alone."

"Where does Brandt live?" Harry took the telescope from Monty.

"See the house up on the hill on the other side of town?"

Harry adjusted the telescope, focusing on a large house overlooking Splendor. "Yeah."

"That's his."

"Whooee. It's a big place." Harry handed the telescope to Milt.

"I wonder if he keeps valuables at home." Milt closed the scope and stepped deeper into the trees, motioning for Harry and Monty to follow him.

"Dammit, Milt. We aren't here to steal. We're here to kill Brandt and Coulter, then ride out before they have a chance to gather a posse."

Milt took a menacing step toward Harry, grabbing the front of his shirt. "We do what I say we do."

Anger flashed in Harry's eyes a moment before he shoved Milt away, causing him to stumble and fall. "Don't ever lay a hand on me again. I don't care if you're my brother or not. Next time, I'll break your neck." Stalking away, Harry swung up on his horse.

Milt straightened, brushing off the dirt. They had two men to kill. Afterwards, he'd find a way to get back at Harry—maybe get rid of him altogether.

"Get your horse, Monty. We have plans to make and a brother to avenge."

Chapter Twenty

Thursday came sooner than Cash expected. He'd wanted to talk to Alison at Bull and Lydia's party, definitely sooner than waiting four days. Then he'd gotten the telegram. Fifty hours later, he tossed out the last of his cold coffee and strapped his gun belt around his waist.

A cool breeze washed across Cash's face as he stepped outside. Shoving his hands in his coat pockets, he walked down the narrow street separating the row of houses from the businesses. Besides the house he and Beau rented, Gabe and Lena lived in one while their home was being built, the school teacher lived in another, Betts and her husband were in the one behind their restaurant, and one stood vacant behind the bank. Taking the narrow walkway between buildings, Cash stepped onto the boardwalk, stopping at Alison's front door.

Grasping the doorknob, he twisted, hearing the overhead bell chime when he stepped inside. He looked around, sucking in a breath when he saw Alison sitting at her sewing machine. Other than the two of them, the store was empty.

Alison looked up, a tentative smile tilting up the corners of her mouth. "I'm almost finished. Would you like some coffee while you wait?"

Clearing his throat, Cash shook his head. "Uh...no thanks. Take your time." He wandered about the room, feigning interest in the finished women's hats and rolls of fabric, thinking he'd rather be anywhere than here. He knew the conversation they were about to have wouldn't end well.

Then his gaze lit on a stunning dress of embroidered green silk, prompting a slight grin. "Is this Lydia's wedding dress?"

Glancing up, Alison stood and walked to him. "Yes. I hadn't planned on starting it this week, but I couldn't sleep the last two nights and it seemed like a good way to pass the time."

"It's beautiful."

Alison felt her face heat at his compliment. "Thank you. She'll make a gorgeous bride." Clasping her hands in front of her, she rocked back on her heels. "I'm finished with my work. Do you still want to talk?"

"That's why I'm here." He hadn't meant to sound so harsh.

The tightness in his voice startled her. "All right. Shall we go upstairs?"

"Wherever you'd be most comfortable."

She rubbed the back of her neck in an attempt to relieve the stiffness from working so many hours.

"Are you sore?" Cash stepped behind her, moving her hand aside as he began to massage the tight muscles.

She moaned as his hands worked their magic on her neck and back.

"Am I rubbing too hard?" Cash's fingers stilled.

"No. It feels wonderful." She sighed, tipping her head forward, letting her shoulders relax.

"That's it, Allie." He breathed in her scent, closing his eyes as he continued to work her muscles. Without thinking, he bent to brush a kiss across her neck, then froze when he remembered the reason for his visit. Dropping his hands, he stepped away. "Better?"

Turning, she saw Cash stiffen and wondered what was going through his mind.

"Yes. Thank you." Smoothing her hands down the folds of her dress, Alison caught her lower lip between her teeth, her brows knitting together. "I suppose we might as well get to the reason you're here." She gestured to a pair of chairs several feet away. "I'll be right back."

Cash watched as she dashed up the stairs. Instead of sitting down, he crossed his arms and leaned against the large table she used to cut fabric. He didn't want to get too comfortable or settle into a cozy conversation. Hearing her reasons for hiding behind a false identity and coming to Splendor were critical. Learning why she allowed him to make love to her, knowing he'd discover her deception, might soothe his bruised ego, but would do nothing to lessen his suspicions about her. The sound of footfalls drew his attention to the stairs.

"I thought you might want to try this." Clasping a glass in each hand, she held one out to him, smiling as he took his time studying the liquid inside each glass. "I'm not trying to poison you. It's the apple wine I told you about."

Taking the glass, he held it up to study the slightly cloudy liquid, then sniffed the contents, his lips twisting into a wry grin. "Doesn't smell too bad."

"Too bad? I believe I should be offended." Her voice trembled as she failed to hide her anxiety about Cash's reason for coming by. She thought the wine would be a peace offering. Now all she wanted was to get this over with and send him on his way. "How about I take a sip first?"

Narrowing his gaze, he chuckled, bringing the glass to his lips. Taking a swallow, he worked to conceal a grimace.

"Well?" Alison prompted.

"Not bad." He took one more sip, then set the glass on the table. "It's a little sweet for me." His expression changed, the amusement in his eyes gone. "We need to talk, Allie." He waited for her to take a seat, then moved his chair closer and sat down. "I need to know who you really are and why you came to Splendor."

Placing her glass next to Cash's, she clasped her hands in her lap. "All right. My name is—"

The bell over the door startled her as Bernie Griggs shoved it open and dashed inside, his breath coming in gasps. "Beau said you'd be here, Cash. He needs you to come quick. The prisoners are causing trouble."

"What kind of trouble?" Cash stood, sending a frustrated glance at Alison.

Bernie glanced at Alison, then back at Cash, lowering his voice. "One of the miners is dead."

Cash burst through the jail door, coming to a stop at the sight of Doc Worthington kneeling next to a motionless body.

"What the hell happened?"

Beau stood a couple feet away, shifting his gaze between the inert body and the men still confined behind bars. "Two of the prisoners got into an argument. By the time I got back here, Galt had his hands around the man's neck. I pulled my gun, ordering him to stop. Instead, he tightened his hold, then shoved the man against the wall. As he fell, his head hit the edge of the bed frame. According to Doc, the blow to his head is what killed him."

"Where's Gabe?"

"He and Lena are having supper with Noah and Abby. I knew you were close, so I asked Bernie to get you first, then Gabe." Beau relaxed for a moment, his features softening. "I think Bernie likes helping us out. Gets him out of the Western Union office for a while." He smiled, remembering how Bernie's face lit up when he asked him for help.

"What happened?" Gabe walked in and shrugged out of his jacket, looking at the body.

"The man died from a blow to his head." Doc continued putting his instruments away, not looking at Gabe. "I'll need help getting him to the clinic."

"Beau and I will follow you over, Doc." Cash took the man's legs while Beau grabbed the shoulders. "Be careful, Gabe. Galt's the one who killed him. We'll come back and sort out what to do."

"Take your time. They aren't going anywhere." Gabe took a quick look at the cells to see Galt in a whispered conversation with another prisoner. "Move away, Galt, or I'll take you out and chain you to a post."

Storming to the bars, Galt wrapped his hands around them, his face contorted in rage. "You'll pay for putting us in here, Evans."

"No, Galt." He nodded toward the blood on the cell floor. "You'll be the one paying, and it will be my pleasure to watch."

"I need to talk to you after we check back with Gabe." Cash walked beside Beau as they returned from delivering the body.

"We can talk at the jail."

"No. Alone." Cash didn't like keeping anything from Gabe, yet he needed to talk to Beau, tell him what he'd learned about Alison. He'd allowed himself to get too close to her, build feelings he should've ignored until he knew more about her. Desire overcame common sense. Passion overcame restraint.

Beau studied Cash, seeing concern etched deep in the lines of his face. "How long since you've slept?"

"Lack of sleep isn't important right now." Cash stepped onto the boardwalk, stopping at the door to the jail.

"We'll encourage Gabe to go home to Lena. We can talk in the front and still keep watch on Galt and the others."

Cash nodded, then walked inside. "Doc's taking care of the body. Why don't you head home to Lena?"

"Cash and I will watch the prisoners." Beau took a look in the back. All seemed quiet.

Standing, Gabe picked up his hat. "If you don't mind, I'll accept the offer."

They waited a few minutes, then settled into chairs. Beau rested his arms on the desk and leaned forward. "What do you want to talk about?"

"We didn't have a chance to talk last night," Cash whispered in Alison's ear, causing her to flinch.

Whipping around, she placed a hand on her chest. "Cash, you startled me."

"Mrs. Burns? You're next."

Alison turned back to face the open teller window.

"I'll wait for you outside." Cash didn't linger, not wanting to draw Horace Clausen's attention. A few minutes later she joined him, opening her parasol to shield her face from the morning sun.

"Did you take care of the crisis? I believe Bernie said you had a dead man at the jail." She started walking down the boardwalk toward the opposite end of town, Cash keeping pace beside her.

"It wasn't a crisis, but there was a body. Doc had already arrived by the time I got there."

Stopping, she shifted to look up at him. "I would think any killing would be considered a crisis."

Knowing her secret, the meaning of her statement was clear. As she started walking again, it took all his restraint not to grab her by the shoulders and shake the confession out of her.

"Any death is tragic, Alison. Most don't create a crisis."

She stopped at the end of the boardwalk, sucking in a breath. "When do you want to talk?"

"Close the shop tomorrow. We'll go to the cabin at Survivor Pass so we won't be interrupted." Seeing the skepticism on her face, he clarified. "Talk only. Nothing more."

Her expression changed for a brief moment. Cash wasn't sure if he saw pain or relief flash across her face.

She looked down at the ground and nodded. "I'll need a horse."

"I've already spoken with Noah about you riding Joker again. I'll be by mid-morning."

Alison knew she should refuse. She owed him nothing—had no reason to tell him the truth and expose the reasons for her lies. Although he hadn't said it, she believed he'd already made up his mind about them and would no longer be courting her. Keeping her secret was the safest decision for her.

"I don't know, Cash. What happened between us can't be changed. It would be best to forget it entirely."

"Believe me, that will not happen. We can meet tonight at your shop, where we might be interrupted, or we can ride out to the cabin. You choose, but you *are* going to talk to me."

Letting out a deep sigh, she nodded. "I'll see you at the shop tomorrow morning."

"Here's how it's going to be. We take care of both men tomorrow." Milt didn't ask for his brother's thoughts or anyone's approval. If they didn't like the way he ran the gang, they could confront him. Or they could leave, but they wouldn't be riding out alive.

Harry walked up to him, crossed his arms, and fixed him with a hard stare. "How do you expect to kill both when we don't know where they'll be?"

"We know. Monty says Noah Brandt works a few hours on Saturdays, then goes home."

"He always leaves at ten o'clock." Monty stepped up next to his brothers, not wanting either's temper to explode.

"We'll get Brandt as he rides up the hill to his house. There's good cover and places where we can position more than one man." Milt's smug grin grated on Harry, but he held his tongue. "I'll send Louis and Clem. They're the best shots and are fast riders. After they do their job, they'll meet the rest of the boys on the trail back to Big Pine."

"And Coulter?"

"You, Monty, and I will set up a surprise at the shack for the deputy. Monty says he rides out after meeting with the sheriff and making his rounds."

"He usually leaves town not long after Brandt closes the livery. I watched both of them for weeks and they seldom change."

"Good job, kid." Milt slapped his youngest brother on the back.

Monty nodded, the haughty grin on his face reminding Harry of Chet. The thought sent a chill through him.

"Sounds like you have it all covered." Harry's gut reaction warned him they'd missed something, but he knew there'd be no changing Milt's mind.

"See, Harry. You gotta have more faith in me. Chet never did and look where it got him."

Harry ignored the comment. Even though Chet was a true S.O.B., he had his reasons for never listening to Milt. "If you're satisfied with what Monty's told you, I can't argue."

"The boy's done good." Milt shot a look at Monty. "You want to be the one to take care of Coulter?"

"Hell yes. Bobby was the best friend I ever had. It's my job to make things right."

"You sure about that, Monty? As I recall, you've never killed a man. Are you sure you want to start with a lawman?" Harry knew that as much as Monty wanted to be like Milt, he also had an aversion to killing. *Squeamish* was what Chet used to call it. He never trusted Monty with a job that might end up in a shootout, saying he couldn't depend on him to finish someone off.

"I'll start with Bobby's killer. I don't care if he's a deputy or not. He deserves to die."

Harry lowered his gaze to the ground and shook his head. "If that's what you want. When do we ride out, Milt?"

"Right after we eat in the morning." He looked at the rest of the gang standing around them, listening. "Afterwards, we meet the rest of the boys on the trail, ride to Big Pine, and relieve the bank of its burden of guarding so much cash."

"Then on to California, right, Milt?" Monty's eager face didn't show a trace of fear, not even with what lay ahead of him.

"Yeah, kid." Milt clasped him on the shoulder. "Then we ride to California."

Chapter Twenty-One

"Think about this, Cash. You're going to be alone with a woman who may be out for revenge." Beau paced around the living room of the house they shared. They'd finished their rounds and had been back at their place for over an hour, talking about Cash's intention to take Alison to Survivor Pass.

"Your confidence in me is touching." Cash continued to sit, sipping his whiskey, watching Beau get himself all worked up.

He stopped his pacing long enough to glare at Cash. "That's not what I mean and you know it. Maybe I should go with you."

"Thanks, but I need to do this alone. She won't talk if you're there."

"She may have no intention of talking at all. I'll follow you out and stay hidden."

"Gabe needs you here, Beau. We don't know if those men rode out or not, and can't take a chance of them coming back with both of us gone."

"I don't know what's tied your knickers up in knots about them. They were a group of drifters who played cards and finished off a couple bottles of whiskey. I'd wager they're into Wyoming or Idaho by now."

"Maybe." Cash pushed up from the chair, pouring one more shot of whiskey before leaning a hip against the counter.

"You feel that strongly about them still being around?"

Cash nodded, rolling the shot glass between his fingers. "I can't tell you why. It's just a feeling I have."

"We've always done well abiding by your instincts. I don't see any reason to stop now."

"Except there's not much we can do about it. Both of us have ridden out to locate their camp and found nothing. Still, I'm certain they're out there, waiting." Cash tossed back the whiskey, letting the warmth of the amber liquid trickle down his throat.

"I still don't like you riding up to the cabin with Alison. You can't trust her. She's liable to do anything, then ride out before any of us knows what happened."

"Not likely. Alison knows I'll tell you and Gabe where I'm going, and people will see us riding out of town together. Except for what she's wearing, she'll have nothing with her. If she does mean me harm, it won't be on the mountain tomorrow. She'll plan it out, have her belongings ready, and her money out of the bank."

"Maybe she does have her belongings ready and you don't know it."

"Doubtful. I saw her today in the bank making a *deposit*, not a withdrawal." Setting his glass on the counter, Cash turned to the bedroom. "I need to get some sleep."

Beau nodded, not ready to bed down just yet. He had a lot of thinking to do and not a lot of hours to do it.

"Are you riding up alone, Cash?" Gabe looked up from the new wanted posters he'd received that morning. Beau had already left to check on a disturbance down the street, leaving Gabe and Cash at the jail.

"I'm taking Alison with me." He didn't want to give any further explanation, already feeling the guilt of not sharing what he'd learned about her with Gabe.

"Watch your back."

Cash's eyes widened at the warning. "What do you mean?"

Gabe leaned back in his chair, his expression unreadable. "Nothing, except people aren't who or what they appear to be sometimes."

Straightening in the chair, Cash noticed the glint in Gabe's eyes. A wry smile formed on his lips. "You know."

"About who Alison really is? Yes."

"How? I know Bernie would never divulge the contents of a private telegram."

"You aren't the only one with contacts back east. I'm surprised your contact and mine didn't stumble over each other in their quest to learn the truth about Mrs. Burns. Or should I say, Miss McGrath?"

"Hell," Cash mumbled, raking a hand through his hair. "I should've told you."

"Yes, you should have, but you did what you thought was right. Now, how are you going to deal with her?"

"I won't tell you how, but she knows I discovered she isn't a widow."

Gabe released a somber chuckle. "I'll bet that was awkward."

Cash stared at him, realizing Gabe already knew how he'd learned of Alison's deception. "That's an understatement. My reaction wasn't the best."

"Afterwards, you received the telegram about her being Bobby McGrath's sister."

"Right. She's agreed to tell me the truth."

"And she has no idea you already know who she is?"

"None."

"Do you believe she'll come right out and tell you she came to Splendor to avenge her brother's death?"

"I don't know if that's her reason, Gabe. Maybe she came to learn the truth, put his death behind her."

"Then why the lies? She could've traveled out here and stayed at the boardinghouse while she talked to people. There was no shortage of witnesses. Why buy a shop and tie herself down unless she had a broader plan? I think you're deluding yourself if you believe she didn't come here to exact vengeance." Gabe waited. When Cash didn't respond, he forged on. "I'm sure you've talked to Beau and he's already warned you about riding up to Survivor Pass with her. Am I wrong in thinking you ignored his advice?"

"No, you aren't wrong." Cash leaned forward, resting his arms on the desk. "The timing won't be right for her. If she planned to kill me today, she'd be ready to get out of Splendor. Believe me, Alison's made no plans to leave—not yet. She has no idea I know her true identity."

"You sure about that?"

"Yes."

Slapping his hands on the desk, Gabe stood. "The circuit judge is due today. He'll want to have the trial on Monday, so I'll need both you and Beau to help with the prisoners."

"We won't be staying at the cabin the way I usually do. I'll bring Alison back to town by early evening."

"I need to pick up food from Suzanne for the prisoners. Can you stay at the jail until I return?"

"We won't leave for a couple hours. You can be certain I'll be back tonight, Gabe, with the truth about Alison McGrath."

"Are you sure you won't stay home this morning, Noah?" Abby rocked Gabriel in her arms, watching from the porch steps as her husband swung up on Tempest.

"I won't be gone long. Dax is sending someone to town to pick up the tools he ordered. He's probably already at the livery."

"Bull?" Abby guessed, smiling.

"He'd be the logical choice. I'll invite him to the house for lunch."

Noah's heart swelled as he watched the two people he loved most in life standing a few feet away. Gabe, the one other person he held a deep affection for, lived less than a mile away. Soon, he and Lena would have their own place a couple miles away. Noah couldn't imagine a better life, never thinking he'd ever be this happy.

"I'll let Lydia know. I'm sure she'll want to prepare something extra special for you."

"You mean, Bull, don't you?" Reining Tempest toward town, he smiled at Abby's laughter as she stepped back inside the house.

"Are you ready?" Cash stood at the bottom of the stairs as Alison walked down wearing a coat and grasping a small bag.

"What's in there?" He nodded toward the satchel when she'd taken the last step down.

Her face colored. "We didn't have a chance to eat last time, so I packed something."

"May I?" He reached out his hand.

"It's not much." She handed him the bag, wondering why he was so curious about bread, fruit, and cold chicken. "Hope it's all right."

Glancing inside, he handed the bag back, not feeling a bit guilty about confirming what she'd said. "It's fine. The horses are out back. Let's get going." He had no plans to stay at the cabin after he learned the truth. Once she confessed her true reasons for being in Splendor, they'd ride back to town, pack her belongings, and he'd put her on the first stage back east.

He helped her onto Joker's saddle, then mounted Hunter, reining him toward the north end of town. Within minutes, they'd disappeared down the trail. Riding in silence, Cash kept watch. He'd felt a prickling sensation the moment they'd left the boundary of Splendor, yet he'd seen nothing, including any wild animals. The thought had him sitting up straighter.

Foxes, mule deer, raccoons, rabbits, even an occasional gray wolf were common when riding outside of town. Today, he'd spotted nothing. Resting a hand on the butt of his gun, Cash took another look around.

"Let's go this way." Taking a trail to his left, he remained vigilant as they made a steep vertical climb. He'd taken the animal path one other time. Not wide, with patches of ice and snow, it cut some time off his normal ride.

"Where are we, Cash?"

"We're still going to the cabin, just taking a different trail. I thought you might like a change in scenery."

Riding behind him, he couldn't see her eyes roll at the obvious lie. "Since I've been on the other trail so many times," she called to his back, her sarcasm clear.

Glancing over his shoulder, Cash nodded. "Are you doing all right?"

"As good as possible with the narrow, icy trail, and tree limbs slapping me in the face every few seconds. How about you?"

His rumbled laughter sounded good after suffering his disdain for so many days. Ever since what happened at the cabin, she'd been plagued with guilt, remorse, and a sense of loss so great she couldn't sleep. Deciding the time had come to tell him the truth, intense fear wrapped around her as they rode up the mountain. She had no idea how he'd respond, what he'd say, or if he'd arrest her for the plans she'd made so many months ago.

All Alison knew was she'd ruined her chance to gain his trust or have him care about her again. He had cared once. She knew this as certain as she knew her brother would no longer come running through the fields toward her, laughing and holding out his arms for a hug. Her eyes misted at the memory. The reality of why and how he had died hurt more. It wasn't at all as she'd expected. If it weren't for Lena sitting with her one evening, explaining the events of the shooting, Alison might never have learned the truth.

"It won't be long now. The trail may be rough and the snow will get thicker the closer we get to the top, but it takes less time than the trail we took before."

The lump in her throat had dissolved, reforming as a hard ball of ice in her stomach. Reaching the cabin meant they were closer to the time he'd learn her secret—the moment when he'd push her from his life for good and she'd have decisions to make. If he didn't arrest her, would she stay in Splendor to run her business? Or would she leave?

She had little money. What she'd saved in Kentucky was used to purchase the business and move west. Selling the shop and starting over someplace else would be her last choice. But staying to watch Cash move about his days, perhaps falling in love with someone else, held no appeal at all. Both choices felt like a rope around her neck, tightening, squeezing the life out of her.

"Another five minutes, Alison." Cash looked over his shoulder, noticing the glazed look in her eyes. "Are you doing all right?"

Clearing her throat, she nodded. "Yes. Fine." Not long now before her life would change. If only she could see into the future and discover how.

"Can I help?" Bull stood a few feet from Noah, watching as he loaded the tools Dax had ordered.

"Sure. See the stack over there?" Noah nodded toward a box of new tools. "Those go, too."

It took little time with both of them working to load the wagon, feed and water the horses in the stable, and close the livery.

"Unharness the horse and throw a saddle on him. We'll leave the wagon here while we have lunch at the house." Noah saw Bull's brows furrow. "You didn't think you could ride in and out of town without seeing Lydia, did you?"

"Dax mentioned needing the tools as soon as I could get them back to the ranch. I doubt he'd understand me stopping in to see Lydia."

"I believe he *would* understand, but we'll make it a quick visit. I know the ladies have already made lunch, and I'm sure you don't want to disappoint them."

"I most certainly would *not* want to disappoint the ladies." Bull grinned, latching onto any reason to see Lydia. "I'll saddle the horse."

"You move up the trail, Clem. I'll stay here and give the signal after Brandt rides past. We'll get him from the front and back so there's no chance he'll get away."

"What do we do with the body, Louis?"

"What do you think we do with it?" He waited while Clem considered the question, then shrugged. "Nothing, Clem. We ride out as soon as he's on the ground."

"We aren't that far from town. Someone will hear the gunfire."

"That's why we won't hesitate after we take our shots. We can't stick around to check the body or move it off the trail." Pulling out a worn pocket watch, Louis checked the time. "You need to get into position. Brandt should be leaving the livery in a few minutes."

Reining his horse around, Clem rode up the trail before disappearing into a copse of pine trees set around two large boulders. Both would provide excellent cover while giving him the visibility needed to spot his target. Dismounting, he grabbed his Enfield rifle, looked around, then hunkered down near one of the boulders to wait.

Louis secured his horse several yards off the trail. Checking his Whitworth rifle, he smirked. It was more than he needed for this kill. He'd used it for long-range targets as a sharpshooter for the Confederacy. If all went according to plan, Brandt wouldn't be more than a hundred yards up the trail. During the war, his longest hit had been about eleven hundred yards. Granted, he'd marked a group of officers standing in a cluster and he'd hit only one, yet it had been recorded as a kill.

Anticipation gripped him at the prospect of tallying up one more kill of a Union soldier. According to Monty, Noah had been a major in the Union Army, a sharpshooter with a stellar record. After today, he'd be nothing more than a number, his record during the war dying with him.

Noah and Bull rode next to each other as they started up the trail out of town. Noah's house sat on a hill overlooking Splendor. A slow stride would get them there in thirty minutes. Today, they rode at an increased pace, hoping to cut ten minutes off the trip.

Riding side-by-side, anyone who didn't know them might assume they were brothers. Both were well over six feet tall, and with their military background, had a naturally relaxed, upright posture in the saddle.

"Have you and Lydia set a date for the wedding?" Noah glanced over at Bull, knowing his friend didn't want to wait long to claim her.

"Early summer at the ranch. It's where Lydia and I got to know each other. I can't think of a better place. We talked to Reverend Paige last Sunday and he's agreed to ride out with his wife."

"Another big shindig at Redemption's Edge."

Bull chuckled. "Lydia, Rachel, and Ginny are already coming up with ideas. Doubt it will be long before Lena, Isabella, and Suzanne join them." Sighing, he shook his head. "I know the ladies all mean well, but I'd just as soon ride to Big Pine for a quiet wedding and enjoy a few days away."

"Have you said as much to Lydia?"

Bull shot a glance at Noah, his eyes crinkling at the corners. "Do I look like a man with a death wish?"

A deep, rumbling laugh left Noah's lips. "You look like a man with everything to live for. Why, I bet—"

Before he could finish, a loud crack came from behind him, a burning pain searing into his back.

"Noah!" Bull started to reach over for his friend when another shot rang out from in front of them, the bullet knocking Noah off his saddle.

Pulling his revolver from its holster, Bull slid off his horse as more shots hit the ground around them. Grabbing Noah by the collar, noting the blood, he tried to drag him off the trail. He groaned at the effort of moving a man who weighed as much as he did. Seconds before reaching a safe location, Bull heard the crack of two rifles. One bullet whizzed past his head. A moment later, he cursed as the second bullet found its mark. Bull collapsed on top of Noah, taking one last glimpse of the sky before his eyelids grew heavy and the world went black.

Chapter Twenty-Two

Standing on the boardwalk, Clay McCord's hand stilled on the door of the general store. Whipping around, he focused his gaze on the hill behind town. Another shot rang out, confirming what he'd heard moments before.

"Did you hear that?" Bernie ran out of the telegraph office, waving his arms.

"Find Sheriff Evans and Beau. Send them up the hill toward Brandt's house." Jumping off the boardwalk, Clay ran to the stables behind the livery, taking mere minutes to saddle his horse. By the time he started up the trail, at least two more shots pierced the morning air, his chest tightening with each bang. He'd seen the sign saying the livery was closed, knowing Noah left mid-mornings on Saturdays. Sending up a prayer, he spurred his horse on, anxiety gripping him at what he expected to find.

Bernie burst into the Dixie, seeing Gabe and Nick talking near the bar.

"Sheriff! Shots are being fired up the hill to the Brandt place."

Not waiting, Gabe rushed out of the saloon, Nick close behind.

"Clay McCord is already heading up there," Bernie called to their backs, doubting either heard him in the rush to grab their horses.

"Where's Beau?" Nick sucked in a breath as he saddled his horse, working as fast as possible to keep up with Gabe.

"Rode out an hour ago." Swinging into the saddle, he reigned Blackheart around to see several townsfolk clustered outside the stable gate. "Get inside the buildings and wait there," he shouted as he rode past, Nick a few yards behind.

Fear wrapped around Gabe as he encouraged Blackheart up the wide trail toward Noah's house. The ride seemed to take forever, even though only minutes had gone by before he spotted a man kneeling beside two inert bodies. Drawing his gun, he pointed it at the man.

"Put your hands up and step away."

Clay raised his hands, standing, turning so Gabe could see him.

"Clay?"

"I heard the shots and sent Bernie to get you." His rough voice and somber face signaled what Gabe feared. "It's bad, Gabe."

Nick reined to a stop as Gabe slid from his horse, dropping to his knees next to Noah. A feral scream wrenched from his chest at the blood pooling around him. Seeing the other body, he gasped at the sight of Bull, blood covering his shirt.

"Both are still breathing, but we need to stop the bleeding." Clay pressed his hands against Bull's wound, Gabe doing the same with Noah, applying pressure to what appeared to be the most life-threatening wound.

"Nick, we need a wagon. Then get Doc up here and ride to the Pelletier's. We'll need Rachel."

Clay and Gabe did what they could, neither Noah nor Bull responding to their efforts.

"They're both still breathing." Clay's ragged breaths spoke of the effort needed to stop the bleeding. "Just barely," he muttered.

"We will not lose them. We can't," Gabe ground out, ripping off his shirt and pressing it to Noah's wound. *I can't lose you*, he thought, an agonizing pain squeezing his chest. "Hold on, buddy. You can make it. You've *got* to."

"I wonder what's gotten into him." Lydia rocked Gabriel, trying to pacify him. A few minutes before, he'd woken up screaming, his face red, arms flailing.

Abby sat down, adjusted her clothing, then reached out. "Give him to me, Lydia. Maybe he's hungry." A few minutes later she looked up at Lydia, shaking her head. "He's not interested."

"I can take him out in the sunshine and walk with him. He always likes being outside."

"Like his papa." Abby stood, buttoned the front of her dress, then checked the time on the wall clock. "I wonder what's keeping the men."

"You know how they are. Probably got to talking about something and lost track of time. They'll be here." Lydia walked through the front door, taking a seat on the rocker Noah had built for Abby on the porch. Bull had already told her he planned to build one for them. They both loved children and wanted a houseful.

Gabriel began to settle down as Lydia continued to rock. Within minutes, they were both asleep. Which is how Lena and Suzanne found them when they arrived an hour later. Stepping down from the wagon, they glanced at each other, neither wanting the job they'd been given by Nick, yet knowing the news would come best from them.

"I thought I heard a wagon pull up." Abby looked down at Gabriel sleeping in Lydia's arms as she walked through the door. Warmth spread through her as a smile curved her lips.

Glancing at Lena and Suzanne, her smile froze, then slipped completely when she saw the somber expressions on their faces. Her hands began to shake as she walked down the steps to meet them. The men were long overdue, her worry increasing with each passing minute until she'd made the decision to ask Lydia to ride into town and find them.

"What is it?" Abby's voice shook. Reaching out, she latched onto Suzanne's hand. "Tell me."

Suzanne had known Abby since she was a young girl and looked after her for a while after her mother died, until Abby had been sent back east to school. Her heart broke looking at the fear on her face.

"Let's sit down." Suzanne tried to guide her back to the porch, but Abby pulled away.

"No. Tell me."

Her distressed demand woke Lydia. Seeing Lena and Suzanne, she stood, careful not to wake Gabriel. "Is something wrong?"

Lena looked between the two women. They couldn't afford to waste more time.

"Both Noah and Bull were shot and are at the clinic."

"My God." Abby's hand flew to her mouth, her eyes tearing. "We have to go."

"Abby, wait." Suzanne stepped close. "You both need to know. The men are in very serious condition. Doc doesn't know if either will make it."

Lena dashed to grab Gabriel as Lydia's arms began to give out. The young woman's shoulders slumped as panic surged through her an instant before a calm resolve stilled her features.

"We must leave right now." Lydia hurried to the wagon, climbing into the back as Suzanne helped Abby onto the seat, then climbed up next to her.

Lena handed Gabriel to Suzanne, then squeezed herself onto the seat, grabbing the lines. Her throat tightened as quiet sobs came from the back of the wagon. Glancing over her shoulder, she saw Lydia swipe at the tears streaming down her face.

Why? Lena thought as anger spread through her. She felt like screaming at the injustice, knowing her rage would change nothing. Steeling herself, Lena guided the wagon back to town, sending up silent prayers the entire way—for Noah and Bull, for Abby and Lydia, and for the entire town who had become her family.

They rode close to the cabin, finding an area where the snow wasn't as deep. Ground tying Hunter, Cash walked around Joker, reaching up to help Alison down.

"I'm perfectly capable of getting off a horse." She ignored his gesture, tugging up her dress and swinging a leg over the back of the saddle, stumbling a little as she landed. Untying the satchel from behind the saddle, she lifted her hem, strolled past him and through the open doorway. The door still rested where it had fallen the first time Cash brought her here. Glancing at the bed, her face flushed at the memory, wishing she could take that day back and start over.

Cash came in behind her, grabbing the chair and setting it down next to the bed.

"Have a seat, Alison." He gestured toward the bed, then pulled over a chair for himself and sat down.

Pursing her lips, she pulled her coat tighter, taking hesitant steps to the bed, sitting on the edge. Gripping her satchel on her lap, she sucked in a deep breath, letting it out in a slow whoosh. Directing an unwavering gaze at Cash, she began.

"My name is Alison Burns McGrath. I'm twenty-two years old. My father was killed in the war, my mother is still living on our farm in Kentucky, and my brother was killed during a bank robbery in Splendor."

Cash stared at her, his face a mask. She saw no anger, no condemnation, and more surprising, no shock at her confession. Her eyes widened a little before her gaze shifted to the floor, then back up to his face.

"You knew all this already, didn't you?"

Cash could barely talk for the relief he felt. She'd laid it all out, didn't try to hide behind more secrets. Her candor stunned him.

"Yes, I knew."

She leaned forward. "Yet you wanted to ride all the way to the cabin to hear me say it?"

"We needed privacy."

"I could've told you all this at the shop."

He stood, closing the distance between them, holding out his hands. Setting the satchel on the bed, she placed her hands in his, allowing him to help her up. Hope surged through her for a brief moment at the look he gave her, so much like what she saw in his eyes when they'd made love.

Wrapping an arm around her waist, he drew her aside, opening the latch on the satchel with his other hand and reaching inside.

"Do you always travel with a Colt .45, Allie?" Not loosening his hold around her waist, he held up the gun. "Fully loaded, I see. What were your plans for this?"

With a strength she didn't know she possessed, Alison wrenched herself free, taking several steps away. "I know you won't believe me, but I brought it for protection."

"Protection?" His voice oozed with sarcasm. "From who?"

"You." She took another step away, seeing his cocky smile slip.

He placed the gun on the bed, then turned to face her. "Why would you need protection from me?"

Grasping her hands in front of her, she licked her lips. "You shot Bobby. I thought..."

The fear on her face hit Cash for the first time as he realized what she was telling him. He stepped toward her, only to watch her back up against the wall.

"I'd never hurt you, Allie."

A grim laugh escaped her lips. "You already did when you refused to listen to my explanation. I knew you were angry at the way you discovered I wasn't a widow, but I thought you'd at least give me a chance to explain." She placed a hand on her heart, as if the gesture would still its pounding.

"You're right. I should have given you a chance to explain. It was my mistake pushing you away." He glanced at the bed behind him. "That still doesn't explain the gun."

She pushed away from the wall. "I didn't know what to expect from you today...riding out of town to a cabin no one but you visits."

"You didn't come here to kill me?"

"What? No. I lov..." She clamped her mouth shut, realizing what she'd almost admitted.

Closing his eyes, he mumbled a curse, scrubbing a hand down his face before looking at her. Taking a step toward her, he held up his hands, palms out, when she looked as if she wanted to run.

"Come here, Allie."

She shook her head, refusing to move.

"Allie, please. Come here."

Lifting her chin, she walked forward, stopping a couple feet away. "What?"

"Closer."

"I don't need to be closer to hear what you have to say."

"Allie, come closer."

Letting out a frustrated breath, she crossed her arms and glared at him. "Why?"

The smile spreading across his face caught her by surprise. Moving to within inches of her, he rested his hands on her shoulders.

"Because I don't want to tell you I love you from across the room."

Her jaw dropped, her eyes flying open. Recovering, she stared at him. "You love me?"

"I do. Please tell me I'm not alone."

Her head spun. She'd never expected to hear those words from him, never thought she'd ever be alone with him again after today.

"Allie?"

Her mind clearing, she looked into his eyes. "I love you, too, Cash."

Wrapping her in his arms, he drew her close, lowering his mouth to hers.

"Well, now. Isn't that the sweetest thing you ever heard, Harry?"

Breaking the kiss, Cash pulled Alison behind him, recognizing the two men from the wanted posters.

"Milton and Harrison Penderville. What a surprise." Cash backed up toward the bed. Alison backed up with him, as if she knew he wanted her closer to the gun.

"He knows us, Harry," Milt sneered. "Guess our reputation is getting around."

"Let me be clear, Penderville. It's not a good reputation." Cash let his arms hang loose at his sides.

Harry's gaze narrowed. "Take out your gun and lay it on the floor."

"No." Cash ignored Alison's gasp at his refusal.

"We'll kill you if you don't."

"You're going to kill us whether I remove my gun or not, Milton."

"It's Milt. Now, get rid of the gun."

"Not going to happen." Cash knew he could take one of them, even with guns already in their hands. He didn't know if he could keep Alison out of the crossfire. "I'm surprised you came all this way up the mountain. I'd have thought you'd take the opportunity to rob the bank while I'm out of town."

"We care nothing about the small amount of money in your bank. We're here because you killed one of our men. A good friend of our brother." Milt stepped aside, letting Monty move next to him.

"Hello, Deputy Coulter."

Cash's eyes narrowed. "Brother?"

"Thought you'd be surprised." Monty drew his gun and walked forward. "I asked a lot of questions while working for Silas. I needed to know who killed my best friend, Bobby McGrath. Imagine how I felt when I learned it was you."

Leaving the safety of Cash's body, Alison glared at Monty. "Bobby would never have been friends with a group of killers."

All three brothers laughed before Monty responded. "We were friends all right. Real good friends."

"I don't believe you. Bobby wasn't a killer. He wasn't like you." Alison's voice trembled as she tried to deny the truth about her brother.

Monty's face hardened, the smile he always wore disappearing. "I'll tell you what Bobby was. He rode with us for months. Robbed banks and used his gun. He did everything my brothers asked, never flinching. You may believe your baby brother was a saint, but he wasn't." He shot a hateful look at Cash. "He still didn't deserve to be executed by a lawman."

"There was no execution, Monty. I gave Bobby several chances to lower his gun. It didn't matter what I said, he still refused to toss it aside. He gave me no choice." Cash stepped in front of Alison, attempting to shield her from the gunmen. "Your friend didn't *have* to die that day. He *chose* to die."

"Shut up, Coulter. Bobby didn't choose anything. You shot him in cold blood." Monty raised his gun. Like Bobby, his hand shook, but he didn't fire.

"Shoot him, Monty." Milt stood beside him, his voice cold and unemotional.

"Do it, kid. It's what he deserves." Harry watched Monty's gun shake as sweat formed on his brow. "You know it's what Bobby would've wanted."

"That's. Not. True." Alison's shout echoed in the cabin as she took a step away from Cash.

"Alison, get back," he ordered, praying she'd listen.

Before either could say another word, a shot slammed into Harry, sending him sprawling. Cash drew his gun, firing a shot at Milt, hitting him in the chest. Before he had a chance to fire at Monty, Alison moved in front of him, aiming her Colt at Monty.

"Drop the gun, Monty," Cash warned, trying to nudge Alison aside.

"You killed my brothers." His voice was flat, devoid of emotion as he stared at Milt and Harry, both dead at his feet. Whipping his head up, he aimed the gun at Cash. "It's your turn, Coulter."

Cash pointed his gun, but before he could fire, a shot rang out. Monty staggered backward, looking down at the red stain growing on his chest. Eyes wide, he sent an unbelieving look at Alison.

"But...he killed your brother..." Whatever else he wanted to say died on his lips. His knees buckled, his body convulsed, then Monty Penderville joined his brothers.

Turning to Alison, Cash saw tears streaming down her face, her arm shaking from holding the heavy weapon in front of her. Putting a hand on her shoulder, he reached out to her with the other.

"Give me the gun, Allie."

She didn't look at him, her gaze fixed on the men in front of her.

"I killed him." Her trembling voice cut through him.

"I know, sweetheart, but it's over now. Give me the gun."

She blinked several times, her entire body shuddering as her knees started to give way.

Wrapping his arm around her waist, he tightened his hold, grasping the gun a moment before her grip gave way. Turning her to him, he tucked her head under his chin, listening as quiet sobs wracked her body. Looking up, his gaze landed on Beau standing in the doorway.

"I had a feeling you'd follow me."

Beau kicked each of the bodies, making sure the job was complete.

"Couldn't let you leave me as the only deputy in Splendor." He nodded toward Alison. "She going to be all right?"

Cash stroked her hair, placing a kiss on the top of her head. "Yes. She's going to be fine."

Chapter Twenty-Three

"How long do we wait, Louis?" Clem and the rest of the gang waited at the agreed upon location. Milt, Harry, and Monty were to join them long before now.

"I don't know, but we can't wait much longer." Slapping his hat against his leg, watching as the dust drifted in the breeze, he let out a string of curses. "There weren't supposed to be two men riding up the trail."

"Wish we'd known which one was Brandt."

"They looked like brothers. We had no choice but to shoot them both." Louis had accepted his role in the gang a long time ago. Milt or Harry told him who to kill and why, and the job was done. Brandt deserved to die for killing Chet. The other man happened to be in the wrong place at the wrong time.

Looking at the sun's descent into mid-afternoon, Louis made a decision.

"We know where Milt wants to camp outside Big Pine. I say we ride there and wait for them to join us. Staying so close to Splendor isn't safe."

"What if they never show up, Louis?" Clem took another glance behind them, hoping to see a cloud of dust signaling the Pendervilles were close.

"We'll give them two days. After that, we've got to assume they've been arrested...or are dead."

Doc Worthington hadn't taken a break since Noah and Bull had been rushed into the clinic, grateful Rachel hurried inside not long after their arrival. She'd come as quickly as possible, along with Dax, Luke, and Ginny, who kept watch on young Patrick.

What Doc and Rachel hadn't expected was Clay McCord staying to work alongside them. His quick, efficient movements had them glancing at each other more than once, brows raised. By silent agreement, they decided to save their questions until later.

The three worked in quiet unison, saying little, letting their experience guide them. Neither Noah nor Bull had woken, delaying the need for chloroform.

"Rachel, I need more hot water and morphine." Since her friends had been brought in, she'd kept a nearby table stocked with bandages, laudanum, opium pills, morphine, chloroform, whiskey, and brandy. A few precious bottles of a new antiseptic, carbolic acid, had arrived weeks before, which they used to sanitize Noah's and Bull's wounds and soak the dressings before applying.

"Got it," Clay mumbled as he pulled out a bullet from Noah's chest, depositing it in a bowl on the table. "Rachel?" He didn't have to say more before she helped clean the opening with carbolic acid, then prepared the bandages and suture thread, soaking them in the same liquid. In a matter of minutes, they'd become a team.

"Uncle Charles, are you all right?" Rachel hurried around the table toward him when he stumbled backward, catching himself against the counter. Putting an arm around him, she noticed his shaking hands and sweat-laden brow. "You need to rest for a bit."

"I can't. Noah and Bull need me, Rachel."

"You aren't any good to them if you collapse."

"She's right, Doc. Rachel and I can handle this for a while." Clay stepped away from the table after finishing stitching Noah's third wound. "I can't quite grasp how none of the bullets hit a critical organ or artery on either man. The odds are remarkable."

Doc Worthington lowered himself into a chair, letting out a tired breath. "They are a long way from being out of danger, Mr. McCord. Or should I call you *Doctor* McCord?"

Clay didn't respond, although his hands stilled at his sides.

"Where did you learn to perform surgery? Or am I wrong in believing you have considerable experience?" Doc leaned back in the chair, his weary gaze focused on him.

Rachel continued to clean Bull's chest, then applied another bandage to a wound which bled profusely, listening to her uncle's questions. Clay's quiet chuckle had her glancing at him.

"I worked in Union field hospitals during the war." A sheepish smile lifted the corners of his mouth. "In truth, I worked with you at several battle sites."

"That can't be true. I'm certain I'd remember a man of your talent."

"It would be a miracle if you recognized me from the war. I had a mustache and thick beard, and wore spectacles most of the time. Not to see, but to keep the blood out of my eyes."

Doc Worthington's jaw dropped. "Your eyes...I should've figured it out hours ago. The blue-gray color lined with deep brown always struck me as intense, belonging to a man of high intellect."

Clay laughed at the description. "Not sure about high intellect, but I've been accused many tines of being too intense."

A painful moan drew their attention to Noah in time to see his eyes flutter open. He blinked several times as he attempted to focus before he tried to roll to his side.

"Oh no, you don't." Rachel dashed to his side as Clay gently pushed him back down on the table.

Noah's gaze latched onto Rachel's, his eyes reflecting fear and confusion.

"You were shot—more than once."

He blinked, his hand coming up to rub across his forehead. "When?"

"A few hours ago. You and Bull were ambushed, left for dead." Rachel had to hold him still as a look of panic crossed his face.

"Bull...is he..." Noah tried to sit up again.

"Noah, you must stay down." Doc's stern words caused him to lie back. "Bull is right here." He nodded to the table next to Noah. "He's in a little better condition than you, but not much."

Noah licked his lips. "I need water."

Rachel picked up a glass while Clay lifted Noah's head.

"A small amount, Noah." Rachel held the glass to his lips, letting him swallow little more than a tablespoon before moving it away.

Lowering Noah's head to the table, Clay watched as his eyes closed and he drifted off to sleep.

"Good. He needs as much rest as he can get. Clay, are you able to stay?"

"For as long as you need me, Doctor."

Worthington placed a hand on Clay's shoulder. "I'd appreciate it if you'd call me Charles."

"All right...Charles."

"Good. Now I think it's time to let everybody know what's going on in here."

"I'll stay in here while you and Rachel talk to them." Clay put a hand to Bull's forehead, noticing the fever subsiding. "He's cooling some."

"Come on, Rachel. Let's go talk to them."

Worthington opened the door, letting Rachel precede him to face a room full of her friends and family. No one spoke as Doc stepped next to her. Taking a deep breath, he looked at each face, understanding the pain he saw in their eyes.

"We removed three bullets from Noah. He's sleeping now. If there's no infection, he has a good chance of making it." He looked at Abby, reaching out to take her hand in his. "Noah was quite fortunate. None of the bullets hit a vital organ, but there is one problem."

Gabe walked up next to her, putting an arm around her shoulders. Abby swallowed, her eyes damp as she waited.

"There was considerable damage to his right arm. He may not regain full use of it."

She glanced at Gabe.

"He's alive, Abby. We could've lost him," Gabe whispered. "I'll do whatever I can to help him with his arm."

"We'll all help, Abby. Whatever he needs." Dax stepped next to them, sending a quick glance at Rachel, who responded with a grateful smile.

"Can I see him, Doc?"

"Not yet. We'll see about you visiting him for a few minutes when he wakes up." The room quieted before he heard a soft voice.

"What about Bull? Is he..."

Doc's gaze landed on Lydia. Her pale face and trembling lips cut through him. "He's alive, Lydia."

"Oh God." She brought her hands up to cover her face, trying to muffle deep sobs.

Luke, Bull's closest friend, put an arm around her shoulders, pulling her close, then looked at Doc. "Will he recover?" he asked.

"We removed one bullet and the wound is clean, so yes, he should recover as long as he avoids infection. If all goes well, he can probably go home in a couple days."

"He'll stay with us, Doc." Abby looked at Lydia, who nodded as she swiped away the dampness on her face.

"Who is in with them now?" Gabe dropped his arm from Abby's shoulders.

"Well now, it seems Splendor has another doctor in town." Doc glanced over his shoulder toward the patient room. "Clay McCord was a surgeon for the North during the war."

"What?" Dax and Luke said together.

"He never said a word." Lena's brows lifted. She'd never considered him to be more than a quiet drifter.

"We may never have known if Noah and Bull hadn't been shot. Clay's good. Real good." Doc directed his comment at Rachel, knowing she'd get his meaning.

"Charles, Bull is awake." Everyone turned when Clay stuck his head out the door to make the announcement. Gabe made the first move, extending his hand.

"Thanks for helping save them, Doctor McCord. I can't tell you how grateful we all are."

Clay felt his cheeks flush as he accepted Gabe's hand. He'd never been comfortable with praise. In his mind, he'd done what anyone trained in medicine would have under the circumstances.

"I just followed Doctor Worthington's lead."

"Now, Clay, you're being too modest." Worthington walked past him to check on Bull. Seeing him trying to sit up, he put a hand on his shoulder. "Not yet, Bull. You have some healing to do before I can let you leave."

Bull turned his head toward the other bed, his voice tight. "How's Noah?"

"He's as lucky as they come. We pulled a few bullets out of him. He'll recover if the wounds don't become infected." Doc checked Bull's dressings.

"I feel fine, Doc. I'd rather head home."

"Not today, Bull. Until the fever goes away, you won't be going anywhere. Did you meet Doctor McCord?"

Bull saw Clay standing next to the doctor and nodded. "He said something about helping you and Rachel today. Guess he forgot to mention being a doctor."

"It seems he didn't plan to tell anyone. Then he found you and Noah." Doc shot Clay a look he couldn't quite decipher.

Clay stepped forward. "Just needed some time to sort a few things out in my head. Today made me realize how important my skills are."

"And they shouldn't be wasted, young man."

"No, Doctor, they shouldn't."

Clay broke off the banter when Noah groaned and tried to turn over.

"Hold on, Noah. Let me take a look at your wounds."

As Clay checked the bandages, Noah spotted Bull. "You look like hell," he muttered, trying to mask the agony flashing through his body.

Bull's attempt to laugh turned into a grimace as pain shot through him. "We're alive. I figure that's what matters."

Noah closed his eyes and nodded. A moment later, he'd drifted back to sleep.

"He'll be sleeping a great deal during the next few days, as should you." Doc pulled a blanket from a chest and placed it over Bull. "I have a woman out in the waiting room who's anxious to see you."

Bull pursed his lips. "I don't know if Lydia should see me like this."

"Believe me, she won't care about anything except you being alive. Clay, would you let Lydia know she can come in?"

"Of course." Opening the door, Clay motioned for Lydia. "You'll only have a couple minutes with him before he'll need to rest."

She nodded, a mixture of hope and happiness crossing her face. "I'll take any amount of time you can give me."

Cash, Alison, and Beau stabled their horses before walking to the jail. They'd buried the bodies in a shallow grave, planning to return with a wagon the following day to bring them back to town.

"I'll make some coffee." Beau picked up the dented coffee pot and grabbed a tin of coffee.

"I should go home, Cash. A bath and clean clothes are all I need right now."

He placed a hand on the small of Alison's back. "I'll walk you home, then I need to find Gabe."

They hadn't made it to the door before Bernie came dashing inside. "Did you hear about Noah and Bull?"

"What about them?" Cash's eyes narrowed, his voice gruff.

"They're at Doc's. Both were shot."

"So it was the Penderville gang." Gabe paced to the front window, then turned around. "I should've listened to you, Cash. You always thought there was a connection."

"It's not your fault, Gabe. I had a gut feeling, nothing more. There wasn't a shred of proof those men were tied to the Pendervilles. Besides, Beau and I searched several miles outside of town and never saw a trace of the men we saw in the saloon."

"It was a bold plan, and it almost worked. The ambush of Noah and Bull, then the attempted shootings of you and Alison weren't coincidences." Beau pushed away from the wall. "I need to get back to the jail, check on the prisoners. The circuit judge is supposed to arrive today for the trial on Monday. It can't come soon enough."

"I'll come back to sit with Noah and Bull after I take Allie home," Cash offered.

"No need. We have plenty of people who've offered to stay. Get some sleep." Gabe clasped Cash's shoulder. "Glad Beau talked me into letting him follow you."

Cash smirked. "Me, too, Gabe."

Cash escorted Alison to the shop, following her upstairs. After learning about Noah and Bull, then telling Gabe their story about the Pendervilles, neither felt as tired as they had when they rode into town. Alison busied herself making coffee while Cash paced around her home. Placing the pot on the wood stove, she turned toward him.

"If you're hungry, I have a few eggs and some potatoes."

His gaze moved down her body before locking on her face. He needed to leave, put some distance between them. What he wanted to do was stay, wrap his arms around her and never let go.

"I should let you get some sleep."

"I'm not tired." She took a few tentative steps toward him.

"A lot has happened today, Allie." He narrowed the distance between them. "It would be best if I left."

Stepping to within a few inches of him, she placed her hands on his chest. "I think you should stay."

Clutching his hands into fists, he held his arms rigid at his sides. "You're tired and not thinking straight. Besides, a lot of people know I walked you home. We need to consider your reputation."

"I'm not worried about it."

Cursing under his breath, Cash relaxed his hands, moving them up to grip her shoulders.

"*I* care about it, but you're making it hard for me to do the honorable thing."

Smiling, she moved her hands in slow circles on his chest. "You didn't do the honorable thing a few weeks ago."

His breath hitched as her hands created a heat which ripped through his body. Each stroke chipped away at his resolve to take it slow, court her, make sure he was who she wanted.

"Did I misunderstand when you said you loved me?"

"No," he ground out, raising his hands to cover hers. "You heard me right." His eyes smoldered, darkening to a deep emerald green when she let her leg travel up his. "Allie, you're making this difficult."

She raised onto her toes, brushing a kiss across his mouth.

"Do you want me, Cash?" Moving her hands from under his, her fingers trailed a sensuous path up his arms. Wrapping her arms around his neck, she aligned their bodies, feeling a shudder pass through him a moment before a deep growl escaped his lips.

Losing the battle, Cash scooped her into his arms, walking the short distance to the bed. He gently eased her down, bracing himself on his elbows, hovering above her.

"Is this what you want, Allie?"

"Yes," she breathed out, her heart pounding.

"Are you sure?" His lips made a path from the corner of her eye to her jaw, then down the smooth column of her neck.

"Yes." She felt fevered, as if she'd explode if he didn't give her what she wanted.

Moving up to her mouth, he hovered an inch above it. "There are conditions this time." His hand stroked a path down her arm, resting on the curve of her waist.

"Conditions?" She squirmed against him.

"Do you want to hear them?" His hot breath washed against the sensitive skin below her ear.

"I, um...yes, but hurry."

He chuckled at her impatience, glad she wanted this as much as he did.

"First, no more lies. Not ever."

"No more lies," she agreed.

"Second, you'll tell our friends about your past."

"Fine. I'll tell them. Please, Cash..." Her voice trailed off as he sucked lightly at the hollow of her neck.

"So impatient." He lifted his head to stare into her eyes. "Third, and this is the most important condition, Allie."

Her eyes widened, her breath coming in gasps. "All right."

"Marry me."

Epilogue

Two months later...
Cash watched Allie move about the crowded yard of Redemption's Edge, hugging people she barely knew who'd come to celebrate their marriage. His love for her had swelled each day since she'd agreed to become his wife. Some thought his decision to wed her had been too quick. He knew differently.

Not one to believe in love at first sight, he always thought the woman he married, if he ever did, would be someone he'd known for months, maybe years. A friend who turned into a lover. His thoughts changed the moment he met Allie.

"You look like a man well and truly caught." Noah held a cane in his left hand, bracing himself, letting his right arm hang loose at his side. He'd spent two weeks in Doc's clinic before being released. The last six weeks had been dedicated to recovering the use of his right arm and hand. He'd had a small measure of success each day.

"Is that how you felt when you married Abby?"

"I felt that way within moments of my first glimpse of her." Noah chuckled, remembering their rocky courtship. "I just never thought I'd be lucky enough to win her."

Cash's gaze moved over the crowd once more, resting on Bull standing with his arm around Lydia.

"Bull seems to be recovering." Cash knew he'd gone back to work at the Pelletier ranch a week after the shooting. "Alison told me they've set a wedding date."

"He told me early summer." Noah shifted his weight, grimacing at the pain. "It'll be a great day when I can throw away this cane. Dang thing reminds me how much work I have ahead of me." He glanced at Cash, seeing the confusion on his face. "I'm doing everything Doc recommends. So far, I don't see much improvement."

"It's going to take time, Noah. If anyone can turn this around, it's you." Cash thought of his friend, Stephen, having only one leg and an arm which hung limp at his side, knowing there was no hope of ever getting full use back. At least Noah had hope, and Cash knew he'd do all he could to recover what he'd lost.

Noah returned a grim smile, his eyes reflecting the true burden he faced to get back the life he had before the ambush.

Cash opened his mouth to say something more when he spotted Alison and Abby walking toward them.

"Gabriel is asleep, Noah. I thought you might want to ask me to dance." Abby slipped her hand in his and squeezed, even though he couldn't return the gesture.

"Abby, I—"

"No excuses, Noah Brandt. You can do anything you put your mind to. Right now, your wife wants to dance with her husband. So put your mind to it."

Cash draped an arm over Allie's shoulders, both laughing as Abby dragged Noah toward the band.

"Where do you think the orphans are off to?" Cash asked, seeing Lydia's younger sister and brother, Selena and Sam, dash toward the bunkhouse with Billy and Margaret Zales. All except Billy had been living at Redemption's Edge since a group of men, including Bull and the Pelletiers, found them living in a cave over a year before.

"Seems they're just being kids, Cash. Having a great time at our wedding."

He nodded, ignoring the prickly sensation which always signaled danger.

"You aren't worried about them, are you? They're at our wedding. What could possibly happen?"

Shaking off the unnerving sensation, Cash smiled. "You're right."

Allie reached up, stroking a finger along his jaw. "Let's not think of anyone except us the rest of today, Cash."

Clasping her hand in his, he brought it to his lips, kissing each finger, then burning a trail across her palm to her wrist. Shifting her in front of him, he placed a kiss on the tip of her nose.

"Concentrating on you the rest of the day sounds real good, Mrs. Coulter." Hearing the band start a new song, he smiled. "Will you dance with me?"

They found an open spot on the dance platform next to Bull and Lydia, who seemed too lost in each other to notice anyone else. The band broke into a lively number, people whooping and clapping as the dancers tried to keep up with the beat.

Cash pulled Allie to him as laughter filled the air. Ignoring anyone who might be watching, he brushed a kiss across her lips, then repeated it until she placed her palms flat on his chest to stop him.

"Mr. Coulter, I do believe you're trying to seduce me." She flashed him a brilliant smile.

"You would be right, Mrs. Coulter." Cash started to lower his head again when ear-piercing screams had him stepping away, pulling Allie behind him.

"Help! Someone help us!" The panicked cries came from behind the barn.

"My God, Cash. It's the children." Allie started to dash toward the barn when Cash pulled her back.

"You stay here, Allie. Let me see what's happening." Cash didn't wait for a response as he, Bull, and most of the men took off at a run.

Rounding the barn, they stopped at the sight before them. Billy lay on the ground, blood flowing from a gash on his head.

"Somebody get Doc Worthington," Dax shouted as he dropped to a knee next to Billy, checking his pulse, then tearing off his shirt, holding it to the wound. "He's alive."

Jack, Lena and Gabe's seven-year-old son, stood ramrod straight, his gaze focused on the horizon, pointing. Selina, Lydia's eleven-year-old sister, stood beside him, her face streaked with tears.

"Jackson?" Gabe knelt beside him, drawing the boy to him. "What is it, son?"

Jack's vacant gaze moved to Gabe.

"They took him," Selena sobbed.

"Who, Selena?" Bull asked, kneeling down, turning her toward him.

Her panicked face, flushed and wet with tears, tore into Bull.

"Sweetheart, tell me what happened," Bull coaxed in a soft voice as Lydia ran up to them, placing an arm across her sister's shoulders.

Glancing around, Lydia's heart began to race when she didn't spot her brother, fifteen-year-old Samuel. Her voice shook as she turned Selena to face her. "Where is Sam?"

A haunted look crossed Selena's face. "They took him, Lydia," she choked out. "The Indians took Sam."

Thank you for taking the time to read Survivor Pass. If you enjoyed it, please consider telling your friends or posting a short review. Word of mouth is an author's best friend and much appreciated.

Please join my reader's group to be notified of my New Releases at:
www.shirleendavies.com

I care about quality, so if you find something in error, please contact me via email at:
shirleen@shirleendavies.com

About the Author

Shirleen Davies writes romance—historical, contemporary, and romantic suspense. She grew up in Southern California, attended Oregon State University, and has degrees from San Diego State University and the University of Maryland. During the day she provides consulting services to small and mid-sized businesses. But her real passion is writing emotionally charged stories of flawed people who find redemption through love and acceptance. She now lives with her husband in a beautiful town in northern Arizona.

I love to hear from my readers.

Send me an Email: shirleen@shirleendavies.com
Visit my Website: www.shirleendavies.com
Sign up to be notified of New Releases:
www.shirleendavies.com/contact-me
Check out all my Books:
www.shirleendavies.com/books.html
Comment on my Blog:
www.shirleendavies.com/blog.html
Follow me on Amazon: www.amazon.com/shirleen-davies/e/b00dw9lusw

Other ways to connect with me:

My Facebook Fan Page:
www.facebook.com/shirleendaviesauthor
Twitter: www.twitter.com/shirleendavies
Pinterest: www.pinterest.com/shirleendavies
Google+: www.gplusid.com/shirleendavies.
Tsu: www.tsu.co/shirleendavies.

Other Books by Shirleen Davies

http://www.shirleendavies.com/books.html

Tougher than the Rest – Book One
MacLarens of Fire Mountain Historical Western Romance Series

"A passionate, fast-paced story set in the untamed western frontier by an exciting new voice in historical romance."

Niall MacLaren is the oldest of four brothers, and the undisputed leader of the family. A widower, and single father, his focus is on building the MacLaren ranch into the largest and most successful in northern Arizona. He is serious about two things—his responsibility to the family and his future marriage to the wealthy, well-connected widow who will secure his place in the territory's destiny.

Katherine is determined to live the life she's dreamed about. With a job waiting for her in the growing town of Los Angeles, California, the young teacher from Philadelphia begins a journey across the United States with only a couple of trunks and her spinster companion. Life is perfect for this adventurous, beautiful young woman, until an accident throws her into the arms of the one man who can destroy it all.

Fighting his growing attraction and strong desire for the beautiful stranger, Niall is more determined than ever to push emotions aside to focus on his goals of wealth and political gain. But looking into the clear, blue eyes of the woman who could ruin everything, Niall discovers he will have to harden his heart and be tougher than he's ever been in his life…Tougher than the Rest.

Faster than the Rest – Book Two
MacLarens of Fire Mountain Historical Western Romance Series

"Headstrong, brash, confident, and complex, the MacLarens of Fire Mountain will captivate you with strong characters set in the wild and rugged western frontier."

Handsome, ruthless, young U.S. Marshal Jamie MacLaren had lost everything—his parents, his family connections, and his childhood sweetheart—but now he's back in Fire Mountain and ready for another chance. Just as he successfully reconnects with his family and starts to rebuild his life, he gets the unexpected and unwanted assignment of rescuing the woman who broke his heart.

Beautiful, wealthy Victoria Wicklin chose money and power over love, but is now fighting for her life—or is she? Who has she become in the seven years since she left Fire Mountain to take up her life in San Francisco? Is she really as innocent as she says?

Marshal MacLaren struggles to learn the truth and do his job, but the past and present lead him in different directions as his heart and brain wage battle. Is Victoria a victim or a villain? Is life offering him another chance, or just another heartbreak?

As Jamie and Victoria struggle to uncover past secrets and come to grips with their shared passion, another danger arises. A life-altering danger that is out of their control and threatens to destroy any chance for a shared future.

Harder than the Rest – Book Three
MacLarens of Fire Mountain Historical Western Romance Series

"They are men you want on your side. Hard, confident, and loyal, the MacLarens of Fire Mountain will seize your attention from the first page."

Will MacLaren is a hardened, plain-speaking bounty hunter. His life centers on finding men guilty of horrendous crimes and making sure justice is done.

There is no place in his world for the carefree attitude he carried years before when a tragic event destroyed his dreams.

Amanda is the daughter of a successful Colorado rancher. Determined and proud, she works hard to prove she is as capable as any man and worthy to be her father's heir. When a stranger arrives, her independent nature collides with the strong pull toward the handsome ranch hand. But is he what he seems and could his secrets endanger her as well as her family?

The last thing Will needs is to feel passion for another woman. But Amanda elicits feelings he thought were long buried. Can Will's desire for her change him? Or will the vengeance he seeks against the one man he wants to destroy—a dangerous opponent without a conscious—continue to control his life?

Stronger than the Rest – Book Four
MacLarens of Fire Mountain Historical Western Romance Series

"Smart, tough, and capable, the MacLarens protect their own no matter the odds. Set against America's rugged frontier, the stories of the men from Fire Mountain are complex,

fast-paced, and a must read for anyone who enjoys non-stop action and romance."

Drew MacLaren is focused and strong. He has achieved all of his goals except one—to return to the MacLaren ranch and build the best horse breeding program in the west. His successful career as an attorney is about to give way to his ranching roots when a bullet changes everything.

Tess Taylor is the quiet, serious daughter of a Colorado ranch family with dreams of her own. Her shy nature keeps her from developing friendships outside of her close-knit family until Drew enters her life. Their relationship grows. Then a bullet, meant for another, leaves him paralyzed and determined to distance himself from the one woman he's come to love.

Convinced he is no longer the man Tess needs, Drew focuses on regaining the use of his legs and recapturing a life he thought lost. But danger of another kind threatens those he cares about— including Tess—forcing him to rethink his future.

Can Drew overcome the barriers that stand between him, the safety of his friends and family, and a life with the woman he loves? To do it all, he has to be strong. Stronger than the Rest.

Deadlier than the Rest – Book Five
MacLarens of Fire Mountain Historical Western Romance Series

"A passionate, heartwarming story of the iconic MacLarens of Fire Mountain. This captivating historical western romance grabs your attention from the start with an engrossing story encompassing two romances set against the rugged backdrop of the burgeoning western frontier."

Connor MacLaren's search has already stolen eight years of his life. Now he is close to finding what he seeks—Meggie, his missing sister. His quest leads him to the growing city of Salt Lake and an encounter with the most captivating woman he has ever met.

Grace is the third wife of a Mormon farmer, forced into a life far different from what she'd have chosen. Her independent spirit longs for choices governed only by her own heart and mind. To achieve her dreams, she must hide behind secrets and half-truths, even as her heart pulls her towards the ruggedly handsome Connor.

Known as cool and uncompromising, Connor MacLaren lives by a few, firm rules that have served him well and kept him alive. However, danger stalks

Connor, even to the front range of the beautiful Wasatch Mountains, threatening those he cares about and impacting his ability to find his sister.

Can Connor protect himself from those who seek his death? Will his eight-year search lead him to his sister while unlocking the secrets he knows are held tight within Grace, the woman who has captured his heart?

Read this heartening story of duty, honor, passion, and love in book five of the MacLarens of Fire Mountain series.

Second Summer – Book One
MacLarens of Fire Mountain Contemporary Romance Series

"In this passionate Contemporary Romance, author Shirleen Davies introduces her readers to the modern day MacLarens starting with Heath MacLaren, the head of the family."

The Chairman of both the MacLaren Cattle Co. and MacLaren Land Development, Heath MacLaren is a success professionally—his personal life is another matter.

Following a divorce after a long, loveless marriage, Heath spends his time with women who are beautiful and passionate, yet unable to provide what he longs for . . .

Heath has never experienced love even though he witnesses it every day between his younger brother, Jace, and wife, Caroline. He wants what they have, yet spends his time with women too young to understand what drives him and too focused on themselves to be true companions.

It's been two years since Annie's husband died, leaving her to build a new life. He was her soul mate and confidante. She has no desire to find a replacement, yet longs for male friendship.

Annie's closest friend in Fire Mountain, Caroline MacLaren, is determined to see Annie come out of her shell after almost two years of mourning. A chance meeting with Heath turns into an offer to be a part of the MacLaren Foundation Board and an opportunity for a life outside her home sanctuary which has also become her prison. The platonic friendship that builds between Annie and Heath points to a future where each may rely on the other without the bonds a romance would entail.

However, without consciously seeking it, each yearns for more . . .

The MacLaren Development Company is booming with Heath at the helm. His meetings at a partner company with the young, beautiful marketing director, who makes no secret of her desire for him, are a temptation. But is she the type of woman he truly wants?

Annie's acceptance of the deep, yet passionless, friendship with Heath sustains her, lulling her to believe it is all she needs. At least until Heath drops a bombshell, forcing Annie to realize that what she took for friendship is actually a deep, lasting love. One she doesn't want to lose.

Each must decide to settle—or fight for it all.

Hard Landing – Book Two
MacLarens of Fire Mountain Contemporary Romance Series

Trey MacLaren is a confident, poised Navy pilot. He's focused, loyal, ethical, and a natural leader. He is also on his way to what he hopes will be a lasting relationship and marriage with fellow pilot, Jesse Evans.

Jesse has always been driven. Her graduation from the Naval Academy and acceptance into the pilot training program are all she thought she wanted— until she discovered love with Trey MacLaren

Trey and Jesse's lives are filled with fast flying, friends, and the demands of their military careers.

Lives each has settled into with a passion. At least until the day Trey receives a letter that could change his and Jesse's lives forever.

It's been over two years since Trey has seen the woman in Pensacola. Her unexpected letter stuns him and pushes Jesse into a tailspin from which she might not pull back.

Each must make a choice. Will the choice Trey makes cause him to lose Jesse forever? Will she follow her heart or her head as she fights for a chance to save the love she's found? Will their independent decisions collide, forcing them to give up on a life together?

One More Day – Book Three
MacLarens of Fire Mountain Contemporary Romance Series

Cameron "Cam" Sinclair is smart, driven, and dedicated, with an easygoing temperament that belies his strong will and the personal ambitions he holds close. Besides his family, his job as head of IT at the MacLaren Cattle Company and his position as a Search and Rescue volunteer are all he needs to make him happy. At least that's what he thinks until he meets, and is instantly drawn to, fellow SAR volunteer, Lainey Devlin.

Lainey is compassionate, independent, and ready to break away from her manipulative and controlling fiancé. Just as her decision is made, she's called into a major search and rescue effort, where once again, her path crosses with the intriguing, and much too handsome, Cam Sinclair. But Lainey's plans are set. An opportunity to buy a flourishing preschool in northern Arizona is her chance to make a fresh start, and nothing, not even her fierce attraction to Cam Sinclair, will impede her plans.

As Lainey begins to settle into her new life, an unexpected danger arises —threats from an unknown assailant—someone who doesn't believe she belongs in Fire Mountain. The more Lainey begins to love her new home, the greater the danger becomes. Can she accept the help and protection Cam offers while ignoring her consuming desire for him?

Even if Lainey accepts her attraction to Cam, will he ever be able to come to terms with his own driving ambition and allow himself to consider a different life than the one he's always pictured? A life with the one woman who offers more than he'd ever hoped to find?

All Your Nights – Book Four
MacLarens of Fire Mountain Contemporary Romance Series

"Romance, adventure, cowboys, suspense— everything you want in a contemporary western romance novel."

Kade Taylor likes living on the edge. As an undercover agent for the DEA and a former Special Ops team member, his current assignment seems tame—keep tabs on a bookish Ph.D. candidate the agency believes is connected to a ruthless drug cartel.

Brooke Sinclair is weeks away from obtaining her goal of a doctoral degree. She spends time finalizing her presentation and relaxing with another student who seems to want nothing more than her friendship. That's fine with Brooke. Her last serious relationship ended in a broken engagement.

Her future is set, safe and peaceful, just as she's always planned—until Agent Taylor informs her she's under suspicion for illegal drug activities.

Kade and his DEA team obtain evidence which exonerates Brooke while placing her in danger from those who sought to use her. As Kade races to take down the drug cartel while protecting Brooke, he must also find common ground with the former suspect—a woman he desires with increasing intensity.

At odds with her better judgment, Brooke finds the more time she spends with Kade, the more she's attracted to the complex, multi-faceted agent. But Kade holds secrets he knows Brooke will never understand or accept.

Can Kade keep Brooke safe while coming to terms with his past, or will he stay silent, ruining any future with the woman his heart can't let go?

Always Love You– Book Five
MacLarens of Fire Mountain Contemporary Romance Series

"Romance, adventure, motorcycles, cowboys, suspense—everything you want in a contemporary western romance novel."

Eric Sinclair loves his bachelor status. His work at MacLaren Enterprises leaves him with plenty of time to ride his horse as well as his Harley...and date beautiful women without a thought to commitment.

Amber Anderson is the new person at MacLaren Enterprises. Her passion for marketing landed her what she believes to be the perfect job—until she steps into her first meeting to find the man she left, but still loves, sitting at the management table—his disdain for her clear.

Eric won't allow the past to taint his professional behavior, nor will he repeat his mistakes with Amber, even though love for her pulses through him as strong as ever.

As they strive to mold a working relationship, unexpected danger confronts those close to them, pitting the MacLarens and Sinclairs against an evil who stalks one member but threatens them all.

Eric can't get the memories of their passionate past out of his mind, while Amber wrestles with feelings she thought long buried. Will they be able to put the past behind them to reclaim the love lost years before?

Hearts Don't Lie– Book Six
MacLarens of Fire Mountain Contemporary Romance Series

Mitch MacLaren has reasons for avoiding relationships, and in his opinion, they're pretty darn good. As the new president of RTC Bucking Bulls, difficult challenges occur daily. He certainly doesn't need another one in the form of a fiery, blue-eyed, redhead.

Dana Ballard's new job forces her to work with the one MacLaren who can't seem to get over himself and lighten up. Their verbal sparring is second nature and entertaining until the night of Mitch's departure when he surprises her with a dare she doesn't refuse.

With his assignment in Fire Mountain over, Mitch is free to return to Montana and run the business his father helped start. The glitch in his enthusiasm has to do with one irreversible mistake—the dare Dana didn't ignore. Now, for reasons that confound him, he just can't let it go.

Working together is a circumstance neither wants, but both must accept. As their attraction grows, so do the accidents and strange illnesses of the animals RTC depends on to stay in business. Mitch's total focus should be on finding the reasons and people behind the incidents. Instead, he finds himself torn between his unwanted desire for Dana and the business which is his life.

In his mind, a simple proposition can solve one problem. Will Dana make the smart move and walk away? Or take the gamble and expose her heart?

No Getting Over You– Book Seven
MacLarens of Fire Mountain Contemporary Romance Series

Cassie MacLaren has come a long way since being dumped by her long-time boyfriend, a man she believed to be her future. Successful in her job at MacLaren Enterprises, dreaming of one day leading one of the divisions, she's moved on to start a new relationship, having little time to dwell on past mistakes.

Matt Garner loves his job as rodeo representative for Double Ace Bucking Stock. Busy days and constant travel leave no time for anything more than the occasional short-term relationship—which is just the way he likes it. He's come to accept the regret of leaving the woman he loved for the pro rodeo circuit.

The future is set for both, until a chance meeting ignites long buried emotions neither is willing to face.

Forced to work together, their attraction grows, even as multiple arson fires threaten Cassie's new home of Cold Creek, Colorado. Although Cassie believes the danger from the fires is remote, she knows the danger Matt poses to her heart is real.

While fighting his renewed feelings for Cassie, Matt focuses on a new and unexpected opportunity offered by MacLaren Enterprises—an opportunity that will put him on a direct collision course with Cassie.

Will pride and self-preservation control their future? Or will one be strong enough to make the first move, risking everything, including their heart?

Redemption's Edge – Book One
Redemption Mountain – Historical Western Romance Series

"A heartwarming, passionate story of loss, forgiveness, and redemption set in the untamed frontier during the tumultuous years following the Civil War. Ms. Davies' engaging and complex characters draw you in from the start, creating an exciting introduction to this new historical western romance series."

"Redemption's Edge is a strong and engaging introduction to her new historical western romance series."

Dax Pelletier is ready for a new life, far away from the one he left behind in Savannah following the South's devastating defeat in the Civil War. The ex-Confederate general wants nothing more to do with commanding men and confronting the tough truths of leadership.

Rachel Davenport possesses skills unlike those of her Boston socialite peers—skills honed as a nurse in field hospitals during the Civil War. Eschewing her northeastern suitors and changed by the carnage she's seen, Rachel decides to accept her uncle's invitation to assist him at his clinic in the dangerous and wild frontier of Montana.

Now a Texas Ranger, a promise to a friend takes Dax and his brother, Luke, to the untamed territory of Montana. He'll fulfill his oath and return to Austin, at least that's what he believes.

The small town of Splendor is what Rachel needs after life in a large city. In a few short months, she's grown to love the people as well as the majestic beauty of the untamed frontier. She's settled into a life unlike any she has ever thought possible.

Thinking his battle days are over, he now faces dangers of a different kind—one by those from his past who seek vengeance, and another from Rachel, the woman who's captured his heart.

Wildfire Creek – Book Two
Redemption Mountain – Historical Western Romance Series

"A passionate story of rebuilding lives, working to find a place in the wild frontier, and building new lives in the years following the American Civil War. A rugged, heartwarming story of choices and love in the continuing saga of Redemption Mountain."

Luke Pelletier is settling into his new life as a rancher and occasional Pinkerton Agent, leaving his past as an ex-Confederate major and Texas Ranger far behind. He wants nothing more than to work the ranch, charm the ladies, and live a life of carefree bachelorhood.

Ginny Sorensen has accepted her responsibility as the sole provider for herself and her younger sister. The desire to continue their journey to Oregon is crushed when the need for food and shelter keeps them in the growing frontier town of Splendor, Montana, forcing Ginny to accept work as a server in the local saloon.

Luke has never met a woman as lovely and unspoiled as Ginny. He longs to know her, yet fears his wild ways and unsettled nature aren't what she deserves. She's a girl you marry, but that is nowhere in Luke's plans.

Complicating their tenuous friendship, a twist in circumstances forces Ginny closer to the man she most wants to avoid—the man who can destroy her dreams, and who's captured her heart.

Believing his bachelor status firm, Luke moves from danger to adventure, never dreaming each step he takes brings him closer to his true destiny and a life much different from what he imagines.

Sunrise Ridge – Book Three
Redemption Mountain – Historical Western Romance Series

"The author has a talent for bringing the historical west to life, realistically and vividly, and doesn't shy away from some of the harder aspects of frontier life, even though it's fiction. Recommended to readers who like sweeping western historical romances that are grounded with memorable, likeable characters and a strong sense of place."

Noah Brandt is a successful blacksmith and businessman in Splendor, Montana, with few ties to his past as an ex-Union Army major and sharpshooter. Quiet and hardworking, his biggest challenge is controlling his strong desire for a woman he believes is beyond his reach.

Abigail Tolbert is tired of being under her father's thumb while at the same time, being pushed away by the one man she desires. Determined to build a new life outside the control of her wealthy father, she finds work and sets out to shape a life on her own terms.

Noah has made too many mistakes with Abby to have any hope of getting her back. Even with the changes in her life, including the distance she's built with her father, he can't keep himself from believing he'll never be good enough to claim her.

Unexpected dangers, including a twist of fate for Abby, change both their lives, making the tentative steps they've taken to build a relationship a distant hope. As Noah battles his past as well as the threats to Abby, she fights for a future with the only man she will ever love.

Dixie Moon – Book Four
Redemption Mountain – Historical Western Romance Series

Gabe Evans is a man of his word with strong convictions and steadfast loyalty. As the sheriff of Splendor, Montana, the ex-Union Colonel and oldest of four boys from an affluent family, Gabe understands the meaning of responsibility. The last thing he wants is another commitment—especially of the female variety.

Until he meets Lena Campanel...

Lena's past is one she intends to keep buried. Overcoming a childhood of setbacks and obstacles, she and her friend, Nick, have succeeded in creating a life of financial success and devout loyalty to one another.

When an unexpected death leaves Gabe the sole heir
of a considerable estate, partnering with Nick and
Lena is a lucrative decision...forcing Gabe and Lena
to work together. As their desire grows, Lena refuses
to let down her guard, vowing to keep her past
hidden—even from a perfect man like Gabe.

But secrets never stay buried...

When revealed, Gabe realizes Lena's secrets are
deeper than he ever imagined. For a man of his
character, deception and lies of omission aren't
negotiable. Will he be able to forgive the deceit? Or
is the damage too great to ever repair?

Survivor Pass – Book Five
Redemption Mountain – Historical Western Romance Series

He thought he'd found a quiet life...

Cash Coulter settled into a life far removed from his
days of fighting for the South and crossing the
country as a bounty hunter. Now a deputy sheriff,
Cash wants nothing more than to buy some land,
raise cattle, and build a simple life in the frontier
town of Splendor, Montana. But his whole world
shifts when his gaze lands on the most captivating
woman he's ever seen. And the feeling appears to be
mutual.

But nothing is as it seems...

Alison McGrath moved from her home in Kentucky to the rugged mountains of Montana for one reason—to find the man responsible for murdering her brother. Despite using a false identity to avoid any tie to her brother's name, the citizens of Splendor have no intention of sharing their knowledge about the bank robbery which killed her only sibling. Alison knows her circle of lies can't end well, and her growing for Cash threatens to weaken the revenge which drives her.

And the troubles are mounting...

There is danger surrounding them both—men who seek vengeance as a way to silence the past...by any means necessary.

Reclaiming Love – Book One, A Novella
Peregrine Bay – Contemporary Romance Series

Adam Monroe has seen his share of setbacks. Now he's back in Peregrine Bay, looking for a new life and second chance.

Julia Kerrigan's life rebounded after the sudden betrayal of the one man she ever loved. As president of a success real estate company, she's built a new life and future, pushing the painful past behind her.

Adam's reason for accepting the job as the town's new Police Chief can be explained in one word—Julia. He wants her back and will do whatever is necessary to achieve his goal, even knowing his biggest hurdle is the woman he still loves.

As they begin to reconnect, a terrible scandal breaks loose with Julia and Adam at the center.

Will the threat to their lives and reputations destroy their fledgling romance? Can Adam identify and eliminate the danger to Julia before he's had a chance to reclaim her love?

Our Kind of Love – Book Two
Peregrine Bay – Contemporary Romance Series

Selena Kerrigan is content with a life filled with work and family, never feeling the need to take a chance on a relationship—until she steps into a social world inhabited by a man with dark hair and penetrating blue eyes. Eyes that are fixed on her.

Lincoln Caldwell is a man satisfied with his life. Transitioning from an enviable career as a Navy SEAL to becoming a successful entrepreneur, his days focus on growing his security firm, spending his nights with whomever he chooses. Committing to one woman isn't on the horizon—until a captivating woman with caramel eyes sends his personal life into a tailspin.

Believing her identity remains a secret, Selena returns to work, ready to forget about running away from the bed she never should have gone near. She's prepared to put the colossal error, as well as the man she'll never see again, behind her.

Too bad the object of her lapse in judgment doesn't feel the same.

Linc is good at tracking his targets, and Selena is now at the top of his list. It's amazing how a pair of sandals and only a first name can say so much.

As he pursues the woman he can't rid from his mind, a series of cyber-attacks hit his business, threatening its hard-won success. Worse, and unbeknownst to most, Linc harbors a secret—one with the potential to alter his life, along with those he's close to, in ways he could never imagine.

Our Kind of Love, Book Two in the Peregrine Bay Contemporary Romance series, is a full-length novel with an HEA and no cliffhanger.

Colin's Quest – Book One
MacLarens of Boundary Mountain – Historical Western Romance Series

For An Undying Love...

When Colin MacLaren headed west on a wagon train, he hoped to find adventure and perhaps a little danger in untamed California. He never expected to meet the girl he would love forever. He also never expected her to be the daughter of his family's age-old enemy, but Sarah was a MacGregor and the anger he anticipated soon became a reality. Her father would not be swayed, vehemently refusing to allow marriage to a MacLaren.

Time Has No Effect...

Forced apart for five years, Sarah never forgot Colin—nor did she give up on his promise to come for her. Carrying the brooch he gave her as proof of their secret betrothal, she scans the trail from California, waiting for Colin to claim her. Unfortunately, her father has other plans.

And Enemies Hold No Power.

Nothing can stop Colin from locating Sarah. Not outlaws, runaways, or miles of difficult trails. However, reuniting is only the beginning. Together they must find the courage to fight the men who would keep them apart— and conquer the challenge of uniting two independent hearts.

Find all of my books at:
http://www.shirleendavies.com/books.html

Copyright © 2016 by Shirleen Davies

All rights reserved. No part of this publication may be reproduced, distributed, or transmitted in any form or by any electronic or mechanical means, including information storage and retrieval systems or transmitted in any form or by any means without the prior written permission of the publisher, except by a reviewer who may quote brief passages in a review. Thank you for respecting the author's work.

For permission requests, contact the publisher.
Avalanche Ranch Press, LLC
PO Box 12618
Prescott, AZ 86304

Survivor Pass is a work of fiction. Names, characters, places, and incidents are either products of the author's imagination or used facetiously. Any resemblance to actual events, locales, or persons, living or dead, is wholly coincidental.

www.ingramcontent.com/pod-product-compliance
Lightning Source LLC
Chambersburg PA
CBHW070743190726
48292CB00002B/394